EBURY PRESS

WRITTEN IN THE STARS

Divya is a product manager who writes product specifications during the day and is an author by night. She gets her best creative ideas when she's hanging upside down doing anti-gravity yoga or doodling. In 2019, she won a Gourmand World Cookbook Award for her first book, *Dare Eat That*. She is also the author of a children's picture book, *I Hate My Curly Hair*. She lives in Bangalore with her husband, Vivek. Follow her at: www.divyaanand.com.

Written in the stars

DIVYA ANAND

EBURY
PRESS

An imprint of Penguin Random House

EBURY PRESS

USA | Canada | UK | Ireland | Australia
New Zealand | India | South Africa | China | Singapore

Ebury Press is part of the Penguin Random House group of companies
whose addresses can be found at global.penguinrandomhouse.com

Published by Penguin Random House India Pvt. Ltd
4th Floor, Capital Tower 1, MG Road,
Gurugram 122 002, Haryana, India

First published in Ebury Press by Penguin Random House India 2021

ISBN 9780143452232

Typeset in Adobe Caslon Pro by Manipal Technologies Limited, Manipal

Printed at Repro India Limited

www.penguin.co.in

To Sathy Thatha for never once saying no when I asked for 'one more book' at the library. I wish I could show you this one.

1

The New Moon Brings
New Beginnings

There are days when the stars align so that everything that can go right in your life, does. Today was most definitely *not* one of those days.

'Shit, shit, shit,' I cursed as I stumbled into Last Call, a brewpub in Koramangala, Bangalore. I was dripping wet, holding one broken slipper in my hand while struggling to pull the other one off without falling flat on my face. After getting the slippers off, I blinked away the water and looked around as my eyes adjusted to the dim lighting inside. I started to shake my head to get some of the water out of my thick, curly hair in a manner not unlike that of a shaggy dog. Drops of water went flying around.

'Hey, watch it!' snarled the guy I had accidentally splashed. He was sitting at a table by the door and peering into his phone as though whatever was on it was the real world, and the world around was merely an annoyance.

'I . . . ' I began, ready to apologize.

'Sorry, sir,' a server cut me off, as he quickly handed the man a bunch of napkins and began wiping the table.

'You don't have to be sorry, *you* didn't cause this deluge,' he said pointedly, still staring at his phone. With that passive aggressive comment, my apologies evaporated almost instantly.

What an ill-mannered grouch, I thought.

It was quite unfortunate that he was such a grouch, because he had the kind of good looks that would've otherwise taken my breath away. I decided that he was one of those handsome men who have a terrible personality. I started to scan the pub for my friends.

It was Last Call's weekly trivia night, and our team, Whiskeypedia, was a regular contender. I had attracted some top quality trivia nerds in my life, and we'd put together a team that could beat Bangalore's best trivia enthusiasts hands down. We took great pride in the width of our knowledge of random trivia. I was the literature expert, thanks to my ability to read while I walked, even if it meant that I regularly tripped and *sometimes* broke my slippers. My best friend Kavya was a 'paparazzi-level' expert of pop culture, with an extensive knowledge of both Bollywood gossip and Meghan Markle factoids. Shirin, my colleague, had the uncanny ability to remember almost every obscure historical fact she'd gathered from the works of Manu Pillai, William Dalrymple, Ira Mukhoty, Alison Weir and the like. My other colleague, Upasana, was our current affairs expert and her brother Krish was our science guy. Krish was also supposedly our sports specialist, since he claimed he had followed cricket all his life. Over time, we realized he spent all his time drooling over cricketers and not paying attention to the actual matches, thus making sports our Achilles heel as the rest of us were equally clueless. We were all good at current affairs, and bonded over 1990s Bollywood music, which should be an official category but generally isn't.

'Sitara! Over here,' I heard Kavya call out.

For once, I was glad they weren't sitting at one of the tables in the centre, but were squished into a booth tucked away into a nondescript corner. I wanted to get to our table without drawing too much attention to the fact that I was creating mini puddles on the clean wooden floor.

'Now that's what they call commitment, folks! *She* doesn't let rain, shine or broken footwear stop her from getting her trivia fix,' said George Cherian, the quizmaster, with a wide grin.

With that, my hopes of sliding into the booth unnoticed went crashing as every head in the place swivelled in my direction. I tried to appear inconspicuous, cursing my decision to wear *jhumkas* with tiny bells on them that morning. Thanks to my fashion choices, I was jingling with every step. I felt like a cow with a bell around my neck announcing my arrival. I shuffled over to the booth and settled in with a sheepish smile while a staff member came by to mop up the mess I'd left behind.

'What happened?' said Kavya, as she took in my bedraggled state. As always, she was perfectly put together

in her fitted shirt and black cigarette pants. She looked
the spitting image of the high-flying, corporate executive
she was—a senior manager of procurement—at a leading
consumer goods firm.

Upasana was already digging around in her bag,
presumably for some kind of fashion appliance or accessory
that could help tame the frizz bubble that was slowly
growing around my head, giving me the appearance of
someone who had accidentally electrocuted herself.

'Worst day ever,' I said breathlessly. 'I got into this
endless meeting with Harsh, and it took forever to get him
to stop talking so I could leave. I was already late, and then
five Ubers cancelled on me back-to-back. I waited for an
hour, and even then, I had to beg the last one to accept . . .'

'That's a day in the life of Sitara. Why're you barefoot?'
asked Shirin, cutting to the chase, as she was wont to do.

'Haven't you seen the jam outside? I got down two
signals ago and began walking. And then, some moron
stepped on my foot, so I tripped and my slipper broke just
as it started to rain. I'm telling you guys, I'm Murphy's
favourite child. I had to run just to get here on time,'
I said as I reached out and took a swig of beer from Kavya's
glass. I needed a drink and while there was a pitcher on the
table, there were no spare glasses. I gestured at a server for
another glass.

'I remember telling you to leave work with us,' said
Upasana in an accusatory tone as she finally emerged from
the depths of her ginormous bag, holding out a large clutch
that actually looked like it could hold up my voluminous

mane. I wondered why someone with a silky straight pixie cut would even own this clutch, but Upasana's bag was like a mini beauty store. I was yet to face a situation where she didn't have a ready solution to a beauty emergency. I took the clutch and began putting up my hair into a bun, thanking my lucky stars that I was saved the fate of looking like the guy from the erstwhile Center Fresh ad.

'Harsh is claiming credit for all your work for his own promotion,' Shirin said. 'And you can't even muster up the courage to ask him for yours!'

'Yeah, Ash has started off with his doomsday speech about how we're low on cash so that our expectations are super low. After all the gloom and doom, you end up feeling like you should be grateful for even having a job,' Upasana sighed.

'Guys, trivia is starting,' I said, desperate to draw attention away from the post-mortem of my dead-on-arrival promotion chances.

Trivia night was supposed to be my way of forgetting about work. And yet, I had recruited people I spent all day with into my after-work escape zone. I really should find some non-work friends beyond Kavya! Upasana started to say something, but the lights dimmed as George began his welcome spiel.

I opened my bag and pulled out pens and sheets of paper. I began handing these out as they collectively rolled their eyes at me. I took my pub trivia very seriously. I looked around the room to size up the competition. There were some regulars like 'Google It', 'We Need No Name'

and 'Smarty Pints', as well as some new faces. Given the
shitty day I'd had, I hoped to win today. Last Call offered
winners one round of free drinks and a pizza on the house,
and since we were regulars, it would be good to get some
vouchers for next week. I was especially glad that our arch
nemeses The Sherlock Homies weren't there. We'd lost to
them three times in the last month, and I didn't want to
deal with them today.

'Round 1 is for our literature buffs.

'Our first question tonight is about a prolific author's
most popular character. The author hated him, and referred
to him as a "detestable, bombastic, tiresome, egocentric
little creep". Name the author and the character,' George
announced.*

Even before he'd finished reading out the question, I
was done writing down the answer on our response sheet.
My mood was slowly but surely improving.

Two rounds in, we were leading by fifteen points and
feeling very pleased. We had also demolished a pitcher of
'Hoptimus Prime', one of Last Call's signature brews, so
I was well on my way to cheering up. Just as I was about
to suggest ordering a second pitcher and look at the list of
woodfire pizzas, there was a commotion. Arnav, Namrata,
Zaina and Satish, also known as The Sherlock Homies,

---

* Agatha Christie, Hercule Poirot

walked in. I glared as the four of them took their seats. Zaina waved at someone by the door, and I saw him approach them. I stared as the cute grouch I'd splashed earlier took a seat at their table.

'Of course Oscar's joining their team,' I muttered to myself.

'Who's Oscar?' asked Kavya.

'Screw Oscar, who is *that*?' said Krish, openly ogling at the guy.

'He's cute,' agreed Shirin.

'He's a grouch. Like Oscar. I may have accidentally drenched him when I entered,' I said as I sank lower into my seat so he wouldn't spot me.

Kavya burst out laughing. 'Only *you* would name a cute guy after the grouchiest muppet on *Sesame Street*!'

I was done talking about Oscar the Grouch. Even if I did forgive him for his rudeness, he was still part of The Sherlock Homies, which automatically made him my sworn mortal enemy.

'Focus! Just because we're leading doesn't mean they can't beat us. We *have* to win,' I said, wishing that George wasn't so lenient about allowing teams to join trivia night midway. I would've loved it if they weren't allowed to participate because they were late.

'We're not here to win, we're here because it's fun,' said Upasana.

'Except, Sitara doesn't do anything for fun. What's our lifetime score against them? I'm sure you're keeping tabs,' teased Kavya.

'I'm not,' I defended myself hotly as I mentally did the maths and realized we were down to thirty-one to twenty-six. Shit.

'He's totally checking you out,' interjected Krish. 'Actually, he's more of a Cookie Monster than an Oscar. He has the same cute eyes . . . '

'Can we *please* focus?' I insisted through gritted teeth.

Thankfully, George called for silence so we could move on to the next round. I sneaked a quick glance at Oscar. Our eyes met and he smiled. Suddenly, it was like someone had switched on a bright light in a dark room. He was one of those rare people whose smile didn't just go up till their eyes, it radiated out. And he had a deep dimple on his left cheek, damn him. He really *was* cute. But then, he was also a complete jackass. I looked away quickly.

There was a raging battle between our teams in the next one hour. Questions and answers flew past as we tried to one-up each other. Our sledging game was on point, with a lot of trash talk that the other teams were enjoying. At the end of five rounds, The Sherlock Homies were ahead by five points. I was in a terrible mood. As Krish gestured for our fourth pitcher, I stopped him.

'No more beer,' I announced as I reached for another slice of pizza.

'Speak for yourself, Mom,' said Krish. 'I'm having another.'

'Thanks to you, the supposed expert, we just bombed the sports round,' I glared at him.

'C'mon, some of my answers were close,' he muttered.

'*Lasagne* is a food item. *Labuschagne* is apparently a person,' I said icily. 'A person that every other team, including The Sherlock Homies, knew as the first concussion substitute in test cricket.'

Krish stuck his tongue out at me.

'Chill, I was close. And we'll catch up . . .'

'You're simply taking your frustration out on Krish. You're mad because you missed the question on Daphne du Maurier and Oscar got it,' said Kavya hitting the nail on the head. I hated it when she was right, which she always was, when it came to me.

'While we're waiting for the scores, here's a bonus question for everyone here, whether or not you're participating in tonight's trivia,' said George. 'Raise your hand to answer, and we'll send a mic your way. Last Call has a giveaway for the right answer.'

'Ooh,' exclaimed Kavya, eyeing the beer mug that George was hoisting over his head as though it was a trophy.

It was definitely ooh-worthy. It had a lovely illustration of a group of people drinking and said 'Thirsty Thursday' on top. I was imagining it as a pen stand on my desk at work. I leaned forward to hear the question, determined I'd take the glass home.

'By the fourth century AD, Rome had twenty-eight public _____ stacked with rolls of papyrus. What am I referring to?' asked George.

My hand shot up. This was *so* obvious. Rolls of paper. There was only one kind of paper that was sold in rolls. That mug was mine!

'Two hands went up almost simultaneously. Sitara raised her hand first, so she gets the first shot. You, sir, in the blue checked shirt get a chance if she answers incorrectly.'

'I have the right answer so you don't have to bother getting up,' I called out as I started to walk towards George.

'Let's not get ahead of ourselves,' I heard a deep baritone ring out. I turned and saw Oscar get up from his spot at the Sherlock Homies's table. Krish began miming an arrow hitting his heart. He was a total sucker for deep voices.

For a second, I wavered.

What if my answer was incorrect?

I quickly dismissed the thought. One of my rules of trivia was to never second-guess myself. Whenever I did that, I always substituted a correct answer with an incorrect one. Besides, the question said 'rolls' and that was a dead giveaway.

I took the mic from George, and confidently announced, 'Rome had twenty-eight public toilets. Stacked with rolls of toilet paper, of course.'

I heard a muffled laugh behind me, followed by Oscar quipping, 'The Romans would have loved it if they had invented toilets in the 300s.'

The comment set off a wave of laughter from the trivia enthusiasts. My cheeks burned as the entire pub laughed at me.

'What my friend here meant to say is that Rome had twenty-eight public *libraries*. The Romans sure as hell weren't wiping their behinds with those rolls of papyrus,' said my new nemesis with a wide grin, as the pub erupted into cheers and George handed him the mug.

I died a little inside. Why didn't I think of libraries! The word rolls had led me directly to toilets. That was probably one of my worst trivia answers in history, and thanks to Oscar, the entire pub was now laughing at me.

I slunk back to my seat, convinced that everyone was still laughing at me.

'*Someone* is trying to catch your eye,' said Kavya.

'Yeah, Oscar is looking at you,' said Upasana.

'You mean he's laughing at me, just like everyone else,' I said glumly.

'He's not! As for everyone else, I'd say you did that to yourself,' laughed Shirin. 'Toilet paper? Really?'

Thankfully, I was saved from having to respond by the start of the next round. I couldn't afford to lose this round or today's trivia to The Sherlock Homies now that their newest member had made me the laughing stock of the pub trivia circuit. I looked over to the adjoining table and saw that Oscar was mouthing something. It was most definitely another joke at my expense.

What a colossal ass, I thought as I turned away.

At the end of the last round, our team was tied with The Sherlock Homies and we were going into a tiebreak. Each team had to nominate one person to answer the question. My team sent me because I was the most sober, and could actually frame a response. The rest of them were wasted and could barely string together coherent sentences, leave alone comprehend a question. I sat down at the front of the makeshift stage, and George handed me a mic. The Sherlock Homies sent Oscar who ambled over and took the seat opposite me.

'OK, here's how this will work. You each have a buzzer. I will read out the question; whoever presses the buzzer first and gets the right answer wins,' said George. 'If it's another tie, I'll ask another question.'

We tested our buzzers, and got ready.

'To win today's Thirsty Thursday Trivia, here's a literature question . . .'

I held my breath. This was too good to be true. I had a winning streak with literature tiebreak questions.

'Much of this book written in the 1980s consists of letters written by a character to God . . . .' George began. 'It . . .'

BUZZ!

I pressed the buzzer hard, nearly jumping out of my seat.

My heart hammered in my chest as I confidently announced, '*Are You There God? It's me, Margaret* by Judy Blume.'

'That's the wrong answer. I'll now complete the question for the benefit of the other team. It won a Pulitzer Prize . . .'

BUZZ!

Oh bloody hell.

I watched miserably as Oscar picked up his mic. Now that George had mentioned the Pulitzer, I knew he would get this.

He looked directly at me, grinned, and said, '*The Colour Purple* by Alice Walker.' The pub erupted into hoots and cheers.

'Of course, you'd be extremely remiss if you didn't thank the lady for jumping the gun on the buzzer,' George said, rubbing salt into my very large and extremely raw wound.

'Are you there, God? Whiskeypedia needs you,' Oscar heckled as the pub erupted into laughter at my expense for the second time that day.

I *hated* the guy. He had made me the laughing stock, again. Of course, it was my fault for giving away the opportunity but there was no need for him to rub it in.

What a dick! I thought as frustrated tears pricked my eyes.

Suddenly, all the laughter and the buzzing in the pub stopped. The pub was so silent, you could hear a pin drop. I looked up and saw Oscar looking as though he had been punched squarely in the gut.

Or worse.

I looked around the room. Every single person was frozen. It was like looking at a sea of shocked statues. At The Sherlock Homies table, Zaina's eyes were shooting daggers at me. Arnav was staring with his mouth open. Even the garrulous George seemed to be at a loss for words.

Shit, shit, shit.

I had just accidentally called him a *dick* out loud.

And my mic was on.

I was mortified. I wished that the earth would open up so I could bury myself within and disappear. Of all the idiotic things I had done in my life, this was possibly the worst.

'I didn't mean . . .' I began as he walked away.

George quickly began announcing the results. The Sherlock Homies went up to receive the voucher for their free drinks and pizza. As everyone began to leave, I ran outside to find Oscar and apologize. He was standing by the door, waving at an approaching Uber.

'Hey,' I started. 'I'm really sorry about what I said. It's . . .'

'This is what happens when someone whose head is stuck in the toilet is handed a mic,' he said as he got into the cab and shut the door on my face.

I stared.

I was right.

He really *was* a dick.

2

Venus Goes into Retrograde

'Are you there, God? It's me, Sitara,' Shirin teased as I entered our bay the next morning.

I ignored her as I walked to my desk. I placed my bag on the floor and raised my desk to standing level. I plugged in my laptop, hopped on my raised chair and started to check my email. Out of the corner of my eye, I saw a Starbucks coffee cup on my desk, with 'STARA' scrawled on it. I looked up to see Shirin grinning at me, with a second cup that said 'SREEN' in her hand. She'd brought me a chocolate macchiato with mint syrup. About a year ago, we'd discovered that convincing the baristas at Starbucks to substitute chocolate for caramel in a caramel macchiato and adding mint syrup created a drink that tasted a lot like our favourite mint chocolate cookies. Upasana insisted that we were drinking toothpaste. But what did she know about our elevated palettes? I picked up Shirin's peace offering and took a sip.

15

'You have to talk to Harsh about your promotion today,' she said.

'Maybe . . . this afternoon, I'm doing a demo of Project Nightshade . . .'

'Is that the one that lets you match the lipstick shade to your skin tone? I can't wait for it!'

'Yeah, so, once the demo is done, I'm going to tell him that if he wants this launched, he better make sure I'm promoted. He's been stringing me along for the past three cycles and I'm done waiting.'

'It's long overdue! Just make sure you don't bomb the demo. Remember Harsh almost shut down your last project when he saw a page full of tampons . . .'

'Is it my fault that creep spends all day browsing through the lingerie section of the app? He got the exact recommendation his browsing behaviour should get. Anyway, don't tell anyone, but I've now "fixed" the results for his profile,' I winked.

'Nice! Have you figured out what to say when he whines that we're running out of money?'

'I'll gently remind him that *itne paise main itna ich milega*,' I replied, using my best Bambaiyya accent as she giggled.

'Still, expect he'll say we can't afford raises or promotions. That's always the first line of defence from our bosses,' she grinned.

Shirin, Upasana and I worked for Glam, an online retailer for beauty, fashion and wellness products. Shirin was a data analyst, which made her our official data beautician. She could make data look so good that the rest of us could prove that anything we were about to launch would change the trajectory of the business. I was a product manager, which meant I was supposed to create a magical unicorn of an app that solved every beauty need arising from the random thoughts that my upper management, a group of clueless men, threw at me every day. Six years ago, as a fresh-faced business school graduate, I picked this start-up thinking this gig would help me create a trailblazing career. Now, after spending six years launching new features, including world-changing solutions to pick lipstick shades, it was time I was promoted. After all, success in the corporate world didn't come from actually doing things, it came from being the 'strategy' person. My boss, Harsh, had been dangling this carrot under my nose for the past two years with no results. This time, I was determined to make it happen.

'Good morning, Ms Srinivasan, Ms Wadia,' said Ash, as he passed by our bay on his way to his office. Ash Bakshi was Glam's business head, which meant both our bosses reported to him. He was known for being a business whiz; he'd worked at a Silicon Valley unicorn, a company valued at 1 billion dollars, before the venture capitalists convinced him to move to India. Like many US-returns, he had a weird twang, and the tendency to refer to himself with an abbreviated first name.

Our team had a long-time bet going to find out what 'Ash' stood for. There was no way that was his name, especially since he was from a small town. So far, our money was on Ashwin, but we hadn't managed to find any sources to confirm it. We had even tried bribing the admin assistants to find out what name he used in his official paperwork but everything from his passport to his Aadhar card only had the mysterious moniker, Ash.

He had a terrible temper, the after-effects of which trickled downwards. We spent our time trying to gauge his mood as that defined our bosses' behaviour for the day. Luckily, a good morning wish that included our surnames was one of the signs of a good day.

'You're in luck,' Shirin trilled, echoing my thoughts. I grinned and got to work.

'And here's the perfect shade for me, MAC's O,' I said, as I wrapped up my presentation.

Our demo had gone well. Things had worked exactly as they were supposed to. I congratulated myself for creating a perfect script and bribing the engineering team with beer so they 'fixed' all the bugs. Whenever Harsh had brought up a tangential question, I had made sure to guide the conversation back to the specific paths we wanted to demonstrate.

I had demonstrated the new feature by taking a photo of my hand, which I had uploaded on to the app. Once I'd done that, the app had recommended this particular shade as it suited my skin tone the best.

'This is amazing,' said Harsh. 'Fantastic recommendation!'

I grinned. I knew that making our algorithms prioritize a brand like MAC during the demo was the right call. Harsh was glad that we were recommending a lipstick at the premium price point. He believed that recommending luxury brands would ensure that our customers spent more money on Glam. He had no clue that I secretly thought this particular colour looked ghastly on me, and would've preferred the original recommendation, Scarlet Drill by Lakme, instead.

'Sridhar, let's launch this ASAP,' he said addressing our chief technology officer (CTO), who looked positively delighted. 'Sitara, get this added to the dashboard for our weekly business review with Ash,' he added.

He left the meeting room and headed to his office. I followed him. He looked startled when I entered, but didn't say anything.

'Harsh, I wanted to chat . . . ' I began.

'Make it quick, I only have fifteen minutes till my next meeting,' he said.

That tiny opening was enough. Immediately, I launched into my prepared speech without giving him a moment to get a word in edgewise.

'As you know, I'm a key member of the team. I've been part of the app redesign and I've since launched multiple features, including the one we just demoed. My launches have resulted in a two-fold increase in acquisitions as well as driven customer engagement. It's time we discussed a promotion,' I said.

Harsh sat with his eyes closed, hunched over his desk, massaging his temples. This was his 'thinking' stance. I waited. Just as I was wondering if I'd have to say something more, he looked up.

'Do you know what's going on with the company?' He continued to press his temples as if I were giving him a headache.

I knew he was going to talk about how the business was strapped for cash, and how it was nearly impossible to manage raises. But this time, I was prepared.

'Harsh, we're fine. The last quarter results were in line with investor expectations. Besides, at this point in my career, I need to see growth. Otherwise, I'll have to make some hard career decisions.'

'Sitara, everyone knows that we got great results last quarter because we ran our end-of-season sale . . .'

Of course, I thought angrily. *If things go well, it's because of the end-of-season sale. If they don't, then it's all my fault. These jackasses will never, ever give us any credit!*

' . . . and we've seen a steady decline in revenues since then,' he continued. 'We are number two in our category and have been at that position for three months. None of your launches have changed our market share. If you want a promotion, come up with an idea that will take us to number one in the two months. If not, forget being promoted, you and I will both be out of jobs because our investors will recommend layoffs as we will be running out of money.'

'But Harsh, this lipstick matching . . . ' I began, determined to argue this one out.

'Isn't the launch that will get you promoted,' he summed up. 'If you want to be a senior leader, think like one. Give me a launch that takes us to number one and keeps us there. Then we'll talk.'

I was seething. Harsh had never launched anything in the five years I'd known him. He was clearly counting on me to come up with something that he would present to Ash, and use to his own advantage.

'Harsh . . .' I began.

'I'm late for my next meeting,' he said as he walked to the door.

Our conversation was over.

I was in a foul mood when I got to the cafeteria. Even the fact that my friends were sitting at a table in the open-air section, which I normally loved, didn't cheer me up.

'It went nowhere,' I announced, slamming my plate on the table.

'Did he say Glam is running out of cash?' asked Upasana, as she took a mouthful of her salad. 'When will they realize that we've all worked here long enough to see the pattern of evasion they practise every year.'

'Things have escalated. Apparently, the investors are putting a lot of pressure because we've been stuck at number two. Harsh wants an idea that'll take us to number one within two months, to stop mass layoffs.'

'Sounds like a case for his promotion,' replied Upasana. 'And what is this new story . . .'

'Actually,' Shirin cut in, 'when Ash last spoke with the investors, they gave him an ultimatum. We need to get our numbers up, otherwise they said they'll take a hard look at costs because we're close to running out of money.'

Upasana and I lapsed into silence. Shirin had a prime seat right outside Ash's office. It was a great location because Ash was loud. Consequently, Shirin always knew what was going on. If she said there was a chance our company could get shut down, she was right. I realized that Harsh was serious.

I was about to ask Shirin if she'd overheard anything about appraisals, when I saw Dhruv and his ever-present shadow Aakash walk up to our table. Aakash was the slimiest member of Harsh's team and Dhruv was in marketing like Upasana. I subtly checked to make sure my hair and clothes were in place. I was wearing an off-white dress, which meant the chances of my having spilled some food on myself were high. Just last week I'd managed to get chocolate on the sleeves of my salmon pink shirt, and while I had convinced myself it was inconspicuous, that slimeball Aakash had drawn everyone's attention to it. I've had a crush on Dhruv for a while, and I didn't want him to realize what a klutz I was.

'What are you ladies discussing?' Aakash said, as he and Dhruv pulled up chairs. I groaned mentally. I didn't want to tell them what we were talking about.

Shirin opened her mouth and I kicked her under the table, hoping to stop her. She grimaced but didn't get the message and ploughed on thoughtlessly.

'Appraisals,' she said. 'Have you guys had the talk yet?'

'You know Harsh. Hasn't brought it up,' said Aakash.

'He won't,' said Dhruv. 'You'll have to, if you want it. Like I am. It's almost in the bag.'

'Really?' I said.

'This one has been Ash's go-to guy in marketing since Azhar left,' said Aakash knowingly. 'He's got Ash wrapped around his little finger.'

'Yeah, and the big boss didn't say no when I hinted that I'm ready,' said Dhruv smugly.

'He didn't say yes either . . .' Shirin pointed out.

'With Ash, not saying no is a big deal. That's his favourite word and his first response to any question,' laughed Dhruv as everyone joined in.

I laughed along but my heart wasn't in it. My mind was racing. Was Dhruv going to beat me to a promotion?

'So, Dhruv and Sitara are in the running,' said Upasana.

'Are you?' Dhruv said, smiling at me.

'I've started sowing the seeds . . . ' I said.

'You know only one of you can get it, right?' Aakash interjected. 'Harsh told me that Ash said only the top-rated performer at every level will get a promotion. So there's no way both of you can get it.'

'Sitara is tough competition,' Dhruv said with a wide grin. The grin threw me off. I expected trash talk, but instead he was being weirdly nice. I could feel the blood rush to my face as I wondered what he was hinting at.

'Yeah, my money's on Sitara,' said Shirin confidently.

'I wouldn't be so sure. The last launch would've gone nowhere without that clutter-breaking marketing campaign,' Aakash argued on Dhruv's behalf.

'As though products don't matter, and marketing will sell anything,' Shirin said hotly.

'Please! If it wasn't for marketing, people wouldn't even know about half of the features on Glam!'

As our friends bickered over who was likely to get the promotion, I decided it was time to change the subject.

'How come you guys are eating outside?' I asked. Aakash and Dhruv didn't usually sit in this section of the cafeteria. I suspected that Aakash didn't like sitting outdoors because the slightest wind could mess up his hair, which was held up in gravity-defying spikes with what appeared to be one kilo of gel.

'It's match day,' Dhruv said, gesturing to the giant projector that was set up on one side of the terrace. I had been so wrapped up in thoughts of my discussion with Harsh that I hadn't noticed that the projector was set to Star Sports.

'Oh God,' Upasana groaned. 'Do we really have to watch this match?'

'Come on, where's your sense of pride?' Aakash asked. 'It's India vs England and we're likely to win!'

He stood up and walked towards the projector. Dhruv followed. They were soon joined by a group of people, all of whom were peering at the screen as if something earth-shattering were about to take place. There was a lot of posturing and preening, and some people were giving long speeches with a knowledgeable air. I disliked cricket with a passion, so I focused on my food.

'Do you think Dhruv has really managed to convince Ash about his promotion?' I asked my friends but I was cut off by a loud cheer.

I looked up, annoyed. Couldn't these people watch their match without yelling and disturbing everyone else?

The projector was displaying the cricket pitch in all its bright green glory as the commentators chit-chatted. Just as I decided it was time to leave the cafeteria, Aakash and Dhruv ambled back to the table. They ended up sitting on either side of me, effectively boxing me in on the long bench. I had no way to leave without asking them to get up.

'You don't seem excited. Not a cricket fan?' Dhruv said.

'No,' I grunted.

He looked shocked, and then stared at me expectantly. I ignored him. I was used to getting this reaction every time I announced my disinterest in India's favourite sport. I had zero interest in telling Dhruv that my ex-boyfriend, Arjun, was a cricketer who had managed to get selected for a few of India's matches. I'd spent years following him around while he was playing and developed a strong aversion to the game after spending time in VIP boxes in stadiums across India.

I stared at the projector disinterestedly, wondering how I could politely get one of them to get up so I could leave. They were absorbed in discussing the game, even though it hadn't started yet. The camera panned away from the field on to the crowd. A line of spectators with the Indian flag colours painted across their cheeks came into view. One guy was busy leading a section of the crowd through their off-key rendition of the song, *Come on India.*

Suddenly, a man stood up in the last row of the stands. As he began dancing downwards in a manner reminiscent of the girl from the old Daily Milk ad, the camera began to follow him. I watched open-mouthed as he danced all the way to the front row of the stands. There was a buzz in the stadium as everyone tried to figure out what he was doing. He danced to the centre of the row, where a petite woman was sitting.

'What on earth is going on?' Upasana said.

I was too busy gaping at the screen to reply. The man had now lifted up a sign proclaiming, 'MARRY ME, PRIANCA!' He got down on one knee in front of the woman and pulled a ring box out of his pocket.

'This is so twee,' said Upasana. 'Who even does this in a cricket match?'

The camera now zoomed in on the woman, who was covering her mouth in a perfect imitation of a beauty pageant winner. She was probably Prianca. A petite woman, with extremely delicate features. She looked like the smallest whiff of wind would blow her away. She started crying and nodding.

'Say yes,' he urged, as the camera finally zoomed in on his face.

My heart stopped.

'YES . . .' she yelled.

He pulled her into a hug. They really didn't need to zoom in so close, the giant rock on the ring he was pushing on to her finger could easily be spotted by all the aliens in outer space.

Suddenly, I couldn't breathe. I leaned forward and began gulping. Upasana jumped up and came over to my side of the table and began rubbing my back.

'Are you OK,' she said. I tried to take a deep breath, but I couldn't.

'I'm . . . I'm . . .' I gasped, unable to get any words out.

I tried taking a sip of water but choked on it. Upasana kept patting my back. Slowly, my heart stopped hammering and my breath came back to normal. I sat back staring at the screen, which mercifully had cut out into an ad break.

'How girly,' Aakash said, unable to tear his eyes away from the screen. 'What kind of wuss comes up with such a proposal?'

'Someone trying to compensate for lacking elsewhere,' Dhruv said meaningfully as he rolled his eyes.

'Someone romantic,' Shirin breathed, all starry-eyed.

I wanted to tell her she was wrong. I knew that the man proposing was definitely not a romantic. Because that was *Arjun*. Back when we started dating, I used to tease him about how I'd recreate the Dairy Milk ad one day when he became a famous cricketer and we were engaged. Instead, he'd spent the last five years out of our nine-year-long relationship insisting that he was a free spirit who didn't want to be tied down by a cumbersome institution like marriage. I broke up with him six months ago when he told me that he didn't think he would ever be ready for marriage.

Well, he was ready now. The problem hadn't been that he didn't ever want to get married. It was that he didn't ever want to get married *to me*. And the bastard had stolen my proposal idea and broadcasted it on national television. I was fuming.

This was the stinky cherry on top of the fly-infested rotting dung cake that was this horrible week.

I wondered what could possibly go wrong next.

3

Jupiter Shines in Your Household

I was in a foul mood on my way home. If you believed Google Maps, I lived twenty minutes away from work, but the actual time it took me to get home on any day was entirely dependent on the vagaries of Bangalore's traffic. The traffic today was exactly what I expected from what was rapidly becoming the worst week of my life. I was stuck in a never-ending jam. As the red lines on Google Maps began to burn a hole into my brain, the cab driver decided to increase the volume on the radio.

I mentally cursed my luck at having found the one cab driver in the entire city who wasn't on an endless phone call for the duration of the ride. Instead, he was rubbing salt and pepper into my open wounds by listening to the radio commentary of that blasted cricket match. I had spent my entire workday making sure to leave the room whenever anyone began discussing it, only to now find myself stuck listening to a blow-by-blow account of what was supposedly a nail-biting finish. I pulled my Kindle out of my bag and opened it, hoping to divert my mind with the adventures of the Shergil Sisters, but I was rudely interrupted by my phone ringing.

I had studiously avoided my phone ever since I'd left the office. I knew none of my friends would call because they all knew just how much I hated talking on the phone. They had all left me WhatsApp commiserations, which I'd left unread, knowing they would understand that I would respond when I felt like it. The only message I had opened was from Kavya, who had texted me a bunch of puke emojis signifying her opinion of Arjun's behaviour. I ignored the call without checking my phone to see who it was, but the person kept calling back.

It had to be my mother. She was the only person who insisted on calling repeatedly until you answered. I had tested her limits before and knew that when she was truly determined, she was capable of hitting redial at least twenty times, if not more. And so, I reluctantly answered.

'Hi, Amma!'* I tried to sound as cheery as possible so we wouldn't have to have a mother-daughter heart-to-heart.

'I just saw the news.'

'I'm on my way home, so I don't know who's threatening to nuke whom right now,' I said, hoping to change the subject.

'Arjun was on the news,' she said pointedly. 'He proposed to his girlfriend at the India-England match.'

---

* Amma is mother in Tamil.

'Oh, *that*,' I said, trying to sound as flippant as I could. 'I saw that. I will send him a message to say congratulations.'

'You're not upset?' she probed. My mother was like a bloodhound on a scent when she decided to get into this mood.

I sighed.

I always knew I would regret dating my mother's best friend's son. Unlike my other boyfriends, I couldn't hide my relationship once Arjun told his mother about us. Back then, my worry was that the two mothers would gang up on me and convince me to have the wedding of their dreams. Instead, I was now stuck talking to my mother about the one topic I didn't foresee discussing with her—my love life, or the lack of it.

'I'm fine, Amma,' I said. Earlier in the day, I had decided that my strategy would be to keep repeating that I was fine until everyone believed me. Maybe I would even begin to believe it myself!

'Well, even if you think you are fine, there will be feelings buried deep within,' she insisted. 'The next time I visit, I will do a pranic healing session to cleanse your auras and clear the emotional damage.'

My heart sank. My mother loved pranic healing, and truly believed that she could exorcise all kinds of illnesses, physical and mental, into a bowl of salt water. I was wary of it ever since I attempted to copy her when I was twelve and ended up with a fever. My mother had insisted it was because I had done it wrong, but I was convinced the entire thing caused more trouble than it was worth.

'My aura is fine and I am not suffering any mental damage,' I said. 'You really don't need to worry . . .'

'Take a vacation,' she cut in, ignoring me. 'Kavya and you should go to that place I told you about, Shreyas. It's a really nice yoga retreat and it's so close to Bangalore.'

'I can't,' I said. 'There is a lot going on at work . . .'

'Stop using work as an excuse to avoid dealing with your feelings. You need to prioritize your mental health and emotional well-being!'

That did it.

'Amma, your voice is breaking . . . ' I said, holding the phone away from my face and making staticky noises through my teeth. 'I'll call you when I get home.'

I hung up without waiting to hear her response.

I looked up to see the Ganesha on the dashboard bobbing his head at me in silent judgement. I mentally apologized to Him for knowing fully well that I had absolutely no plans of calling my mother back tonight. Or ever.

I entered the house and hung my keys in the key holder by the door. Kavya's keys were already there. I envied her work-life balance. In all the time we had lived together, I almost never made it back home before she did in the evening. Kavya and I had been roommates at B-school and we were glad when we both found jobs in Bangalore. We were especially thrilled when we discovered that our offices were close to each other, making it very easy for us to share an apartment.

We had found ourselves a nice furnished two-bedroom apartment in a large housing complex. The apartment was cosy and a great place to hang out, with a balcony attached to the living room. Of course, Kavya was the one who spent most of the time in it. She joked that I was a ghostly presence who only sometimes made herself known. On such days, though, I was thankful that I wasn't coming home to an empty house.

Almost as if she had heard my thoughts, Kavya stepped out into the entryway and gave me a tight hug.

'I was hoping you'd miss the match,' she said.

'I wish,' I said and shuddered. 'I saw the entire proposal live because I made the mistake of sitting in the outdoor area of the cafeteria at lunchtime.'

She handed me a glass of wine, which she'd thoughtfully filled right to the very brim.

'Have I told you I love living with you?' I said as I gratefully took it and walked into the living room. I flopped on the couch, ignoring the fact that our landlady's list of rules included never allowing anyone to put their feet on her precious couch.

'How are you?' Kavya asked, as she took a sip.

'I'm fine,' I said yet again. 'I'm over Arjun. Completely.'

'Even if you are, it's still got to hurt,' she replied. 'Anyway, he was a jackass. Good riddance!'

'Can we talk about something else?' I was so done talking about Arjun. Kavya was someone who gave people their space and was nice enough not to push me any further. We spent the next hour skirting around the issue of proposals as we finished dinner and the better part of a bottle of wine. After dinner, I told her that I was really tired and escaped into my room.

Once I was in my room, I made a beeline to the mirror.

'I'm fine,' I practised in front of it. I didn't sound sure enough I decided. I needed to sound more convincing. 'I'm happy for him. I don't need a man to complete me.'

My reflection looked back at me dubiously.

'Oh, screw it! I hate that bastard and I hope he gets chlamydia. Or worse.'

I felt better. Clearly, I was not meant to be the bigger person.

I changed into my pyjamas and walked over to my bed. I plugged my phone into the charger and finally looked at it. I tried to talk myself out of doomscrolling Arjun's social media profiles, but it didn't help. I cursed my complete lack of self-control as I scrolled through photo after photo of the happy couple, and congratulatory comments from some of my erstwhile so-called friends. I started making a mental list of all the people I would now need to unfriend since they seemed to have taken his side in the break-up. Once I was done with his profile, I moved on to Prianca's. There were more photos, including live updates from what looked like an engagement party. I looked at Prianca's other photos, trying to see if I could find out what about her was so commitment-worthy, when I clearly was so not suited for it.

'Stop it, Sitara,' I said to myself and tossed the phone back on the nightstand.

I closed my eyes, hoping I could convince myself to fall asleep. But my brain kept replaying the photos on slideshow mode. I could not believe that the guy who had convinced me that bringing flowers to a date was too 'rom-com' had suddenly metamorphosed into someone who would propose to his girlfriend at a cricket match. He refused to celebrate an anniversary with me when we were together, but now, he was posting albums full of 'If you like it, better put a ring on it' pictures. I regretted taking the high road when we broke up and pretending that we were 'still friends'. If it wasn't for that, I would've unfollowed him on social media and missed all these mind-numbing, torturous updates.

Then you would've created a fake profile just to be able to see these photos, my inner voice taunted me.

I scrunched my eyes and tried to count sheep so I could fall asleep. But my mind was messing with me. Every sheep looked like Arjun in some way. No matter what I did, I couldn't stop myself from thinking about him.

Deep down, I knew my life was better without him. I loved the fact that I didn't have to justify being busy at work when he wanted to talk. I loved that I could eat chocolates in bed without a lecture on how I would attract ants. I loved that I could watch *Gilmore Girls* on repeat and not pretend that I was interested in yet another superhero movie. I loved that I could read without being interrupted because he felt like I was paying too much attention to my book.

But what about the fact that you missed having someone to snuggle up with while watching TV? Or that going to the park was more fun with company? Or that you didn't have to attend boring parties by yourself? Or that you had someone to give you a head massage at the end of a tiring day? Or, or, or . . . the voice in my head began taunting me.

I'm happy, I told myself.

Maybe if I fell asleep thinking of something else, like *Pride and Prejudice*, I would dream that I had a Mr Darcy of my own.

Isn't that how a well-adjusted, single woman in her late twenties who was happy with her life behaved?

It was, wasn't it?

4

Patience Will Help You Rise Above Odds

I stared in frustration at the blank document. After a weekend filled with half-hearted attempts at avoiding social media, I'd got to work early on Monday morning to put together a 'promotion-worthy', 'business-trajectory-altering' proposal. So far, I had nothing. Or rather, I had listed out some ideas, but they were so terrible I had pressed backspace on everything. And now I was back to square one. I felt like the blank document was mocking me.

'Why is this so hard?' I muttered.

'Talking to yourself? That's the first sign of insanity,' Dhruv said. He had walked up behind me and was now peering at my screen intently. I slammed my laptop shut and turned around.

'Are you spying on me?' I asked with narrowed eyes.

'Here I am, a good Samaritan, inquiring after your well-being, and you are accusing me of spying,' he replied with a mock-injured tone.

'You were trying to see what I'm working on.'

'I don't need to. You're losing your mind. Meanwhile, I have a meeting with Ash today. I'm pitching the project that's getting me the promotion,' he retorted.

'What a coincidence! I'm taking a new project to him today too,' I bluffed. It's not like he knew that all I had was this blank document.

'Really?' He raised an eyebrow. 'I didn't see any invites from you on his calendar.'

Whoops. I forgot that Ash had recently made his calendar public, in an effort to prove that he was 'transparent'.

'Wow! You must be worried if you're snooping around on Ash's calendar for inside info,' I said.

'Never underestimate the competition, as Ash would say,' he grinned. 'Anyway, I'm getting back to my presentation. May the best man or woman win.'

I went back to staring at my blank document.

PING!

Notification: Your monthly Colossal Book Box is out for delivery.

Finally, some good news. I loved this box—every month, I received a curated selection of new books as well as book-related swag. The swag was good, but they were often hit or miss. The books, though, were always a hit. I had discovered many authors like Mhairi McFarlane,

Mira Jacob, Meena Kandasamy, Randall Munroe and more through it. I couldn't wait to get home and see what I'd received this month.

I went back to my blank document, gritting my teeth as I wondered what I could possibly come up with. And then, it struck me.

If I liked my book box so much, why couldn't Glam have a beauty box? We could curate samples and send them out to customers who paid for monthly subscriptions. If they liked the samples, they would buy the products. My mind started to race; people loved discovering new brands, and we worked with new brands who wanted to use our platform to reach new customers. We could partner with them! A beauty box could solve our market share problem. After all, after someone purchased a monthly box from us, they would keep shopping on Glam and that would automatically propel us to number one. I couldn't wait to show this proposal to Ash!

As I worked on the presentation, I wondered if I should first speak to Harsh. But I couldn't bear the thought of letting Dhruv get ahead of me. Besides, if Ash liked the idea, Harsh would be ever-ready to take credit for it and would forgive me for bypassing him. I was desperate, and I needed to take a risk. Once I was done with the presentation, I decided to ambush Ash while he was in his office that afternoon.

I set up the presentation and hurried over to Ash's room.

'Hi, Ash, do you have a minute? I'd like to run something by you,' I said.

'Sure, sure, come in,' he said. I was thrown off to see Ash smiling so broadly. He could be charming when he wanted, but that usually happened after he finished chewing up some poor soul inside out. His charm was basically his way of erasing the trauma he caused when he lost it at somebody. Shirin often joked that we all had Stockholm Syndrome and that's why we're still here. I opened my laptop, and turned it around so he could see the screen.

'So, Ash, I've been thinking about how we've been stuck at number two, and I wanted to discuss this idea to fight back . . . '

'Before we get into that Sitara, tell me, how are you doing?' he said with a beatific smile.

Ash never asked anyone how they were feeling or doing, ever. I blinked at him in surprise. 'All OK with you? How are things with Harsh?' he pressed.

'Everything's good, Ash,' I said. 'In fact, Harsh suggested that I come up with a proposal to address our market share problem.'

'I see. Are you sure there's nothing else we need to discuss?'

'I do have some slides to outline my proposal, we could get into that?'

'OK, let's begin.'

I heaved a sigh of relief and launched into my presentation. To my surprise, Ash was behaving completely out of character. Usually, he got into the details of every slide and asked pointed questions. Today, he was in some kind of trance where he kept nodding and smiling. He didn't ask a single question. I wondered if all this silence was building up into one of his infamous epic rages where he would throw me out of his office for my stupidity.

'To sum up, this beauty box will get us to number one and keep us there,' I ended and looked at him expectantly.

'Interesting . . .' he said, as he stared out of the floor-to-ceiling window behind his desk. I held my breath, hoping he liked my idea. He turned and looked directly at me. 'We should explore this,' he started and I cheered internally. 'But I'm not the right person to take this call.'

Um, what? I stared at him. What did he mean he wasn't the right person to decide? Ash was such a control freak that he would get involved in picking the office lunch menu if he felt like, and now suddenly he was claiming he couldn't take a call on something as big as a new product proposal? I struggled to find the words to ask him what he meant.

'You'll have to wait for a week. Our new marketing head starts on Monday. He's an expert on the subscription business, as he's worked for one of the world's largest e-commerce firms. I'm going to rely on him to decide if this one makes the cut. If he approves, I approve,' he announced.

I had to stop myself from groaning. I would have to deal with a new 'head'? I didn't want a new person, who would take months to understand how anything functioned, to become the one to approve my project. This was really going to mess with my chances of getting promoted.

'Why wait an entire week? I'd love to hear your thoughts right away,' I tried to push Ash into taking a decision.

'I think a beauty box makes sense. But the details have to be vetted by an expert and he decides if we should or shouldn't launch this. Anything else?' he asked pointedly as he opened his laptop and began working.

'Anything else' generally signalled the end of the meeting. I got up and left.

I couldn't believe I would have to wait a full week. And, I would have to convince some new person, whose quirks I couldn't even predict. People from big companies always had a giant chip on their shoulder and took forever to understand how things worked in start-ups. I was walking toward Shirin's desk in a daze when Dhruv suddenly materialized by my side.

'We're getting a new marketing head,' he announced, with the air of someone who was doing everyone a favour by dispensing gossip.

'I heard. Ash says he needs to approve my idea,' I said. 'Who is he? What's his name?'

'Really? I thought Harsh would let your idea fly by while I waited for the new person to join,' said Dhruv, avoiding my question. He clearly didn't want to give me any additional information. 'Why is your project dependent on an approval from the marketing head?'

I shrugged evasively and walked away. I didn't want to engage in a longer conversation with Dhruv on this.

Unfortunately for me, Shirin didn't have any information about the marketing head either, which was

surprising because it was so unlike Ash to manage a new hire silently. When Abhijit, our sales head, was being interviewed two years ago, Ash had forgotten to shut the door to his office. Shirin had ended up overhearing the entire conversation. There wasn't a thing we didn't know about Abhijit's achievements or his eight-figure salary before he joined.

'I have some news,' she said as she waved at Upasana to join us as we walked towards the elevator. There was a Starbucks on the ground floor of our office building, and we often went there to escape the muddy brown concoction our machine passed off as coffee, as well as the prying eyes and ears.

'Guess where Ash went on his ten-day break?'

'I don't know! For the first time ever, he didn't drown us in his usual Insta-spam,' I replied. Ash had a penchant for adding every new employee as a friend on social media, which meant we were treated to about fifty new photos a day every time he took a vacation. He was like one of those LinkedIn gurus who created a life lesson out of their daily activities. On steroids.

'Apparently, he went on a ten-day retreat with some organization called the "Shape of Success". You spend ten days in silence, eat only organic vegan food, and do yoga, meditation and what not. After Azhar cited Ash's anger issues as the reason for his departure, the board mandated him to attend.'

'Are you serious?' I asked. 'Is that why he's behaving weirdly?'

'Yes! How did you miss the new list of commandments on his bulletin board?' Shirin asked.

'I saw a Post-it there,' said Upasana. She scrunched her face up as she tried to remember. 'It had a triangle with three words on each point: Listen, Empathize, Delegate.'

'Yup,' said Shirin, as she took a sip of her coffee. 'That's his personalized three-point triangle, designed by the guruji who runs the organization. You're supposed to read this as LEAD: Listen, Empathize and Delegate. Ash is working on this "Triangle of Tranquillity", and will report on his progress. Everyone gets their own shape, and once they work through their issues successfully, they're inducted into the guru's "Triangle of Triumph".'

'This is bizarre. Tranquillity and Ash? That's trash,' I laughed.

'Whatever it is, expect more bizarre behaviour. I heard him talking to HR about setting up a minicamp for the team.'

Oh God. HR's leadership initiatives were bad enough without Ash adding shape-filled jargon into our lives. If he was so intent on 'delegating' the decision-making on my project, I hoped he would display equal enthusiasm at delegating this Shape of Success workshop. I couldn't see Harsh and Abhijit buying into this mumbo-jumbo, and I figured the new marketing head wouldn't either.

We had no idea what we were all about to get into.

✦✦

'I know I'm late, but my day has been horrible,' I announced as I walked into Nasi and Mee, my favourite Asian restaurant in Koramangala.

I was only ten minutes late, but my sister, Sahana, was a stickler for punctuality. I did not want to be at the receiving end of a lecture on respecting someone else's time. Sahana stood up and gave me a hug. She picked up the bag I had thrown by the side of the table and slung it across the back of a chair.

'Someone could've tripped,' she said.

I ignored her. Sahana was obsessed with 'a place for everything, and everything in its place'. She'd sung that to me through our childhood, and effectively put me off picking up after myself when she was around.

'You saw the match?' I said as I sat down, wanting to shove the elephant out of the room immediately.

She nodded.

'I'm happy for Arjun,' I began, hoping that all the practising in front of the mirror was making me sound sincere. I began reading the menu to avoid her piercing stare, even though I already knew what I was getting. This place had the best pad thai in the city.

'Actually, I'm happy for both of them. Of course, I don't really know this Prianca, but she seems nice. Or rather, she photographs nice? And Arjun is a good person. OK, he's an ok person . . .'

Sahana continued to stare at me.

'Fine. Arjun is a rat-bastard who stole my idea and used it to propose to someone else.'

She gestured to the waiter and placed our order without bothering to ask me what I wanted. I held my breath, expecting her to say something to me, but she still didn't say a word. She just continued to stare. It was a time-tested strategy, designed to get me to spill all my secrets.

'I'm not jealous,' I insisted. I began biting my nails, as I was wont to do when I got worked up.

'It's no big deal that she's younger, looks like a Barbie doll and was described by a newscaster as India's sweetheart. I have a great job, my team is kicking ass at trivia, I have amazing friends, and what does she have? A PR-worthy engagement, followed by a wedding. And, of course, a pretentious spelling for the world's most ordinary name. Congrats, Prianca!'

After that rant, I took a big gulp of water and looked around. It was still early in the evening and there were very few other guests. Sahana and I lived in opposite ends of the city, so we typically met in the middle and timed it to work around the traffic.

'Did I tell you? I think I'll finally get promoted this time. I've figured out just what I need to do! I'm doing much better now that I'm single. Arjun was such a distraction, no?'

Sahana raised one perfectly shaped eyebrow and made a non-committal sound.

'Well? You studied psychology, so you're my counsellor,' I said. 'What's your professional opinion?'

'I may have studied psychology, but I'm a practising chartered accountant. If you want my professional opinion, bring me your tax returns,' Sahana replied.

I blinked at her, finally at a loss for words. The waiter chose this moment to bring over our food—cucumber and avocado sushi for the table, a pad thai for me and a Thai red curry plate for her. There was also a side of honey chilli lotus stem, Sahana's favourite. She immediately reached out to serve herself.

'Come on, Sahana, tell me what you think,' I said, as I struggled with the chopsticks, trying to ensure I got the sushi into my mouth and not splattered across the front of my dress like a toddler who needed a bib.

'As though you'll listen,' she retorted.

'I promise I will. Tell me what you think,' I begged.

'Remember my advice is that of an older sister who is concerned her younger sister has completely lost her mind.'

'Fine. And your advice is?'

'You're overreacting and suffering an extreme case of FOMO, as Inaya would say. You need to get over Arjun.'

'So, your best advice is basically to quote your ten-year-old daughter?' I said.

'I knew she wouldn't listen,' Sahana said sotto voce, as she spooned out rice and curry on to her plate. Only Sahana could find a combo of items that was as close to a home-cooked south Indian meal as possible. It looked like she was eating some version of sambhar and rice with honey-chilli chips.

'Why has nobody ever proposed to me like that?' I insisted as I twirled the pad thai around my fork. 'I mean, it was my idea!'

'Oh God,' she sighed.

Sahana was a great older sister. She was the apple of our parents' eye, and smarter than me but she couldn't help that. She was six when I was born and did not take the news well. Apparently, she had expressly requested a brother. Or a fish. Her exact words were: 'Return this baby to the hospital shop, immediately.' Sadly, our parents didn't comply and I ruined everything. Or so she claimed.

I think she got her own back by picking my name. Thankfully, she only got as creative as 'Sitara', a name that confused many neighbourhood *maamis**, who thought my parents meant to name me 'Sita' and insisted on calling me that, no matter what I said. I shuddered to think what she would come up with now.

'I haven't had a promising date in months,' I whined, wanting to change the subject. 'I've stopped waxing my legs above my knees and I've forgotten how to kiss.'

'It's like swimming and will come rushing back when you're confronted by the moment,' she said dryly. 'And waxing above your knees is overrated. I don't either.'

Ugh. *My poor brother-in-law*, I thought. And then gagged because who needed mental images of their sister having sex?! Ew.

'Sitara, if you wanted to be in a relationship, you would be looking for one. You never fail once you've decided to go after something. Which isn't a compliment!'

I looked at her, my cheeks bulging with noodles.

'Why not?' I asked her, puzzled.

---

* Tamil word for aunties

'Are you coming on Saturday?' she said, delicately dabbing at her mouth with a napkin. 'We can talk in detail. Unlike today when we'll both have to rush immediately after we finish eating.'

'Actually, I have to work,' I began. 'I'm working on this new proposal, and Ash asked me to get the approval of the new marketing head. He hasn't joined yet, so I'm not sure what it'll take to convince him.'

'A project approval from some new marketing head is more important than spending time with your niece?' Sahana said. She gave me the look that I imagined got the accounting teams of companies that she audited shivering in terror and ready to spill all their secrets.

'Do you want me to lie and say I'll come?'

'Your priorities are all wrong,' she said, and I felt a rush of anger.

'My work is important. This promotion is the most important thing in my life right now.'

'Sitara, nothing should be more important than spending time with family. Work will come and go, but family is forever.' I struggled not to point out that she sounded like someone who wrote subtitles for cringey Bollywood movies. That line would work perfectly for a *Hum Saath Saath Hain* remake. Or was it *Kabhi Khushi Kabhie Gham*? At times like this, I couldn't fathom that the two of us were even related.

'Why can't you be supportive?' I whined, hating myself for regressing to the child she made me feel like. 'I've just had to deal with Dhruv rubbing it in my face that his project is likely to get approved overnight. Meanwhile, Ash is sending me on a wild goose chase . . .'

'I get it. Work politics are a lot to deal with, especially when you're up for a promotion. But you have to find balance. Don't go overboard to win. We all know how competitive you can be.'

'All the evidence suggests that I am not being competitive enough at work!'

'Sitara. The school banned you from the relay race in fourth standard because you kicked that other girl in the shins to stop her from participating.'

'Actually, it was a lemon and spoon race. And it was an accident,' I defended myself hotly. 'You keep bringing that up every time you want to have the last word.'

'Was hitting me in the eye with the "Q" tile in Scrabble also an accident?' she went on, making sure to use air quotes for the word accident.

The problem with sisters is that they know exactly which button to push. And then they push so hard, they leave a dent that remains for a few days.

'I have to go,' I said, pulling up the Uber app on my phone. I sneaked a peak at my inbox. Shit. Fifty unread emails. I'd have to do a round of clean-up tonight.

'I'll WhatsApp you about Saturday.'

'You can't disappoint Inaya,' she said, using her ten-year-old as bribe. She pulled out her phone and called her driver.

We went to the front of the restaurant. I looked out and realized that it was raining. As usual, I hadn't brought an umbrella. And I was wearing my favourite white

Anokhi kurta. I would soon be looking like a vamp who'd performed a rain dance in a B-grade movie.

Sahana quietly reached into her bag, pulled out an umbrella and handed it to me. It was definitely Inaya's, since it featured the entire cast of *My Little Pony*. I silently thanked God that it wasn't a Hello Kitty umbrella.

'What about you?' I said, suddenly wondering if my sister was sacrificing her umbrella for me. She pulled out a stylish raincoat with a hoodie. Of course, she had a raincoat *and* an umbrella. I was willing to bet she had spares for both items in her bag too. My sister was the perfect Girl Guide; she was always prepared.

'You're a good sister,' I said as I hugged her. 'Even though you quote your ten-year-old and pass it off as advice.'

'You don't listen to me, so it's pointless to give you any advice.'

'Bye,' I called out, walking towards my cab. 'I'll WhatsApp you about Saturday.'

'No, you'll see me on Saturday,' she said. 'You complete nutcase.'

'I love you too,' I said, blowing her an air kiss as I jumped into the cab.

5

Your Career Will See New Beginnings

'He's here,' Upasana announced breathlessly as soon as I walked into the office.

She looked hassled, which was uncharacteristic for someone who was normally unflappable. Shirin was looking equally flustered. The way they were standing guard by my desk, it seemed they had been waiting for me to arrive. People were clustered into small groups all around our bay. Something was up, but I didn't have the time. I was late and needed to get started with the day. I began checking my email.

'Sitara, he's here,' Shirin repeated, stretching out each syllable so I was forced to pay attention.

'Who?' I asked irritably, without looking up.

'Abhimanyu,' she replied.

'Abhiman-who?' I said, finally looking up.

'The new marketing head! He's been in Ash's office for over an hour. We're waiting for them to surface.'

That got my attention. Clearly, nobody was getting any work done today.

'He's joined on a Tuesday? That's odd,' I said. 'I thought HR made people start on Monday.'

'HR's rules only apply to us minions,' Shirin said dismissively.

She walked over to the centre of the bay where all the groups seemed to be converging. I followed, not wanting to miss out on any of the gossip surrounding this newcomer.

'He was on the thirty-under-thirty list . . .'

'For the start-up he created in college and sold before he even began business school,' Dhruv, who had clearly been researching his boss, said.

'He spent five years at Amazon,' Aakash, not wanting to be left behind, jumped in.

'He's really young,' Shirin cut in. 'He graduated B-school in 2010.'

Suddenly, there was pin-drop silence.

'What?' Dhruv choked out. 'That's not possible. He's the marketing head.'

'And he used to be a director,' Upasana added.

'It's right here on LinkedIn,' Shirin pulled it up on her phone. There it was, staring us in the face. Haas School of Business, 2010. This Abhimanyu was Dhruv's age, only a couple of years older than me. But he was Harsh's peer.

He must either be really good at his job, or the world's most skilled corporate politician, I thought. *Or both.*

We continued to peer at his LinkedIn profile. For some reason, he didn't have a photo.

'Did anyone check his other profiles?' I asked.

'Everything else is set to private,' Aakash said. 'This is all there is.'

'How very un-marketing like,' I replied. 'How's he going to promote anything if he can't even promote himself?'

Suddenly, the door to Ash's room opened. The buzz of voices died instantly as everyone scrambled to get back to their desks. Everyone was peering over their monitors, trying to get a look at the new marketing head. But Ash was playing spoiler by standing by the door and blocking our view. He was gesturing as he continued to speak to the person who was still inside. I squinted to see what I could make out through the frosted glass. The new marketing head was tall, almost six feet tall like Ash. He was lean and had really broad shoulders.

Ash stepped out of the office and began walking in our direction. The new marketing head followed him. By now, everyone had stopped pretending they were hard at work. The entire team was blatantly staring as the newcomer walked out of Ash's office.

Shit, shit, shit.

My heart skipped a beat. And *not* in a good way.

I blinked, hoping I was seeing things, but I wasn't.

It was *him*.

Oscar, the grouch.

'Team, say hello to Abhimanyu Singh, our new head of marketing,' said Ash.

'Oh, shit,' said Upasana and Shirin in unison. With that, any hopes I had that this was merely the trivia dick's doppelganger flew out the window.

Ash went around the bay introducing Abhimanyu to everyone.

'This is Sitara, one of our product managers. She has a great idea around creating a beauty box, so I've asked her to speak with you,' Ash said as he introduced me.

I squirmed.

'Hi Osc—Abhimanyu,' I stuttered.

As Abhimanyu looked directly at me, I wished I could jump out of the glass window leaving only a Sitara-shaped crack behind. I would travel back in time to my worst moments to escape this. I could go back to my grandparents' place during vacations and listen to my grandmother yell at my grandfather for hours. Or to the day I walked around in period blood-stained clothes for half the school day before someone told me about it. I could even go back to the day I accidentally tucked my skirt into my stockings when I visited the bathroom during a date and showed the entire restaurant my underwear. *Anywhere* but here.

I began chewing my fingernail, wondering what he would say.

'Nice to meet you, Sitara,' Abhimanyu said politely.

I gaped. He looked at me like I was just another colleague he'd met this very minute. It was as though he didn't remember me at all.

I wondered if this was a good thing or a bad thing.

⋆⋆

WhatsApp Chat

[11.00 a.m.] Sitara: The dick is the new marketing head!

[11.00 a.m.] Kavya: You mean, the new marketing head is a dick.

[11.01 a.m.] Sitara: No, I mean the new head is THE dick. Abhimanyu, from trivia.

[11.01 a.m.] Kavya: Who?

[11.01 a.m.] Sitara: Oscar!

[11.02 a.m.] Kavya: Oscar? Who are all these people?

[11.03 a.m.] Sitara: Kavya! How can you forget the guy from The Sherlock Homies, the one I was calling Oscar?

[11.03 a.m.] Kavya: Oh, *that* Oscar. Krish is still pining for that dick, if you know what I mean . . .

[11.04 a.m.] Sitara: Very funny. Just so you know, his name is Abhimanyu. And he's our new marketing head.

[11.04 a.m.] Kavya: Holy shit!

[11.05 a.m.] Sitara: Exactly. I called the new marketing head a dick.

[11.07 a.m.] Kavya: Did he say anything when he was introduced to you?

[11.10 a.m.] Sitara: Nothing. He acted like he didn't remember me.

[11.10 a.m.] Kavya: Nobody can forget being called a dick. He probably didn't want to create a scene.

[11.11 a.m.] Sitara: You're right. I'm supposed to get HIM of all people to approve my business plan. The one for my promotion. And he HATES me. I am so screwed!

[11.13 a.m.] Kavya: Oh. What if you apologize?

[11.13 a.m.] Sitara: Or maybe . . .

[11.15 a.m.] Sitara: . . . I pretend the incident never happened?

[11.16 a.m.] Kavya: Won't it be awkward? I mean, you'll see him at work every day. What if he's now a permanent Sherlock Homies member?

[11.17 a.m.] Sitara: Oh God, that would be the worst! But yeah, you're right. I'll have to apologize. Shit.

I sighed as I put my phone away. I was not looking forward to apologizing to Abhimanyu 'Oscar' Singh.

'Hi Abhimanyu,' I began as soon I spotted him at the coffee machine.

I had been looking up every few minutes to catch him when he took a coffee break. I felt a little bit like a low-key stalker. He didn't look up. He went about stirring in a sachet of sugar into his coffee. I took a deep breath and ploughed on.

'Can we talk?' I asked.

He threw the stirrer into the bin, took a sip and finally looked at me questioningly. I decided to go on.

'I'm really sorry about what happened last week. I hope it won't impact our working relationship. I was really frustrated that day, and the words just came out . . . ' I said.

'OK,' he said with what looked like a smirk plastered on his face. It threw me off because I didn't know whether he really meant it.

'OK?'

'Yeah, don't worry. I wasn't offended. I'm just glad you're able to construct sensible sentences now,' he quipped, as I stared at him with my mouth hanging open.

He took another sip of coffee.

After that jibe, there wasn't much I could say. I decided to put the incident behind me and get on with what I really wanted to broach.

'Actually, there is one more thing,' I said.

'I have an idea and Ash asked me to speak to you about it. Can we discuss it today?'

'It's my first day, so I'd like to focus on getting to know my team. Why don't you find an empty slot on my calendar later this week once I've had a chance to speak with Harsh?'

'This is time-sensitive and critical. Ash is really interested in this, so the sooner we discuss it the better,' I pressed.

He pulled out his phone and checked his calendar.

'OK, if I'm going to begin my stint by saving lives on the very first day, let's connect at five,' he said and walked away.

Yes, I cheered to myself silently. I pulled out a bottle of coconut water from the fridge and took a sip.

Suddenly, he stopped and turned.

'Oh, and by the way, I don't appreciate name dropping.'

✦✦
✦

'I've got projections to show how the beauty box will increase our new user base as well as . . . ' I was in the middle of my presentation when Abhimanyu cut me off.

'You scheduled an urgent meeting for this?' he asked incredulously. He picked up a pen and began writing notes in a tiny black notebook. I tried to peer into it but couldn't see what he was writing.

'This is the model that AllureBox has operated successfully . . . '

'You mean, this is the model that resulted in AllureBox declaring bankruptcy! Shouldn't you check if the company still exists before you set up a meeting based on an idea they tried?' He stared at me, brows furrowed in annoyance.

'This idea will work in India,' I said hotly. 'We have the premium customers on our platform. With this, the value-conscious customers will sign up because the box is priced such that they will discover new brands for next to nothing!'

'Yeah, you'll attract a whole new customer segment of bargain hunters! One that will stock up on samples and buy nothing. What's the point?'

He shut his notebook as though it wasn't even worth making notes. My ears were drumming. I was so angry. Abhimanyu was infuriating. He had no context whatsoever, and was talking about all the wrong metrics. I jumped in to correct him.

'Abhimanyu, you're misunderstanding the objective. With this plan, we will attract new customers. We have other features that will drive revenues once they're on Glam,' I argued.

'Sitara, there is no point in bringing in new customers if they're predisposed not to spend money. I don't see any point pursuing this,' he said with an air of finality.

'Ash was convinced. We should really dive into the details . . .'

'In that case, take your proposal to Ash,' he cut in icily.

'What I meant was you're judging this too quickly. I have detailed projections on revenue. Let me take you through them,' I backtracked quickly. I was used to involving Ash because it was the best way to talk Harsh into anything. It was obvious that Abhimanyu was different. Bringing Ash into the conversation was more harmful than helpful. I would have to watch myself.

'I'm here to double Glam's revenues, and with that in mind, I will only focus on plans that have a shot at changing our trajectory. I suggest you focus on something along those lines too,' he said, effectively ending the meeting.

I left, fuming at his arrogance.

Who did he think he was? Even Ash spent more time listening to a proposal before shooting it down. This guy had been disinterested in my presentation throughout. He asked me a few stray questions, but didn't push for details. I was sure he was still mad at me, and he most certainly wasn't letting trivia grudges stay within trivia. He wouldn't give me a fair hearing.

PING!

Glam Office Messenger Group Chat

[#Best-Buds@Glam—5.35 p.m.] **Upasana**: Did you see the email?

[#Best-Buds@Glam—5.36 p.m.] **Shirin**: I know! What is this nonsense?

[#Best-Buds@Glam—5.40 p.m.] **Sitara**: Abhimanyu sucks! I cannot believe we have to deal with such a self-centred ass.

[#Best-Buds@Glam—5.41 p.m.] **Upasana**: Forget him. Check your email!

[#Best-Buds@Glam—5.41 p.m.] **Sitara**: He said my idea is terrible and my time is better spent elsewhere. Upasana, do you know what's going on with Dhruv's project?

[#Best-Buds@Glam—5.41 p.m.] **Shirin**: Sitara, CHECK. YOUR. EMAIL.

[#Best-Buds@Glam—5.45 p.m.] **Sitara**: WTF is this?!

[#Best-Buds@Glam—5.45 p.m.] **Upasana**: Exactly! We're all going through the Circle of Success programme :(

[#Best-Buds@Glam—5.45 p.m.] **Shirin**: Did you see that questionnaire? It's five pages! I have to finish an analysis Harsh asked for, and now I also have to fill this? I'll be here all night.

[#Best-Buds@Glam—5.46 p.m.] **Sitara**: We're all going to be here all night. Not just today, but for the duration of this workshop.

[#Best-Buds@Glam—5.47 p.m.] **Upasana**: I can't believe Ash is pretending we get off at 5 p.m. every day.

He thinks we will do two hours of this programme and then head home? Who will finish the mountains of work we have?
[#Best-Buds@Glam—5.48 p.m.] Sitara: We're so screwed!

I walked to my desk and started packing my things. I had a ton of work, but I couldn't sit in the office any longer. Usually, I avoided working at home. But today was one of those days where I felt like I would get more done if I was lounging on my couch in my pyjamas instead of sitting in the office where I ran the risk of running into that insufferable ass again.

Of all the start-ups in all of Bangalore, *why* did he have to walk into mine?

6

Exercise the Power of Might over Matter

'What the . . . '

I stopped a few metres away from my desk and rubbed my eyes. It looked like a crime scene, with yellow tape criss-crossed in front of it, cordoning it off from the rest of the bay. The cubicle walls had been removed and there were ugly, bright blue plastic sheets hanging in their place. I wondered if I had missed an email about some admin work in the office. But as I looked around the bay, I noticed that everyone else's desk appeared to be untouched.

Why has mine been vandalized, I wondered. *And where are all my things?*

I kept looking around and suddenly spotted a large box in the corner. A familiar sweatshirt was draped around the box. I rushed over and realized that someone had piled all my things into the box in the most haphazard manner possible.

What kind of moron dumps a fat diary right on top of a plant, I wondered as I dived in to organize my things. My poor succulent! It already looked a little traumatized.

'Didn't you check your email?' Shirin asked, as she walked up and handed me a cup of coffee with 'SITAR' written on it.

'No, I was so stressed after filling out that ridiculously long questionnaire last night, I decided to take a break this morning,' I replied. 'What did I miss?'

'They're knocking down this wall,' she said gesturing to the wall behind my desk, which was now covered by blue plastic sheets. 'It will be replaced with a glass door, leading to the room that's behind. That room is now going to be a cabin.'

I blinked. It was going to be so weird having a door next to a row of seats. But whoever was taking that cabin was getting a prime location on the floor. The cabin was tucked away in the corner and had floor-length windows on all sides except the area with the wall that separated it from the cubicles in front.

'What? For whom?' I asked, knowing that it couldn't possibly be for Ash. Ash loved his cabin because it was right by the entrance to the floor, thus allowing him to track all our comings and goings. Plus, it was equally well-lit.

'Abhimanyu,' she said, rolling her eyes. 'He's also asked for his team to move to this bay. Your team is moving to the opposite side, next to the tech team.'

I gasped.

'But Harsh's office is here,' I said gesturing toward it.

'No, Harsh is moving to the other side too.'

'Harsh is *okay* with moving to an office that's away from the windows?'

Harsh had fought hard to get a cabin on the 'good' side of the floor, with floor-to-ceiling windows. If he moved to the other side, he would get a cabin that was right by our cubicles. Those cabins were dingy and didn't get any natural light. I couldn't imagine Harsh taking this move quietly.

'I don't think he had a choice,' Shirin said. 'I heard Abhimanyu stipulated he'd decide where he and his team would sit before he agreed to join. Plus, he told Ash he'd never heard of a product team sitting away from engineering . . . '

'What a diva,' I muttered. But also, what a master player! It was a stroke of genius, telling Ash that all product teams sat next to tech teams. Ash would do anything Abhimanyu claimed his ex-employer did, irrespective of whether or not that was actually true. I was impressed by his ability to play Ash.

I picked up the box with my things and walked to the other side. My heart sank. The product team had been assigned seats right in the centre, away from the windows. The engineers had already claimed the prime spots near the windows. The blinds were drawn, ensuring that not even an iota of natural light touched anything in the vicinity. I had learnt the hard way that engineers were closet vampires who would bite the head off anyone who dared open the blinds, so I didn't dare attempt that. I looked around the dark, dingy space and felt a pang of longing for my old seat which was right by a window.

Suddenly, a group of workers passed by and walked into one of the offices. They were accompanied by Ranjani, the admin head.

'These men are the limit,' she muttered. I looked at her and gave her a tentative smile, hoping to make her feel better. That's all it took for the floodgates to open.

'Nobody realizes how difficult it is for the admin team. One person says he will sit only in that room, which by the way doesn't even exist yet, and wants the entire thing redone overnight. The other one has a hissy fit because he is moved to this side, and is now asking us to instal new lighting to brighten up his office. Meanwhile, Ash wants me to get his office soundproofed. And they want everything done ASAP!!'

She stopped short of cursing but I could see the thoughts flit through her mind. I didn't know what to say, so I just murmured my sympathies. It didn't seem like Ranjani wanted much else. She thanked me, and began barking directions at the workers. I assumed they were the ones meant to 'brighten' up that office, at the behest of Harsh. Ranjani was taking her revenge on Harsh with her choice of lighting. It fit the brief of being 'bright'. But it wasn't cheery or warm. It was the kind of stark white light that was characteristic of hospitals. Instead of improving the lighting in the office, it was making things much worse. I was not looking forward to having meetings with Harsh in that grim space.

I put the box down on the desk with my nameplate on it. As soon as I set up my laptop and opened it, another group of workers walked in and began making a racket as they started drilling and hammering. Even though the drilling was happening on the opposite end of the floor, the sound was bouncing off the walls and starting to give me a headache.

PING!

Glam Office Messenger Group Chat

[#Glaminions—9.45 a.m.] **Sitara:** How are we supposed to work with this infernal racket!

[#Glaminions—9.45 a.m.] **Aakash:** Nobody cares about us. This is just a giant pissing contest among the bosses.

[#Glaminions—9.46 a.m.] **Upasana:** I heard Harsh is getting new lights?

[#Glaminions—9.46 a.m.] **Sitara:** Yes, his office now looks like a hospital. OMG!

[#Glaminions—9.46 a.m.] **Shirin:** What?

[#Glaminions—9.46 a.m.] **Sitara:** Um, Harsh now has minigolf set up in his new office. I guess he's indicating he's now 'senior' leadership?

[#Glaminions—9.47 a.m.] **Shirin:** Then he should consider soundproofing his cabin. There's a bunch of admin guys complaining about having to replace the glass in Ash's cabin. That's the power move.

[#Glaminions—9.47 a.m.] **Upasana:** How will we know what's going on if we can't overhear Ash's conversations?

[#Glaminions—9.50 a.m.] Bhargavi: As if soundproofing could cut out the ruckus Ash makes when he's yelling at someone!

[#Glaminions—9.50 a.m.] Dhruv: Burn!

[#Glaminions—9.55 a.m.] Shirin: Fancy people with their fancy demands! <eyeroll>

[#Glaminions—9.55 a.m.] Upasana: I think Abhimanyu wants to be away from Ash so he can work in peace without Ash ambling in with his ideas.

[#Glaminions—9.56 a.m.] Aakash: He wants his desk to face the door so he can see whether his team is working or not. Micromanager!

[#Glaminions—10.00 a.m.] Bhargavi: Speaking of leadership whims, I think Ash's full name is Ashirwad.

[#Glaminions—10.00 a.m.] Sitara: As in atta?

[#Glaminions—10.00 a.m.] Bhargavi: Why not? I'd want to shorten my name if I was named after a brand of atta. Besides, his parents definitely thought he was a 'blessing'. That explains his sense of entitlement!

[#Glaminions—10.01 a.m.] Shirin: Our quest to get to Ash's real name can't possibly end with atta!

DRRR!

The sound of drilling got louder. There were workers in all three offices on the floor and it was like a drilling contest was on. Each group seemed determined to prove that they were working the hardest, and they chose to show it through the noise they were making. Ash's desire to soundproof his office was kicking off the biggest bout of sound pollution we'd ever witnessed. I decided it was time to head downstairs. Working at Starbucks would be so much more productive than attempting to work at my new desk.

Thanks yet again to that dick, Abhimanyu!

After the bizarre events of the office reorganization that had begun on Wednesday, I was cheered up by the fact that Thursday brought with it trivia night. This time, I was determined to win. I had spent the better part of the previous weekend trying to bring myself up to speed on the latest in the world of sports, so we weren't stuck relying on Krish.

Stalking Arjun's social media does not exactly qualify as 'sports research', the annoying little voice in my head piped up, sounding unmistakably like Kavya. I ignored it.

For once, I entered Last Call with Upasana and Shirin, having managed to leave office together. Kavya and Krish were already there and had got a head start on ordering. The table was loaded with pizzas and a pitcher of beer. They'd even made sure to get extra glasses. I suspected that was Kavya's idea, to make sure I didn't steal sips from her glass until I got my own.

'They're doing something different today,' Kavya said as we settled down. 'Only four teams are here so they're doing a knockout round. Two at a time, and the last one standing wins.'

I shrugged. The format didn't matter, as long as the end result was a win for Whiskeypedia. It sounded easier to win with only four teams in the running. Those vouchers would be ours! I had already chugged down the glass of beer I'd poured myself when I sat down, and now reached out to steal a sip from Kavya's glass. She gave me a dirty look.

I looked around the bar to size up our competition. I spotted a new team, filled with five nerdy looking men who looked like they had crawled out of bed and fallen into Last Call. They were already looking so tipsy that I was fairly certain we would beat them. Where were the other two teams?

'They're not here,' Kavya said, looking directly at me.

'Who?' I asked, the picture of innocence, as I reached for a slice of pizza.

'The Sherlock Homies. Do you really think I'll fall for your puppy dog eyes? They must be coming because George read out the list of teams and they were on it. We're against them in the finals if we beat Sotally Tober and they beat Yer a Quizzer Harry.'

'Well, we'll be beating everyone today,' I announced confidently. I gestured to the waiter. I couldn't keep stealing sips from everyone at the table. I needed more alcohol.

'Do you think he's on their team?' Shirin jumped in.

'Who?' I asked.

'Abhimanyu!'

I shrugged as though it didn't matter to me, even though I was wondering the very same thing. Kavya looked at me and raised an eyebrow. She was seeing right through my fake nonchalance.

'Maybe we should've asked him if he wanted to carpool with us,' Upasana said. 'That way, we could've found out if he was coming.'

'Hey, so which team is Sotally Tober?' I asked.

'That one,' Krish said, pointing at the raucous bunch of men in the corner. They were the ones I'd already sized up as too drunk to compete.

'Let's send them a pitcher and get them as drunk as their name suggests,' I grinned.

'That's called cheating,' Kavya said. 'And don't think I haven't noticed your not-so-subtle change of subject.'

I ignored her. 'I'm just being supportive of their will to chug.'

I looked towards the door and was promptly rewarded with a whack on my arm from Kavya. I rubbed my arm and glared at her.

'Stop looking for Abhimanyu,' she said.

'I'm not looking for him . . . '

'Of course,' she rolled her eyes at me. I stuck my tongue out at her in response. The rest of the table ignored us as they normally did when we regressed into this version of a playground squabble. George suddenly appeared at the front of the pub. He was in deep discussion with someone.

'Hey George,' Krish called out and began to do a little dance to get George's attention. He couldn't bear that George was focusing so intently on someone else, even if it was the person in charge of helping him with the mic and lights for trivia night.

Of course, just as Krish began his twerking routine, Abhimanyu walked in. I wanted to die of embarrassment. I slouched a little lower in my seat as my neck grew hot. Zaina, who was with Abhimanyu, shot me one of her death stares. She was definitely still mad at me over what had happened last week. They sat down at the table on our right. I took a deep breath and poured myself another glass of beer.

'Welcome to our newest edition of Thirsty Thursday,' George boomed, now that he was mic-ed up. He gave a little wink in our direction, which got Krish to stop twerking. 'We realized that the standard format of writing down your answers to the questions was resulting in folks getting some help from their friend Google . . . '

Krish booed loudly.

'And so, tonight, we decided to mix it up. We have four teams, and we'll do a knockout tournament. Each team sends one member up front for every round. You get two points for a correct answer. One point if you correctly answer a question that the other team passes to you. Let's begin with Whiskeypedia and Sotally Tober,' he said.

'What's the category?' Krish yelled out. Thank God someone was sober enough to ask that question. I had been so busy trying to evade Abhimanyu's gaze, I had completely missed considering that the category would decide whom we should send to this round.

'We're starting with a fun one—Art in Popular Culture,' George said. We stared at each other, trying to figure out who would be our best bet.

'Kavya,' I said immediately.

'But what if music is also a category?' she said, chewing her lip thoughtfully.

'Upasana can manage,' I replied. Art in Popular Culture sounded complicated and I couldn't keep our pop culture pundit out of this round.

'No,' Upasana jumped in. 'Don't you remember I thought that Beyonce and Jay Z collectively referred to themselves as Bey-Z.'

'That's a pretty good guess,' Shirin giggled. She served herself a slice of pizza.

'That's not the point. It took me weeks to live it down!'

'Longer than Sitara and toilet rolls?' Kavya said with a cheeky grin.

'Fine,' I said hurriedly. 'Kavya, you go.'

Kavya walked up to the front where George was standing. He had gone through a lot of trouble. There was a mini stage at the front of the bar with two chairs facing each other. He'd also managed to get a floor lamp to create a makeshift spotlight that would shine directly over the competitors' heads. I think he was trying to create an atmosphere of drama. However, it looked less like a quiz and more like an interrogation room. Kavya and one of the guys from Sotally Tober, who looked uncannily like Harry Potter, with his messy hair and round glasses, took their seats. I wondered if the guy realized he was in the wrong team. With his looks, he should've been in Yer a Quizzer, who had all come decked head to toe in Harry Potter gear and were busy waving their wands at the stage.

'Let the games begin,' George said and walked over to the centre of the stage. He gestured to the projector behind him as a picture came up.

'Name this painting,' he said pointing at an image of Phoebe from *Friends* holding up a painting of a truly hideous looking creature that appeared to be escaping from the frame.

'GLYNNIS,' Kavya yelled. Of course, she knew which of the two, Gladys and Glynnis, this picture was. She watched *Friends* on repeat endlessly and could tell you what any character would say next before they did so on the screen.

'But you didn't press the buzzer,' George said. 'So, the question passes. Do you have an answer?' he asked the Potter lookalike.

'Glynnis,' he replied, looking extremely pleased with himself.

We groaned. There was no way he would've got if Kavya hadn't given it away. He had looked stunned until she'd opened her mouth.

Kavya mouthed 'sorry' to us.

'Since 1970, Art Deco posters are used not only in advertising, but also for self-expression and decor. In the late twentieth century, print-based motivational posters were essential office decor in the West. Name the popular character from the award-winning 2005 sitcom who featured these posters on his walls,' George said, moving to the next question.

The Potter lookalike buzzed. George looked at him.

'Um . . .' he tried stalling for time.

'If he doesn't have the answer, it has to pass,' Kavya jumped in, wanting to regain the points she'd lost.

'She's right,' George said. 'What's your answer?'

'Barney Stinson from *How I Met Your Mother*.'

'Right answer,' said George, as we cheered.

'Next question: How did Sleeping Lady with Black Vase by Hungarian artist Robert Bereny become famous in 2009?'

BZZZZZ! Kavya buzzed as the Potter lookalike looked completely lost.

'It was used as a prop in *Stuart Little*,' she announced confidently.

'That can't be right,' her opponent burst out. His team heckled and yelled.

'Why not let George tell you if I'm right or not?' Kavya said. She leaned back in her chair and crossed her legs, looking quite regal.

'She's right,' George chimed in, looking impressed that she knew this obscure fact.

As the round went on, Kavya decimated the other team with her answers and witty quips. The Potter lookalike looked more and more out of his depth with every question. He kept looking at the clock as though he was counting down to the time when his humiliation would end. George, on the other hand, looked like he was questioning whether he'd put in enough thought behind the questions. Kavya walked off the stage amidst much applause. Before she got back to the table, someone bought her a beer as a thank you for her entertaining performance.

The next round was Literature. I chugged an entire glass of water to clear my head before I went up. I sat on the stage, squirming at the sharp light that was almost blinding me. I blinked a few times to clear my vision. Damn George and his weird set-up. My opponent, another member of Sotally Tober, stepped on stage—a tall, lanky guy with a pretentious goatee. He seemed a little more sober than the one Kavya had trounced. He slouched in his chair with an arrogant expression on his face.

They sent a girl, he mouthed at the rest of his all-male team. Ah, these guys believed women couldn't quiz. You'd think that after Kavya's performance, they would change their assessment of women and trivia. Clearly, he needed to have his behind handed to him to truly learn that lesson. I couldn't wait to show him just how well 'girls' could quiz.

'Where does Emma Corrigan work,' George asked, looking mighty pleased with himself.

BUZZ!

'Panther Cola,' I said. My team whooped. I swear, I saw George wink at me. He probably didn't appreciate Mr Tober's stance any more than I did and had purposely begun with a question featuring the lead from a Sophie Kinsella novel.

'This 2003 mystery thriller opens with a murder at the Louvre . . .'

BUZZ!

'*The Da Vinci Code*,' I announced confidently, earning my team two more points. I couldn't believe that George had included such an easy question. This was more a game of quick reflexes than trivia.

'What's the longest book ever written?'

BUZZ!

'Marcel Proust's *Remembrance of Things Past*,' said Mr Tober. He looked mighty confident.

But I knew he was wrong. I jumped in immediately. 'George, you asked for the longest book, not novel. The longest book is the Bible,' I argued.

'Quiz master rules. I give him the points,' George said.

I pouted. My team booed.

'No heckling. That won't get you any points,' George said.

'Next question: This children's book only has fifty words in it, because the author took on a dare from the editor that it would be impossible to write a book in only fifty words.'

BUZZ!

'*Green Eggs and Ham*,' I said. This was one of my favourite children's books of all time.

'Would you eat them in a box? Would you eat them with a fox?' my team yelled from the audience, quoting the book for everyone's entertainment.

'And for a bonus point, the author . . . ,' George began.

'Dr Seuss,' I quickly jumped in before Mr Tober could process what was going on.

The quiz went on and our teams were neck to neck. I was starting to feel the pressure. It wasn't just about winning any more, it was about beating this arrogant ass. Every time he got a correct answer, he smirked and stroked that ridiculous goatee. I wasn't leaving here without beating him fair and square. I glared at him and pushed my hair away from my eyes.

'You can visit the author's family home in Concord, Massachusetts. She reluctantly moved from Boston in 1868 to write this book. Name the book.'

BUZZ!

I pressed the buzzer so hard, I almost fell out of my chair.

'*Little Women*,' I said confidently. I have been a fan of Louisa May Alcott and the March girls since I was a girl. I'd visited the family home when I'd last travelled to the US, annoying my family who didn't want to be dragged to see some 'random old house' as my mother succinctly put it.

George nodded and said. 'And for a bonus point, which character in the book is actually the author herself, as evidenced by the fact that she writes the book eventually . . .'

BUZZ!

'Jo,' shouted Mr Sotally Tober.

'Correct,' said George. 'Your teams are tied.'

I stared at him in shock. He didn't just say that, did he? My team screamed in frustration.

'That's wrong,' I burst out. 'That's from a scene in the movie. There was *nothing* in the original book to suggest that Jo wrote *Little Women*!'

'My decision is final,' George began, but he was cut off as Krish jumped on stage waving a phone in his face. I found Google results to back up my claim. George kept shaking his head, leading to more of my team members clambering on to the stage.

'You're not paying attention to the research,' Kavya insisted as she stood in front of George with her hands on her hips.

George looked shaken to see a group of four tipsy trivia enthusiasts now crowding his stage. He took a few steps back, to put some space between him and Kavya. Unfortunately, he didn't notice the wire connecting the floor lamp to the power outlet and tripped on it. He fell directly on the lap of a woman sitting in the first row, who looked completely scandalized, as the lights went out in perfect synchronicity.

'Get away,' she yelled as she pushed George off her lap and on to the floor.

Soon, there was a mini riot as people argued on which answer was correct. The argument escalated, and suddenly, pitchers were being upended on the floor. A server came running to clean the mess. He was still holding a tray in his hand. He slipped on the puddle of beer, sending bowls of peanut masala flying into the air. There was a lot of shouting, some colourful cuss words and a whole lot of commotion. Within minutes, the entire lot of us, including George, was politely escorted outside and trivia night ended rather unceremoniously with no real winners. As everyone began to scatter in different directions to head home, I continued to defend myself rather hotly.

'It's the principle of the thing. That wasn't even a book question. And it was the second time that he got his trivia wrong . . . ' I ranted as Kavya looked at her phone, trying to find us an Uber.

Something warm trickled down my forehead. I mopped it with my hand and realized I had beer in my hair. Oh well, it would add shine. I began shaking my head to get rid of it, and in the process ended up sending some errant peanuts that were trapped in my thick curls flying out.

'Oh,' I heard someone exclaim from the side.

Whoops! I may have mauled someone with the peanuts. I turned towards the person so I could apologize.

'How is that every time we meet here you send refreshments flying my way?' I heard him say.

My brain froze.

Of course, it was just my luck. There he was, grinning at me with that familiar half-smirk on his face, and some peanuts in his hand.

Abhimanyu. How the man managed to always be around at my most embarrassing moments, I didn't know.

He flicked the peanuts into a dustbin by the side of the road and turned his back towards me again.

With that, any hope of getting into the good books of Glam's marketing head went right out the window.

7

The Zodiac Timekeeper Says the Clock Is Ticking

'#MeTooGlam', Dhruv announced with a wide grin, looking extremely pleased with himself.

We were in our weekly 'Innovation Exchange' meeting, Ash's brainchild to get the team to come up with new ideas. One of the rules of this meeting was that we were supposed to 'diverge', which was corporate speak for telling us we weren't allowed to shoot down ideas. This generally meant that we had to maintain a straight face, irrespective of how absurd an idea may seem.

Thanks to this ridiculous guideline, I was forced to stifle a groan when Dhruv mimed a hashtag with his hands. *This* was his big idea? A marketing campaign where beauty influencers would give makeovers to women who had spoken out against harassment? He claimed it would inspire our customers to be more comfortable in their own skin.

'#JumpOnTheBandwagon,' I saw Upasana scribble in her notebook.

She'd doodled Dhruv looking smug and happy while riding a wagon. I tried not to laugh. Upasana's doodles were classic and the only thing that helped us survive many of our long, meandering meetings that were a case of death by PowerPoint. This meeting was filled with people trying to prove how their projects would change the world. I hoped that Ash would see through Dhruv's ridiculous plan.

'#MeTooGlam. It's got quite the ring to it,' Ash said with a smile. My heart began to beat so fast, the valves made a 'kerplunking' sound. 'Let's roll this out!'

Oh, crap.

I couldn't believe that Ash was in such a benevolent mood. Dhruv had chosen the perfect meeting. Ash wouldn't refute anything while he was preaching to the rest of us that we needed to be open to new ideas. Dhruv's idea was moving forward so smoothly. Meanwhile, Abhimanyu was refusing to even listen to me! It was infuriating. I tuned out wondering how I would manage to get ahead of Dhruv.

Next, Aakash launched into a long spiel about some new way to improve the payment experience on Glam. I kept nodding to indicate I was paying attention, all the while weighing my options and wondering how to corner Abhimanyu. Aakash tended to go on once he started on a pitch, so it gave me time to drift off completely. Suddenly, my attention was yanked back into the room by Upasana stifling a giggle.

'. . . this is a must-must project,' Aakash was saying.

Must-must? Was he now coining new terms to make people take him seriously?

My eyes were drawn towards Upasana's sketchbook. True to form, she had now doodled a caricature of Aakash dressed in Akshay Kumar's outfit from *Mohra*, with the black turban-like headgear and sunglasses. He was holding a mic and singing '*yeh idea bada hai must-must*'. I bit my lip to stop laughing as she quietly began humming the tune of '*tu cheez badi hai mast mast*'. I was so focused on her doodle, I stopped paying attention again. I was rudely jolted out of my thoughts when Harsh spoke.

'Sitara, why don't you go next?'

What? I stared at Harsh, wondering what on earth he wanted me to share. I shook my head trying to get the '*pa, ni, sa*' refrain from the song out so I could focus on Harsh.

'Sitara,' he repeated. 'Share your idea.'

'Sitara can't share her idea,' Abhimanyu cut in. 'The beauty box concept isn't ready.'

'Actually . . .' I began, all ready to defend myself now that Abhimanyu had questioned my idea. I may not have been prepared, but I wasn't going to lose a chance to bring it up with Ash when he was in his 'all ideas are welcome' mode.

Ash frowned at Harsh and Abhimanyu who were staring at each other like two boxers in a ring. He cut in, 'Harsh, Abhimanyu, Sitara, I'd like to talk this through with the three of you. The rest can leave.'

The team shuffled out of the room as soon as the words were out of his mouth. I saw the entire group head towards the elevator and knew they were going to get their post-meeting coffee. Meanwhile, I was stuck in this freezing conference room with two of my least favourite people and Ash.

Harsh stood up, wanting to take control as was his typical style when Ash was around. He loved to act like he was in charge. The minute Ash left the room, Harsh would immediately tune out since he was no longer trying to parade his 'excellence'.

'So,' Harsh said, 'if the concept isn't ready, we should start by taking a step back.'

I cringed. 'Taking a step back' was one of those typical corporate moves that Harsh adored. He liked to pretend that we were zooming out and looking at a problem from all perspectives, but all it meant was that he would write a bunch of random keywords on the whiteboard and take credit for anything that came out of anyone's mouth.

True to form, he went to the whiteboard and began writing in block letters—CORE CUSTOMER PERSONA. I groaned internally. Just last month, we had paid an external consulting firm a bomb and they had spent weeks telling us about Glam's 'core customer persona'—a woman in her mid to late twenties named Tania who worked at a corporate much like ours.

The concept had struck Ash and ever since he kept asking us, 'What would Tania do?' Tania was now the mythical beast that roamed the halls, trying to get us to guess her whims and fancies.

As soon as Harsh wrote 'What would Tania want' on the board, Ash nodded sagely. This encouraged Harsh. He began listing out Tania's likes and dislikes, needs and wants and so on. I resisted the urge to ask him why he was listing this information out when all of it was listed out in a giant poster that was stuck on one of the walls of the conference room. The only thing the whiteboard was lacking was the photo of Tania herself, which was also on the poster in its grinning, stock photo glory.

'The thing is, Sitara,' Harsh said, turning around and looking pointedly at me, 'you need to channel Tania. Think like a working professional, a woman around twenty-five to thirty years of age.'

Ash nodded in agreement as if this were the wisest thing anyone had ever said. I bit my tongue to stop myself from reminding them that I literally *was* Tania. I was the same age, had the same demographic profile and was the real-life embodiment of that poster minus the toothy grin and shiny hair.

I wondered how I'd got myself in this mess. Ash's tacit approval seemed to embolden Harsh even more.

'I think the key question here is what women *really* want,' Harsh announced.

Commissioning research at Glam isn't going to solve your dating issues, I thought ungraciously.

Harsh seemed to think that working on a woman-centric category would somehow make him magically attractive to women. I had to put a stop to this nonsense before this group of men told me what women like me wanted out of our app.

'Harsh, a beauty box is exactly what the customer wants! It'll help them discover new brands they can add to their beauty routine,' I jumped in to stop the conversation from disintegrating.

'I don't think you've got into the mind, heart and soul of this customer,' he dismissed me. 'This is a woman who's moved away from home and lives alone in a big city like Bangalore. We need to understand what her key need is. For instance, if she were taking a cab, her key need would be safety.'

I wanted to scream out in frustration. We had already identified all our key customer needs with our quarterly research, which Upasana had presented to both of them barely a month ago. I wondered if Harsh appreciated the irony of what he was saying.

'I think we need more research,' Ash announced. He leaned forward and helped himself to a cookie from a plate that was kept in the centre of the table.

'We already have all the research,' I tried again. 'Our last insight study clearly suggested that customers are looking to discover new brands.'

'She's right,' Abhimanyu said. I'd almost forgotten he was in the room, because he'd been so silent. 'We have the research but we need to think beyond the same old ideas.'

He looked at me meaningfully. I bristled. Was he saying my beauty box idea was old?

'We need to consider the impact the project needs to deliver,' I said. I stared, willing him to back down.

'OK. We have twenty minutes left,' Abhimanyu said. 'Let's hear your idea.'

Whoops. I wasn't expecting him to put me on the spot! I chewed on my fingernail, wondering how I could buy time.

'As we've discussed, our objective is to drive new user growth,' I began. Abhimanyu leaned forward, picked up a cookie and stared at it as if it were the one talking.

'We need an idea that will bring in users to Glam and keep them hooked so they wouldn't want to shop anywhere else.'

Harsh smiled encouragingly. Ash began making circling motions with his forefinger in the air, signalling me to get on. Apparently, Harsh had used up all our time for 'stepping back', 'setting context' and going on about the fictional Tania. I would now have to come up with solid ideas because Ash was impatient.

'So one idea I'd like to discuss is . . . ' I looked at Abhimanyu and saw that he was giving me a blank stare. He wasn't moving, just staring directly at me with a poker face. 'One idea would be that we create a "Shazam" for make-up. You scan a photo and it pulls up the product.'

Abhimanyu made a face. 'Isn't this an extension of your lipstick shade picker? What else?'

So much for 'divergent thinking'!

I looked at Harsh and Ash. Neither of them was willing to comment now that Abhimanyu had summarily dismissed the idea. I had to buy time and come up with ideas to save face. I took a deep breath and opened my notebook pretending to evaluate from the promising list of potential ideas I had written down, when in reality I was staring at the grocery list Kavya had given me that morning.

'We could create a universal shopping cart. Let customers add and purchase products from any app, not just ours . . .'

Ash choked on his coffee, and quite rightly so. Even someone with the most 'open-minded' approach to ideas couldn't digest sending customers to shop on someone else's app.

'Next,' Harsh snapped.

'I still think we should explore the idea of a beauty box,' I began.

Immediately, Abhimanyu fixed me with a cool glare. 'Do you have any other ideas? We've agreed the beauty box isn't worth pursuing. And your other ideas are just as bad.' He looked down pointedly at his watch. I realized we had only ten minutes to go.

I looked at my notebook again, hoping an idea would magically emerge out of the shopping list. All I could see was dosa batter, eggs, kasoori methi and curd. Unless my idea involved creating a face pack with those ingredients that would become the next beauty trend, I needed to move on fast. I took a quick flip through my notebook, hoping to find something else—there were a ton of scribbles from my doomed attempts to come up with ideas and multiple doodles by Upasana as we came up with combined jokes. A cold sense of dread gripped me. I could not afford to let them think I didn't have a plan. Dhruv was ahead and I was very close to making a fool of myself.

'Sitara,' Harsh's voice cut through the tension like a knife slicing through a slab of butter.

'OK, so the beauty box in itself will not drive someone to become a regular customer. But what if we create a subscription programme?' I blurted out.

Abhimanyu leaned forward and raised his eyebrows.

I ploughed on. 'We can price it so customers pay a subscription fee, monthly or yearly to be part of this programme. In return, they get a range of benefits—samples of new products, additional discounts, faster delivery . . .'

'Free makeovers, maybe a personal stylist . . .' Abhimanyu jumped in, looking mildly interested.

I held my breath. Was the man finally coming around?

'We can come up with a list of benefits. The key is to ensure that you can't easily put a price on them so the customer always feels that our programme is giving them more value than the price they've paid,' I said.

'So this is basically Glam Prime,' Abhimanyu smiled.

Harsh gasped. It was difficult to figure out if it was in joy or despair.

Ash sat up straight and grinned. 'Now that's the kind of concept we need.'

Immediately, Harsh rearranged his expression to look interested and involved. With Ash sounding interested, he knew what reaction he needed to give me. The man had no mind of his own! I struggled to stop rolling my eyes.

'It's a good concept, but it needs work,' Abhimanyu cut in, ever ready to bring my hopes crashing. 'I'll need details to decide if we should pursue this. Put together a deck and let's review it.'

'Oh, don't worry about the roadmap. I've evaluated tech feasibility with Sridhar and we can do it . . . ' Harsh said grandly.

I stared at him. How did he evaluate the feasibility of an idea I pulled out of my backside barely five minutes ago? He could go to any extent to pretend he was calling the shots!

'Even so, we need a detailed plan,' Ash said. 'Ms Srinivasan, you have your work cut out. I look forward to seeing what comes out of this.'

With that, he stood up and swept out of the room. Abhimanyu followed.

'Good work,' said Harsh, his chest puffed out like a peacock. 'A subscription programme. All you need is a name with a good ring to it! That's all these marketing folks look for. Come up with a good hashtag too.'

'Thanks, Harsh,' I said through gritted teeth. I wasn't ready to forgive him for putting me under so much pressure by bringing up the beauty box in the team meeting. It had ended well now that I'd hit upon an idea that Abhimanyu seemed mildly interested in, but it could easily have backfired.

'Don't worry about approvals,' he continued. 'I can intervene if you need it.'

Yeah, right, I thought. *Try 'intervening' with Abhimanyu, I'd like to see how that ends!*

I was going to do this myself. After all, this could be my ticket to the promotion.

8

The Full Moon Is a Tough Cookie

Every time I stepped into the bylanes of Malleshwaram, it felt like I had stepped away from real life into the pages of an R.K. Narayan novel. I was walking to my sister's place after being dropped off nearby just so that I could enjoy the Saturday morning weather. I studiously avoided making eye contact with the long line of people bingeing on vadas and pongal from Veena Stores as my stomach growled rebelliously. Sahana would murder me if I said I had already eaten.

I wondered how our roles had got reversed over time. As teenagers, Sahana had been the rebellious one while I was the strait-laced one. She'd got tattoos (including a misguided butterfly on her hip), stolen alcohol from our father's stash, had an inappropriate boyfriend and barely attended college. She'd even got a tongue piercing which lasted an entire week before my mother noticed and promptly made her get rid of it. And yet, here I was outside her two-storeyed house in a residential street in Malleshwaram. The house was next to a temple, a school and even a yoga class that took place in a refurbished cowshed. She had managed to achieve all my mother's dreams in one fell swoop—a husband, a job in an 'acceptable' profession and two children. Meanwhile, I was still floundering around with nothing to show for myself.

I went up to the front door and realized it was slightly open. As soon as I pushed it open, Ram, Sahana's husband, materialized in the doorway. He gestured that I should walk inside silently, by pressing his fingers to his lips and looking mildly panicked.

'The baby is asleep,' he whispered hoarsely, as I stepped in and removed my chappals. I adjusted my dupatta, thanking my lucky stars that I hadn't worn the jhumkas with bells on them. They wouldn't have been received favourably. 'Sahana is with Amma* and Appa** in the living room.'

Ugh! I thought I was early, but of course, they had been expecting me to show up earlier. My parents had taken the Shatabdi from Chennai the previous evening. Sahana had suggested I should come for breakfast, but I had convinced her I would stop by for lunch. I was sure that my father would hold me responsible for delaying his meal, and I would have to endure a lecture on discipline.

---

* Mother in Tamil
** Father in Tamil

'Look who's finally here,' my father said as soon as I entered. He peered at his watch and added, 'you're just in time for lunch.'

'Actually, I'm early,' I said, as I leaned forward to give him a hug, followed by my mother. Now that he'd pointed out I was late, he disappeared behind the pages of *The Hindu*.

'We said we'd eat at twelve thirty,' Sahana said. 'I thought you'd be here an hour earlier.' I didn't allow the polite smile on my face to fade, even though my cheeks were beginning to hurt.

'Did you really want my help with cooking?' I asked, as I entered the kitchen and deposited the box of kaju katli I'd bought on her pristine kitchen counter. I wasn't known for my cooking skills and besides, my sister hated having anyone else cook in her kitchen.

Sahana frowned, as she tucked her curly hair back into the severe bun she wore. The time she'd spent in a hot kitchen had left it completely frizzy and there was a halo of stray curls sticking up around her head. I wondered if this was a good time to suggest she used the bottle of curl cream I'd given her two months ago. Just as I was wondering why I was putting myself through this, Inaya, my kooky niece and the reason I couldn't stay away, stuck her head into the kitchen and gave me a wide grin.

'Chithi,'* she exclaimed, as she rushed at me and enveloped me in a hug. 'I thought you said you couldn't come when I messaged you!'

---

* Aunt, mother's younger sister in Tamil

'I said I *might* not come,' I corrected her.

Her message was the reason I had decided to show up. After all, how hard-hearted would I be to refuse an invite accompanied by a GIF of Fluttershy with a puppy-dog expression saying 'PLEASSSSEEEE'.

I picked up a dish of sambhar and followed Sahana out of the door as she began setting the table.

'It took us a long time to reach last night,' my mother said. 'There was a terrible jam right outside the railway station. I told Appa we should take the metro, but of course, he didn't agree.'

My mother loved public transport and would do anything to take the metro instead of relying on a cab or any other mode of transport. Unfortunately for her, my father wasn't a fan of switching metro lines or even walking to the metro station, especially when luggage was involved. Amma joined Sahana and me in the dining room and pulled out a chair, with my father and Ram following close behind.

'*Kuzhanthai innuma thoongarthu?*'* my mother asked Sahana. She was whispering in the sing-song lilt that people used when they were talking to babies, even though the baby wasn't even in the room.

'Yes, Patti,** he's asleep,' said Inaya. 'I told Amma I also want to take a nap, but I'm not allowed. *He* can sleep the entire day but I have to do homework, and go to art

---

* Is the baby still asleep?
** Grandmother in Tamil

class and . . . ' she trailed off, frowning at the injustice. She scraped her chair over to sit near me with a loud screech, causing both her parents to glare at her. Ram seemed to hold his breath as he stared at the baby monitor by his plate. Thankfully, the baby didn't stir.

'*Nee ellam** big girl,' my mother informed Inaya. 'Chak is a baby, and they need to sleep.'

Chak. One year ago, Sahana had her second child and decided to give him half a name. Apparently, it was the rage to give your child an 'international' name and not a 'boring, old-fashioned one that sounds like they're named after someone's grandmother'. Except, my sister had picked a name off her favourite parenting app without realizing it was an abbreviation. I tried telling her that 'Chak' wasn't a name, that at the very least it would be 'Chakrapani' or 'Chakravarthy' but she wouldn't listen. She said it meant 'brilliance', according to the app. I refrained from reminding her that the same app had convinced her to name her daughter 'Taana' because it claimed the word meant 'encourage' without any indication of the provenance of this weird interpretation. I had argued with her for months that 'Taana' was only used in the negative sense, and meant 'taunt' in Hindi. Unfortunately for Chak, I wasn't as successful. I even tried telling her that to be truly international, she should consider 'Chuck', which was also an abbreviation, but you try telling a post-partum mother anything without getting your head bitten off.

---

* 'You are' in Tamil

I hoped she'd begun an SIP for the therapy he'd have to undergo to get over being teased. The Brilliant Boy with Half a Name.

'Did you know Sitara is up for a promotion?' Sahana said, as she entered with freshly made curd. Of course, she served home-made curd in a traditional pot. Meanwhile, I was lucky if I remembered to buy a packet. The last time my parents visited, I didn't have any curd and the store was shut. After that, we'd come to a tacit understanding that we would meet at Sahana's house whenever they visited Bangalore.

'All this focus on work, but no thought about her future otherwise,' sniffed my mother, shaking her head in disapproval.

'How many people will you manage if you're promoted?' my father asked, finally putting away his paper and looking at me with some interest.

We began passing the dishes.

'I've told you this before, Appa. We have a flat structure. I won't have any people reporting into me yet. I need to be more senior for that.'

'So you do all this work for nothing? Back in my day, one didn't stay at a job for years without having people to manage. . . . ' my father launched into one of his stories about how companies used to function while I tuned out. In my father's world, the title 'manager' meant that you managed people. I had given up trying to explain my job or my title. As far as my parents were concerned, I was a glorified beautician, and if I had a team they'd probably equate me with the manager of a salon!

'It's not for nothing,' I said. 'A promotion is a step in the right direction.'

'You need job security,' he said. 'These new-fangled start-ups don't know what they're doing. See, even today, there's news about that "Blluee" app shutting shop. You should've taken the job at P&G,' he said. My father had been devastated when I had turned down the chance to join P&G as a management trainee six years ago. He couldn't believe I would pick some unheard-of start-up over one of the world's leading consumer goods firms. He had been predicting Glam's demise ever since.

'I wouldn't have managed to do the kind of work I get here,' I said.

'So what? Everyone knows P&G, it's stable. Who has heard of Glam?' he asked.

I opened my mouth to defend myself. But my mother jumped in, every ready to defuse yet another father-daughter blow-up in her own inimitable style.

'So, where's this kurta from? I hope you didn't get it from one of those Fab India, Anokhi type places. Those are quite costly.'

And off we'd jumped from the frying pan directly into the fire. I took a deep breath. It was going to be a long lunch.

★★

Thankfully, we managed to get through the rest of the meal without further disagreements. Everyone focused on the food—my father on his favourite sambhar rice and potato fry, Ram on the kaju katli I'd brought, and me on Sahana's excellent lemon rasam. Of course, the tentative peace was too good to last.

'That Arjun's proposal keeps playing on TV,' my mother said as she picked up another katli from the box. I tried to look nonchalant.

'I don't think there's anyone left in the country who missed it! He must've spent a fortune on that ring,' said Sahana, ever the chartered accountant.

'This is what happens if you only focus on work. That could've been *you*,' my mother said accusingly. Yet again, I wondered what had ever possessed me to date my mother's best friend's son. Even if he was the cutest guy in college, I should've looked the other way. My parents didn't know about his commitment phobia and I was routinely blamed for our break-up.

'You should've stuck it out. If that had been you, Ram and I could've been in a VIP box watching a match live tomorrow,' my father said.

'I'm so sorry I ruined *your* life,' I said pointedly. I stared at my plate, wishing it would open up a portal into another world so I could escape this conversation.

'Inaya, show Chithi your project for the weekend,' my sister jumped in, giving me a way to leave the room. I mentally thanked her. Inaya immediately jumped up and grabbed my hand. She began pulling me towards her room.

'It's a secret project,' she whispered to me in a conspiratorial tone. 'I don't show it to just about anyone.'

'Aw, thanks for showing me,' I said, as we left the room.

'Amma and Appa usually make me go away if they're talking about me,' said Inaya. 'Or if they're talking about something they don't want me to tell people. Amma says I have no filter. What's a filter, Chithi?'

I delicately sidestepped her question, 'They're probably talking about me today, so you don't have to worry.'

She opened the door to her room. I gasped. I blinked a few times to make sure that I wasn't seeing things. Inaya's room was normally ultra-neat and organized. Right now, it looked like a tornado had hit it. I wondered if she'd suddenly decided to play Dorothy in the *Wizard of Oz*. That would explain the state of her room, as well as the baggy overalls she was wearing. There were mountains of clothes, stationery, books, toys, and other odds and ends piled up in the room.

'Today is Kondo-day,' Inaya announced as she walked right into the centre of the mess.

'What day?' I asked.

'Not what, Chithi, who! Marie Kondo. You know about the KonMari method, don't you?'

'Um, how do you know about Marie Kondo?' Our family had an obsessive cleaning trait, but I hadn't expected it to percolate in this manner into my ten-year-old niece.

'I've read the book,' she said matter-of-factly. 'All you have to do is pick up an item and model it. I will decide if it sparks joy or not. If it does, I'll keep it. If it doesn't, I'll give it away.'

'Hmm, so things that don't spark joy are given away,' I said. I spied a giant garbage bag in the corner that was presumably being used to collect these objects.

'Yes, when we get rid of things that don't spark joy, we find inner peace and happiness,' she replied seriously. I wondered if it was time to introduce her to the new and improved Ash and his guru. She probably could give them a few tips.

'In that case, how do I get rid of your Thatha*-Patti?' I asked. 'They're not sparking any joy!'

'Chithi,' Inaya squealed with laughter. 'It's not for *people*! I said things. You're being mean.' I took my place in her assembly line and began passing her things. As we sorted through her stuff, we continued talking.

'I'm still not used to being ten. I feel so old,' she said as she passed me some books that she claimed she was too old for.

'Well, you'll always be my baby niece, no matter how old you are,' I replied.

'That's because you're VERY old,' she said brutally. 'Appa says you will soon be so old that no one will want to marry you.'

And there was that filter Sahana had told her about. *Thanks a lot for the vote of confidence, Ram!* I thought.

---

* Grandfather in Tamil

'Marriage isn't everything,' I told her. 'It's not even the most important thing in life. There are other things that are more important.' I didn't want Inaya to grow up thinking that the sole purpose of her existence was to get married and have babies.

'I know. I'm going to get married though. To Rohan, from my class,' she announced. 'He's so cute. All the girls have a crush on him.'

I tried to keep a straight face.

'Looks aren't everything, Inaya.' I hoped to teach her not to fall for the best-looking guy in class, unlike myself. The best-looking ones weren't always the smartest and I had learnt that the hard way after being routinely bored out of my brains.

'But Rohan is the best at maths and he can do the fastest cartwheels in school. And he always exchanges his lunch with me if I have something boring,' she defended her crush. I couldn't really argue with her logic. I had dated people with fewer accomplishments.

'Anyway, Chithi, you should add lavender oil to your bath water,' she said, producing a bottle from a mountain of essential oils that she'd already moved to her 'spark joy' pile. 'It reduces stress and makes you smell good.'

'Are you trying to tell me I smell bad?' I asked as she giggled.

'NO! It's for stress. Thatha said you never call, and then Amma said it's because you are always stressed about work.' My niece believed there was an essential oil to solve each and every one of life's problems. She handed me the bottle. I took it, knowing that she didn't give these away lightly.

'Also, Chithi, if you're becoming a sprinter, then you need to use clove oil to relax your muscles. Especially since you're really old. Your knees will hurt with so much running,' she continued.

Sprinter? I was vehemently against running of any kind so I wondered where she'd got that from.

'Um, Inaya, who told you I'm becoming a sprinter,' I said.

At first, she didn't reply. I willed her to spill the beans.

Slowly, she said, 'I heard Appa telling Amma. They don't know that sometimes I go out into the landing and spy on them when they're talking to each other.' She looked extremely pleased with herself.

And then the penny dropped.

'Are you sure they said sprinter and not spinster?' I asked her.

'Maybe,' she said dismissively. 'I wonder if there's an essential oil to help spinsters? I'll find it for you!'

For the second time that day, I hoped that my sister was investing in SIPs for her child's future therapy needs. Even if Chak survived the trauma of his name, Inaya most definitely would need to get over the impact of all the 'lessons' she was imbibing from her incessant eavesdropping.

★★

My parents left right after lunch, much to Sahana's dismay and my joy at having successfully evaded Amma's attempts at a pranic healing session. They said they had a bhajan to attend at their friend Vrinda Aunty's house. Amma insisted it would be impossible for Vrinda Aunty to manage all the arrangements. Appa said that he didn't want food to go waste as they'd already confirmed their attendance. Personally, I knew he was looking forward to dinner as Vrinda Aunty was a fantastic cook who never skimped on ghee, sugar and everything else that my health-conscious mother rationed. I didn't know why Sahana was bothered—our parents were staying at her place for two weeks, so she would have a lot of time with them. I had originally planned to leave after my evening cup of chai, but she convinced me to extend my visit. Before I knew it, it was well past 9 p.m. and Inaya was getting ready for bed.

'Stay over,' said Sahana. 'I'll set up the sofa bed for you. Amma Appa are also on their way back, we can spend the day together tomorrow.'

'Yes, stay,' said Ram half-heartedly while he turned the page on the book he was reading.

'No, I have an early start tomorrow. It's much easier to get back tonight,' I said.

'Ram, drop her. It's really late,' Sahana said. Ram slowly stood up and reluctantly began rifling through the key holder near the entrance for his car keys.

'No, don't worry,' I cut in. 'I'll share my ride with you so you'll know I got home safe.' I picked up my bag and looked inside it to make sure my phone was there. I needed to check my messages. I shuddered to think of how many e-mails I would've missed today.

'Remember that Appa's surprise birthday dinner is next weekend,' Sahana said as she gave me a hug.

I didn't reply.

'You *cannot* skip it,' she said, giving me a look.

'Nothing will stop me from attending,' I lied.

She raised an eyebrow at me. As always, she could see right through my stories. I avoided her gaze and looked down at my phone. Hallelujah! My cab was right outside the door.

'I have to go, Sahana! I'll see you soon,' I said.

'Text me once you're in your apartment,' she replied. 'And don't you dare come up with a last-minute excuse to skip the party!'

As if I would *ever* do such a thing.

9

Surprising News Is on Its Way

I couldn't believe this was how I was spending a 'productive' Wednesday evening. If I had a choice, I would have been working on my new subscription programme, but instead I was stuck at this ridiculous workshop. My only consolation was that Dhruv was also stuck, so he wasn't getting ahead either.

It turned out that the giant questionnaires that we'd all filled indicated that the entire team was under enormous stress, something that anyone with eyes could've figured out without putting us through the stress of filling it! Thanks to that, day 1 was called 'Centre of Calm'. So far, we'd been through an intense round of yoga and were now going to be part of a meditation routine that would help us de-stress. I wondered if Ash realized that the FOMO of not being able to check our phones for almost three hours was causing more stress than all the yoga and meditation could effectively address. But apparently, this was going to help us become more 'centred'. I wriggled from my position on the yoga mat trying not to wince as I got a whiff of what was likely someone else's dried up sweat.

'Relax and relaaaax. Totally relax your whole booodddyyy,' the guru sang.

I struggled to stifle my giggles. From the muffled noises I heard by my side, everyone else was having the same problem. I wondered how Ash managed to stay at a two-week-long retreat run by this guru. The man definitely dressed the part, with bright orange robes and a long, scraggly beard. However, I wasn't convinced he was an actual enlightened soul, what with his unerring habit of referring to himself in the third person as well as his demands that we show our respect to him. He had yelled at us at the start of the session because we didn't stand up when he first entered the room. As he droned on, I tried to focus on my breath. Unfortunately, I was perennially distracted by the pins and needles on the underside of my foot. If only I hadn't listened to the instruction to put my weight on my feet while doing the Downward Dog!

'Only Ash would find a guru who looks completely Indian but has a Texan twang,' Upasana muttered under her breath.

'He's an NRI,' Shirin whispered back. 'He went to business school with Ash and then gave up his corporate career to become a corporate guru.'

I shushed them both. We couldn't afford to have one of the guru's flunkies identify us as troublemakers; he'd already given Abhijit a dressing down for not being 'serious' earlier.

'You will now enter the phase of deep relaxation,' the guru's drawl broke into my thoughts. 'Free your mind of all cares . . .'

As if.

This three-day workshop and the time it was taking away from my work was the biggest care I had. The easiest way for me to free my mind would be to quit the workshop. I wondered if the Circle of Success worked like PT class at school, and if I could excuse myself by claiming it was that time of the month.

RRRRRR!

The silence was shattered by the sound of loud snores. I opened one eye to spot the snorer. I wasn't the only one. There was a lot of shuffling and some muffled whispers as everyone tried to surreptitiously look around. I wondered what fate would befall a person who converted the 'centre of calm' to the 'centre of a storm'.

Surprisingly, the guru ignored the snoring and slowly wrapped up the meditation session. Once we had all opened our eyes, I realized that the snores were emanating from Harsh who was still curled up in the foetal position and was fast asleep. Aakash reached out to touch his shoulder, but moved back when he saw that the guru was glaring at him.

'Harsh is in a deep, meditative trance and should not be disturbed. He will open his eyes when he's ready,' the Guru pronounced.

'Inner peace, inner peace,' someone mumbled in the back.

I smirked. I turned and spotted Abhimanyu sitting in the lotus position looking as though he was perched on top of a mountain. I tried to stop myself from staring at his six-pack abs and lean, toned body. His eyes were closed and he was doing a brilliant impression of someone in a deep, meditative trance. Every time Harsh snored, he muttered 'inner peace' to the tone and pace of the snore. When this happened for the fourth time, I couldn't help myself any more and burst into giggles. The guru glared at me, but by this time more people had begun to giggle. He sensed that he was fast losing his grip on the audience and decided to move on.

DONNNNNNNGGGG!

He struck the giant gong hanging by the side of the stage.

Harsh snorted but remained asleep. I marvelled at his ability to sleep through that sound.

'Feel the vibrations from your head to your toes,' the guru said. He struck the gong again and this time Harsh stopped mid-snore. He quickly sat up, trying to appear as though he'd been up all along.

'Good morning, Harsh,' sang Abhimanyu.

The entire room erupted into laughter.

'Does Ash stand for Ashwatthama?' Bhargavi asked, as she shook the Magic 8 Ball.

'How do you come up with these names?' Upasana replied.

'Come on, he's hidden the origin of the name so well, I'm sure it isn't as obvious as Ashwin,' Bhargavi retorted.

She peered at the Magic 8 Ball and then glumly read, 'My sources say no.'

'Maybe it's Ashwagandha,' Aakash said. 'You know like the herb?'

'A herb known as poison berry,' Shirin said, looking at her phone. 'I don't think his parents thought Ash was poisonous, no matter what we think!'

'What are you discussing?' Abhimanyu's voice broke into the conversation as he approached our table with a coffee in his hand. Yet again, I had to struggle to tear my eyes away from him. It should be illegal for someone with that build to wear a fitted shirt!

'Oh, we're just asking the Magic 8 Ball silly questions,' Upasana said nonchalantly. We couldn't afford to have someone from senior management discover our obsession with finding out Ash's real name.

'Will the guru lose his temper again?' Upasana continued, and shook the Magic 8 Ball. Abhimanyu sat down as she stared at the answer.

'You may rely on it,' she read. The entire table burst out laughing.

'Come on, he knows how to re-laaaax and relaaax,' Abhimanyu said, with a near perfect imitation of the man himself, replete with the twang.

By this point, we were clutching our stomachs and laughing. One of the servers looked over. They were probably wondering how to get rid of this rowdy bunch creating havoc in the middle of Starbucks. A group of us had stopped after the session to grab some coffee and snacks for the long night of work. Unlike the other bosses who disappeared as soon as the session ended, Abhimanyu had joined us. I didn't know whether I was more surprised by the fact that he seemed to enjoy slumming with the minions, or by the fact that the dour, Oscar-like man actually had a fun side.

'Me!' Shirin leaned over and grabbed it. Upasana owned the Magic 8 Ball. We liked playing with it whenever we were bored and wanted to pass some time. Of course, none of us really believed in it. But it was really funny to see what the ball came up with, so we kept going.

'Magic 8 Ball, will I manage to complete the competitor analysis tonight?' she asked.

'Don't count on it,' she read out loud and groaned. She took a sip of the coffee that was placed in front of her.

'As if you needed a Magic 8 Ball to tell you that,' Dhruv said. 'Ask an interesting question.'

'OK, will this be the year I move to Delhi?' Shirin had been threatening to quit Glam and move back home for as long as I'd known her.

'Better not to tell you now,' I read out for her as we all laughed. I picked up my chocolate croissant and took a bite.

'Will I get a raise?' Aakash grabbed the ball.

'Deep question,' Dhruv said. 'Do you really think a Magic 8 Ball can answer that?'

Aakash shook the ball hard as if he was hoping he could shake it into giving the response he wanted.

'Cannot be certain,' he read out and frowned.

'I could've told you that, why waste it on the Magic 8 Ball?' I laughed.

'Actually, Aakash, your chances will be better if you move your desk,' Abhimanyu said. He took a bite of his sandwich and chewed thoughtfully.

'I have the perfect seat,' Aakash insisted. 'That giant pillar behind me ensures that no one can sneak up on me!'

Abhimanyu looked as though he was weighing the pros and cons of what he was about to say. He took a sip of his coffee. Suddenly, he seemed to make up his mind. He leaned forward and put his elbows on the table.

'Sitting behind a pillar is bad *vaastu*. It will outweigh any other benefits of that location,' he said.

Aakash looked stunned. I began to laugh, as did a few others at the table. Why on earth would he believe in this kind of mumbo jumbo? I wondered if he was teasing us for our Magic 8 Ball game.

'You can laugh, but this is important,' Abhimanyu said. He looked directly at me in a way that made me stop midlaugh. 'Where you sit in your workplace has a big impact on how well you do. Why do you think I moved my seat? And my team's location too?'

I stared.

'No way,' Shirin said. 'HR wouldn't agree!'

My mind raced. I would've had more respect for Abhimanyu if he had admitted that all the office reorganization was a power move. Doing it because he was looking for 'vaastu-appropriate' seating seemed random.

'Boss, next you'll say you also believe in horoscopes,' Dhruv joked. He was grinning, knowing fully well that being able to say this to his boss in front of a table full of subordinates would make it clear that he had an exceptionally good relationship with Abhimanyu. What a show-off!

'Well, my family astrologer is pretty accurate,' said Aakash. He got a dirty look from Dhruv.

'Yeah, mine too,' Bhargavi said shyly. 'She predicted I would get married in six months, and while I thought it was absurd, I met my husband within a week of her prediction. And we were married six months later.'

I choked on my croissant. I reached out for my coffee and took a sip, hoping to stop myself from coughing out loud. I hadn't realized just how many people at this table believed in astrology.

'I also find Bejan Daruwalla's app to be pretty good,' Aakash piped in again. 'It said that I would try something new today. And I did yoga for the first time.'

'I read the one in the paper every morning,' Bhargavi said. 'It's decent for the most part, though it doesn't always get everything right.'

'I'd recommend checking out the AstroZone app,' Abhimanyu said as he reached out and took another bite of his sandwich. 'She doesn't just give you a generic horoscope, she also points out specific dates that are good or bad in the month. I use that to plan my schedule and it works fantastically.'

'What?' Dhruv said, with his eyes wide open. He took a giant gulp of his coffee, looking as though he wished it was an Irish coffee and not just fortified with regular caffeine.

'Yes,' Abhimanyu replied calmly. 'If I'm feeling uncertain about a project, I use it to schedule leadership reviews based on the dates it recommends. Hasn't failed me yet!'

I resisted the urge to point out that maybe he did well because of his own efforts and not because of some app. But I didn't think he would take it very well. It seemed like he was really sold on this app. Aakash and Bhargavi pulled out their phones and began looking it up.

'Sounds far-fetched,' Shirin said, pragmatic as always. 'How can a single horoscope be accurate for so many people.' She peered into Aakash's phone. 'So if this app says the 31st is a bad day, we assume every Taurean will have a terrible Friday?'

Aakash looked concerned. 'Shit, I have a review with Harsh on Friday,' he burst out.

Abhimanyu patted him on the back. 'Don't worry, it's not all Taureans. Only the ones with a moon rising in Saturn.' Either he was a Taurean himself or such a fanboy of this app that he had mugged up the details of all the star signs. I couldn't believe what I was hearing.

'You've got to be kidding, Abhimanyu,' Dhruv said. Clearly, I wasn't the only one wondering what warped parallel universe we'd suddenly woken up in.

'You don't have to believe in this,' Abhimanyu said. 'But as far as I'm concerned, I would never schedule a meeting or pick up something important on a day that the app warned against. I can't risk that again.'

He shuddered slightly. I wondered what 'again' referred to, but it didn't seem like he would share details with a table full of people, some of whom were already judging him for his love for astrology.

'Wait, so does this mean you approved the #MeTooGlam campaign because I pitched it on the right day?' Dhruv asked.

'You'll have to check your horoscope to know for sure,' grinned Abhimanyu.

Wait, what?

The team continued to ask Abhimanyu questions about the app, but I was no longer listening. Last week, I assumed that while Dhruv's campaign plan sounded good to Ash, he would still have to get Abhimanyu to approve the finer details. Now, it seemed he had already managed that. His campaign would launch fairly quickly now. Meanwhile, I was still planning my project and hadn't got very far.

Shit, shit, shit.

I had a mental image of Dhruv running towards a finish line labelled 'promotion', while I was still dawdling behind the starting point. I was being left well and truly in the dust.

If only I could kick him in the shins and take him out of this race, I thought.

It's too bad that nothing in adult life worked the way it did in lemon-and-spoon races in class four.

10

The Planet of Surprise Brings Delight

'Wow! This is cool,' Kavya said, as she finished scrolling through my presentation on the subscription programme. 'I would definitely sign up for this!'

Kavya and I often bounced ideas off each other at home. Since this was one of my biggest presentations yet, I just had to show it to her. I had spent the last week getting it ready so I could get Abhimanyu's approval. Now that Dhruv had announced he would be launching his campaign soon, I was running out of time. I had put in a lot of effort and I was glad that Kavya liked it. I felt as ready as I would ever be.

'Maybe we can clone you,' I laughed. 'Preferably such that each version buys a subscription. Then I'll get promoted for sure.' I shut the laptop and began serving myself breakfast.

'Does that mean you'll finally start going out again?' Kavya asked.

'Hmm,' I shrugged non-committally.

'You aren't even coming to trivia tonight,' she said. 'Or is that because you started a brawl last week?'

'Attending trivia tonight has nothing to do with work. Or rather, it does, but it's because we have to attend that ridiculous workshop,' I said as I took a huge bite of my omelette.

'Come on, Sitara,' Kavya said. 'You've been killing yourself with work, starting trivia arguments and obsessing over Arjun. You need a break. Maybe take a day off?'

I shook my head and smiled. 'You know what it takes. You went through this last year! It's fine, this entire thing is just temporary. Once I get this promotion, I promise I'll relax. Maybe we can finally go on that trip to Greece we keep talking about!'

'If you say so,' Kavya replied, taking a sip of chai. 'All work and no play will make Sitara a crazy cat-owning spinster. Minus the cat.'

I smiled and took another bite.

'I'm serious,' she insisted. 'Maybe you should consider going on a date. Get on Bumble, and have some mindless sex!'

I choked on the sip of chai I had just taken.

'Um, what?'

'Mindless, meaningless sex. That's just what you need to take your mind off work and relax a little,' she repeated, proving that my best friend had well and truly lost her marbles.

'No thanks,' I said.

'Really? So are you going to let your parents look for a guy?'

I considered all the 'relationships' I knew. Krish and his unrequited crush on George, Kavya and her revolving door of Bumble and Tinder matches, Upasana and her long-distance boyfriend who saw each other only twice a month. Compared to that, my parents' arranged marriage almost seemed like a roaring success. Almost.

'Maybe,' I said. 'But I'm busy with work. I need to get this project approved.'

'Maybe you should check that app of Abhimanyu's to see if there's any sex in your future,' she suggested mischievously. 'What was it called?'

'Wait . . .' I said as a sudden realization struck me.

She swallowed and took another sip of chai.

'I was joking,' she replied. 'I'm not trying a modern version of sending a *jadagam** your way by suggesting you use an app to decide when to start dating again!'

'Forget dating! The app could still work,' I said. My mind was racing with the possibilities.

'What?' She looked at me like I was crazy. I rubbed my eyes so hard, one of my contacts fell out. It was a good thing I wore disposables, the way I treated my contacts!

'Abhimanyu believes in that ridiculous app. And Abhimanyu has to approve my proposal. What if I use the app and find the right time to pitch this?'

---

* Horoscope in Tamil

'Please tell me you aren't saying what I think you're saying,' she said. She reached out and grabbed my hand, something she did when she thought I was being impulsive.

'It's perfect,' I said. 'If he believes the app when it says a date is good or bad, then all I have to do is read his horoscope every day and time my actions based on it.'

She stared at me.

'Firstly, that sounds extremely far-fetched. Do you even know his star sign? What if there are no good days this month?' she challenged.

I ignored her as I pulled out Facebook to see if I could find his birthday. I scrolled through his sparse timeline before realizing his birthday wasn't there. I went to Instagram next with no success. Finally, out of desperation, I went to LinkedIn and that's where I hit the jackpot. For some reason, an old colleague had left Abhimanyu a message on his birthday five years ago. I thanked the overly enthusiastic Mr Sharan Shekhawat for doing me a favour and helping me discover that Abhimanyu was an Arien. I opened up the app store and began searching for the AstroZone app.

'I hope there are some good days soon. Otherwise, I'll have to abandon this plan . . . ' I muttered to myself.

'Secondly,' Kavya cut in, stressing on the word so I'd look up. 'This is super manipulative.'

'All's fair in love and corporate politics,' I said as I willed the app to finish downloading.

'When this kooky scheme of yours ends in tears and tantrums, remember I reserved the right to say I told you so,' she said as she got up and walked into the kitchen with her empty plate and mug.

I was too busy reading Abhimanyu's horoscope to respond.

'Jaanusirsasana,' the guru barked as we all scrambled trying to remember which of the numerous asanas he'd taken us through corresponded to that name.

I had to stop myself from giggling as I recalled Upasana's cartoon versions of each asana. She'd drawn a version of the warrior pose that she'd termed 'deadline warrior' and stuck it on my cubicle. It depicted me struggling with the warrior pose, while using my arms to stick a Post-it on my desk. It was funny and stressful all at once.

'*Jaanu meri jaan . . .*' I heard Abhimanyu humming in the background as Ranjani began to giggle.

The HR and admin posse would laugh at just about anything, I thought as I finally remembered the pose and struggled to touch my knees with my head. These days, they giggled every time Abhimanyu passed by their bay. Upasana, Shirin and I were convinced that one or more of them were already in love with him. I couldn't completely blame them, especially when he was able to do even the most complicated yoga pose without breaking a sweat, muscles rippling on his arms and legs.

' . . . *jaane saara hindustan,*' the song continued to play in my head, even though Abhimanyu had stopped humming.

'Thanks for the earworm,' I muttered to myself.

'One must not speak while the guru is instructing . . . '

I got a dirty look from the guru and put on an innocent face. Shirin had overheard that he was not just a corporate guru, but also a 'life coach'. The orange robes were to give him more of an 'Indian' look in the foreign circles that he typically targeted. We'd joked that the exalted status he received at his corporate retreats abroad explained his deep desire to always be respected, but despite all the jokes, I did not want to anger him. After all, who knew how pissing off the spiritual adviser of your super boss could impact your career?

I struggled to keep up. I hoped nobody was looking at me, because I was likely the most uncoordinated person there. Upasana was possibly the best because she was super flexible. She was able to perform every asana with ease, contorting her body in all kinds of poses as though she had rubber in the place of bone and muscle. Shirin was giving me competition in the clumsiness department, struggling to balance herself in some of the harder poses. Thankfully, neither of us had fallen flat on our faces yet. I heaved a sigh of relief as we moved into Bhujangasana. This was easier than some of the earlier contortions.

DRRRR-POP!

The sound was quickly followed by the smell of what was unmistakably a fart. Suddenly, I didn't feel like I was the worst at yoga any more.

Yet again, everyone struggled to keep a straight face. I wondered if I could spot the source of the fart but the noxious fumes had permeated the entire room. Whoever it was, they had definitely had a heavy, oily lunch. My stomach roiled at the thought.

'If you are feeling uneasy, move into Pawanmuktasana,' the Guru intoned. 'As the name suggests, the wind relieving pose will . . . '

The entire room burst into laughter and I flopped on to the mat, giving up on all pretence that I was holding the asana. I was beginning to see how yoga could be calming for the mind. Or even entertaining.

As soon as the session ended, I ran to catch up with Abhimanyu.

'I've updated my proposal,' I told him. 'I now have a detailed list of the benefits we can offer and also some thoughts on potential partnerships. For instance, now that Korean beauty is catching on so much, Innisfree could be a great marquee partner.'

I paused as he mulled over what I was saying.

'You'll need more than one brand,' he replied.

'I do. I would like to take you through the updated presentation. Can I bring it to you on Friday?' According to the app, Abhimanyu could expect a 'good idea from unexpected quarters' on Friday. I was counting on being that unexpected quarter.

'You can find a free slot on my calendar. But remember, don't bring it to me unless you've got everything in place. This will be a go/no-go call as far as I'm concerned.'

'Of course,' I replied.

Operation AstroZone was officially in effect. I couldn't wait to see what the 'stars' had in store for me.

11

Don't Let Your Focus Waver

'I'm not strategic? How dare they!' Shirin burst out as she looked at the evaluation she had received from the Shape of Success programme. 'Women get this feedback when they're so good at executing that they're loaded with execution tasks and not given time to be strategic. This is Glam's fault not mine!'

'The results are fixed,' Upasana said. 'The guru was so mad at us for giggling that he's given us the worst feedback. He did say that we deserved Circle of Cynicism,' she reminded us. She began peering at her phone screen, while I handed Shirin a Starbucks cup with SERENE written unironically on it.

'He probably got zeroes in school and hasn't exited those circles yet,' Shirin muttered.

'I got Circle of Connections,' I said with a shrug. 'Apparently, I need to work on my people skills.'

'Really?' Upasana said. 'I thought your last few performance evaluations claimed you were too nice and not pushy enough.'

'I think I may have worked on it too well,' I said as I rolled my eyes. 'Either that or it's a case of damned if you do and damned if you don't.'

'As always, women have to work twice as hard to be thought of as half as good,' Shirin said.

'Pentagon of Patience,' Upasana announced, as she tossed her phone on Shirin's desk. 'OK, this evaluation was definitely created by a man. It's like a rulebook for How to Check Your Unconscious Bias.'

Shirin took a sip of her coffee. 'This'll be like all our mandatory workshops—the results won't be used. These evaluations must be lining Ranjani's dustbin already!'

'Yeah, the dustbin is circular,' Upasana winked. We all laughed.

'Listen, can you swap your meeting slot with Abhimanyu tomorrow?' Shirin suddenly asked me. 'I have a meeting on Friday, but I need to take the day off for a doctor's appointment.'

I had carefully booked the slot after poring over Abhimanyu's horoscope, and tomorrow was the best day for this presentation this week. I had even sweet-talked Ranjani into letting me book 'Mt Everest', his favourite meeting room even though I hated it because it was the coldest.

'I need to get the approval as soon as I can,' I tried stalling.

'I know! This shouldn't make a difference,' she replied. 'My meeting is first thing on Friday morning so you're only losing a couple of hours. Please! I can't move my appointment,' she pressed.

'You know how well I cope with last-minute changes,' I attempted to crack a weak joke.

She arched her well-shaped eyebrow at me. Upasana quietly walked away. Damn, I could've used some support. But Upasana never took sides. Shirin also seemed to have expected Upasana to take her side. She gave Upasana's retreating back a cold stare.

'Actually, why don't you find a slot next week?' I said as Shirin continued to glare at me. I couldn't look her in the eye, so I stared at the Starbucks cup as if the letters would suddenly morph into something I could say to smooth things over.

'I've to go over the marketing metrics for last month. I need to get all the department leads to sign off and get it to Ash this week. He won't be okay if I postpone this,' she insisted.

I bit my nail. I didn't know what to say, but I really couldn't give her my slot. I wondered if there was an easy way to end this conversation on an amicable note.

'Well?' she challenged. Something in her tone set me off.

'If it's that important, you could've blocked the slot yourself,' I said, coming off a little sharper than I had intended. 'It's not like you didn't know about the review or your doctor's appointment!'

'This appointment was sudden,' she said, biting her lip. She pushed her wavy hair back behind her ear and glared at me. 'Anyway, how is it OK that you can schedule a last-minute meeting for an idea that barely existed a week ago, but I need to plan my meetings better? Wow, it looks like that ridiculous evaluation was right. You *should* work on your Circle of Connectivity!'

Before I could reply, she tossed her empty coffee cup into the wastebasket and stormed away.

Oh crap.

Generally, Shirin was easy going, so I wasn't expecting such an extreme reaction. I hoped she would forgive me for this soon. I decided I would tell her why I was so vehement about this after I got the promotion.

If this whole horoscope thing worked, that is.

I rubbed my eyes as I blinked at the screen. I'd been staring at my laptop for hours. Earlier in the evening, we had spotted ominously dark rain clouds in the horizon. Immediately, people had started to leave the office to avoid getting stranded in the endless traffic jams that came about when it rained. Normally, I would've been one of them too, but today I wanted to complete my presentation, and so I'd decided to risk it and stay. Thankfully, it hadn't started raining yet.

My stomach grumbled unhelpfully, reminding me that it was almost dinner time. Kavya was going out today so I couldn't rely on her. I made a mental note to place a Swiggy order as soon as I got ready to leave so that the food would arrive by the time I got home. Once again, I'd given up on my resolution to eat healthy. It was bad enough that I barely got any exercise and now my erratic eating habits would further exacerbate things.

'Someone's hard at work,' Dhruv's voice broke into my thoughts. I was surprised to see him. I had assumed I was the only person still here.

'You know how it is,' I said evasively. My throat felt scratchy and my voice sounded hoarse. I picked up my water bottle to take a sip, but it was empty. I walked towards the water cooler, hoping he'd leave. He followed me.

'I think you need something stronger than water,' Dhruv said. 'Want to grab a beer?'

Um, what? Was he randomly asking me out on a Wednesday evening? If I agreed, my 'square of spontaneity' would no longer be non-existent. I filled my bottle and took a sip.

'OK,' I said tentatively, surprising myself. Suddenly, the rumbling in my stomach was replaced by a rush of butterflies. My cheeks were getting warm. I quickly took another sip of water.

'Let's go,' he said. I walked back to my desk and began packing up my stuff. 'You can tell me about your nefarious plans to beat me to the promotion.'

'Don't you wish,' I said as I followed him out.

★ ★
★

The square of spontaneity wasn't working very well for me. Dhruv and I were at Byg Brewski, a pub that was frequented by almost all the office goers in the Sarjapur area. Even though it was the middle of the week, it was buzzing with activity. Almost every table was occupied, and with groups that advertised their IT-worker status through the unofficial uniform of jeans or shorts with ratty T-shirts. We settled down at a table by the fake pond in the centre of the pub. The string lights all around made it feel very date-like.

This isn't a date, I told myself sternly.

'I really like this place,' Dhruv said as he slung his leather Tumi bag on the back of the chair. He even had his initials monogrammed on it. He definitely had fancy tastes and was attempting to project a 'leadership' vibe. I looked at my overstuffed backpack that was beginning to rip at the seams.

Definitely not a date.

'What should we get?' I asked as I flipped through the menu.

'Oh, definitely the Amber Ale. I've tried all the specialities and that's the best.' I ordered that for him and a wheat beer for myself, and some nachos for the table.

'How nice to hang out with a woman who's not on a health kick,' he grinned as he added onion rings to our order.

'What's the point of eating out if you skip nachos or fries,' I retorted. He laughed out loud at that.

'So, what's keeping you late at work?' he asked.

'Just my proposal. But I'm not telling you about it,' I replied.

'Not even after a few drinks? What if I tell you what's happening with mine?' he asked.

'Nice try!'

'We're both going to hear about each other's projects eventually,' he pointed out as a server brought our order to the table. 'My campaign is nearly ready to launch. It'll come up in the next monthly business review.'

At that, my heart started beating faster again. I was glad I hadn't swapped slots with Shirin. I was definitely behind in this race. I kept a straight face.

'So, am I allowed to ask how far you've got or is that off the table?' he pressed. I took a giant gulp of beer so I didn't have to answer right away.

'Do people tend to talk shop while they're out on a date?' I said cheekily.

'A date?' he said as he leaned forward. The butterflies were back as he looked into my eyes. I thought he would look away but his gaze didn't waver. 'I was just asking a colleague for a friendly drink. Glam doesn't have a policy against employees dating, but does that make this a date?'

If he was trying to see which of us would look away first, I wasn't going to be the one to lose. I started back at him, ignoring the fact that my neck was getting hot and my cheeks were bright red at this point. Out of the corner of my eye, I spotted a group of women at a nearby table ogling at him. With his chocolate-boy looks, he was the best looking of all the pot-bellied, bearded Neanderthals in the place. I wondered what they thought of me.

'I don't fraternize with the enemy,' I said. 'I was merely commenting that dates should be free of any agendas.'

He grinned.

'Why are you laughing at me,' I burst out as he finally broke eye contact to wipe his eyes.

'Sorry, sorry! I'm just messing with you. Seriously though, how far ahead is your project? Am I going to hear about it soon?'

'As if Aakash hasn't told you all about it,' I retorted.

'You've managed to keep this one pretty close to your chest,' he said. 'Sounds like you're betting on winning this.'

'I'm confident. Unlike you, the picture of arrogance.'

He pretended I'd hurt him, by miming an arrow to his heart. It was a cool Bangalore evening, but suddenly I couldn't stop fanning myself. I was feeling really warm.

'Aw, don't say that! I'm just betting that the best person gets the promotion. And that's usually me,' he said with a broad smile. 'But don't worry, you still have a few weeks to get your grand plan approved by Abhimanyu.'

Ah. So he did know where I was stuck. I wondered if Abhimanyu was giving him details of just how much he was jerking me around for this approval.

'Don't count me out yet,' I said, way more confidently than I felt.

'So, if this were a date, what would be on your agenda?' he asked, suddenly changing the subject.

'Another drink,' I replied, to avoid answering. 'What about you?'

'One more for me too,' he said. 'I'm going to head to the restroom. I'll place the order on my way.'

As he walked away, I tried to clear my head. I needed to figure out if this evening was his unsubtle way of going on a date with me, or whether he wanted to get me drunk so he could get the details of my project.

'Excuse me, can I take this chair,' one of the girls I'd spotted eyeing Dhruv broke into my thoughts. I nodded and bent to pull out my phone so I wouldn't have to engage with her.

'I love your earrings,' she said. I was wearing pink terracotta earrings that had a pair of eyes that stared you down. Kavya called them my '*buri nazar wale, tera mooh kala*' earrings.

'Thanks,' I said, hoping she would take the hint and go away, now that I was staring intently at my phone.

'We also loved your boyfriend's T-shirt,' she said. 'Homer saying Doh-sa, so funny!'

Ah. They were trying to play the 'is he your boyfriend game'. I opened my mouth to say that he wasn't my boyfriend, when an evil thought crossed my mind. Just because I knew we weren't dating didn't mean I needed to offer him up on a platter, did it? I liked flirting with him when he wasn't being an arrogant ass. In fact, if I were being completely honest, sometimes I liked flirting with him even when he was being an arrogant ass.

'Oh Dhruv,' I said as she smiled hopefully. I could see her mentally making a note of the name. 'He's not my boyfriend, he's gay!'

I saw her smile fall as she quickly picked up the chair and ran to inform her friends.

'Enjoy your evening,' I called out as they all avoided eye contact with me. I noticed that they were drinking the house wine, the worst the bar had. They were going to have terrible hangovers.

Not one of them looked up or replied.

Dhruv walked back to the table with our beers and grinned, 'Were you talking about me?'

'No, she was just borrowing a chair,' I replied nonchalantly. I was amazed at the self-confidence it took to assume that every conversation was about him. Even if this one had been.

As we had our second drink, he began probing me about my project again. I tried deflecting his questions as best as I could. Finally, out of desperation, I decided to change the subject.

'It's such a lovely evening, must we really waste it talking about work?' I asked.

'I believe we were going to talk about your agenda for the date earlier, but you didn't seem to want to talk about that either,' he said, leaning forward.

Oh. Was he trying to flirt with me?

'We already established this wasn't a date,' I replied. I attempted to toss my hair, the way magazines always claimed was seductive, but somehow ended up giving myself a crick in my neck.

'This one may not be, but maybe next time, it will be?'

He was definitely flirting with me. I was at a loss for words.

'Tell me, Sitara, why do I get the feeling that you don't like me?'

Suddenly, Kavya's advice flashed back into my mind. Maybe I should put myself out there, be more open to having a fling.

'What makes you think I don't like you?' I said, attempting fake nonchalance that I didn't feel. I wished I remembered more of those magazine tips on flirting, but I was drawing a complete blank.

'You don't trust me enough to tell me what's going on with you,' he said, seriously. My cheeks were growing hotter and I could feel the tips of my ears burn.

'I don't know you that well Dhruv,' I said, purposely misunderstanding him.

'Well, why don't we get to know each other now?' he said.

I smiled shyly. And then he leaned forward and reached out for my hand. I wondered if I should pull it back, but I could hear Kavya telling me to go for it. I let him hold my hand as he looked deep into my eyes.

I took a deep breath. Dhruv was holding my hand! I was expecting to feel a sudden spark of electricity or some sort of connection with him. I realized I felt . . . nothing. I could've been holding anything in my hand.

Slowly, I pulled away my hand. It was getting a little too awkward. Besides, I didn't want him to think he could lean in and kiss me. I shuddered at the thought as I remembered he'd been attacking the onion rings he'd ordered with gusto.

'Did I do something wrong?' he asked.

'No,' I said, reaching for my bag. 'I think I heard my phone ring.' I peered intently at the screen, pretending that something very important had come up. 'Looks like my flatmate is locked out of the apartment. I'm going to have to rush to let her in!'

He looked a little disappointed, but didn't make a move to stop me. I quickly left a few bills on the table to pay for my share as I collected my things and got ready to leave.

As I walked out, I wondered if I should let the girls know that Dhruv was available. I knew with utmost certainty that I no longer had a crush on him.

12

The Sun Is a Harbinger of Good Luck

Today was the day I truly started believing in horoscopes. Other people's horoscopes at any rate.

'Good work. We definitely have something,' said Abhimanyu, as I wrapped up my presentation.

I heaved a sigh of relief.

Finally. *Finally.*

'I'm on board, but we will need Ash to sign off,' he added.

Sometimes, I wondered whether he got entertained by raising my hopes and then dashing them all in one breath.

'Ash already said he was on board as long as you approved it,' I said, attempting to defuse this new roadblock.

'Come on, Sitara,' he said with that infuriating half-smirk that always made my hackles rise. 'You've worked at Glam for long enough to know that Ash will still want to go over the final presentation before you start executing.

Speaking of which, the execution details aren't completely there yet.'

I wondered where this was leading. I thought the execution section was great. I had spent time with various people on the team to ensure he wouldn't be able to pick any flaws. My confusion must have shown because he began to explain.

'Most of what you have is great. However, this is a project that will require strong marketing support. What you have right now isn't enough. We need a much stronger plan before we pitch this to Ash,' he said and walked to the door. He beckoned one of his team members over. I held my breath, hoping it was Upasana.

I wasn't so lucky.

In walked Dhruv, looking mighty pleased with himself. As soon as he realized I was in the room, his eyes widened. We had been avoiding each other since our 'friendly drink' two days ago. I didn't trust his motives after he'd tried to get me to tell him about my project, and I especially didn't want to be near him after our awkward hand holding.

'Dhruv, I need a detailed marketing plan for Sitara's proposal. You should work with her,' Abhimanyu said.

I opened my mouth to protest. I did not want to work with Dhruv. For one, he would have way too many details of my project. For another, it would be awkward. As I was debating how I could steer Abhimanyu away from this train of thought, Dhruv replied.

'Abhimanyu, I'm occupied with my new campaign. I don't have the bandwidth to take on another large project.'

I was grateful, but also surprised. Given the way he had probed me about my project, I assumed he would jump at the chance to get as much insider information as he could. Maybe he also didn't want to talk about the other night.

'Let's discuss your bandwidth in our weekly meeting. I'm sure we can deprioritize a few things to give you time,' Abhimanyu said. His voice held a warning note, designed to quell any questions. I knew how hard it was to get Abhimanyu to change his mind when he was in this zone. After all, I had been on the receiving end of it all this while.

'This is a great proposal and it would benefit from a solid marketing plan. You should ensure it's set up for success,' he continued.

'Sure, Abhimanyu,' Dhruv said.

He smiled to diffuse the tension. I opened my mouth again, to see if I could change Abhimanyu's mind, but Dhruv had already left. I wondered what was going on with Dhruv.

Was he mad at Abhimanyu for forcing him to work on my project? Or was he mad at me?

'Oh my God! We're going to see a blue moon tonight,' Kavya teased as I entered Last Call with Upasana and Shirin in tow.

'Very funny,' I said.

I sat down beside Kavya. I almost wished I hadn't come. I really wanted to tell Kavya about the world's worst awkward Uber ride, but it would have to wait. Upasana had sat uncomfortably in the middle as I had attempted to draw Shirin into a conversation. Shirin steadfastly ignored me. Even Upasana's attempts to break the ice didn't work. I hoped the trivia session would force Shirin to talk to me.

'One of us should go up to the bar to get the beer. They seem really busy,' Kavya said, gesturing to the bar area. It was packed, with people trying to push their way to the front. Every server in the room looked harried. I volunteered to get the drinks, so I'd get a few minutes away from Shirin's icy stares.

I walked to the bar, surreptitiously tugging at my black and white polka-dotted dress to make sure it hadn't bunched up awkwardly while I was sitting. I got to the bar and noticed Abhimanyu standing there, trying to create a semblance of a line, while others swarmed around him.

'Hi,' I said.

'Hi,' he smiled. I thanked my lucky stars that the lights in the bar were dim so he couldn't see that his smile had made me blush. The man had a killer smile. Even in a dim bar like this, it lit up the space he was in.

'Ready for tonight?' he asked.

'I think so,' I replied. 'What about you?'

He shrugged. 'We're as ready as we always are. Zaina has a bad cold so she decided to stay home. And of course, the others are running late as usual.'

My heart sank a little when he mentioned Zaina. The way she stared daggers at me, I wondered if they were seeing each other. But if they were, why was he here?

'Shouldn't you be with Zaina if she's unwell?' I asked, shamelessly fishing for gossip.

He peered at me with an odd look on his face. 'Why would I? We've known each other since we were in school, but I don't think that warrants 24/7 assistance while she's unwell. Besides, her husband would find it odd,' he laughed.

'Oh,' I racked my brains for a sensible response. 'Cool.'

The minute I said this, I felt like my brain had thrown up its hands in despair and its own stupidity. It now crawled away into a corner to sulk. *I'm no longer a part of this if your runaway mouth won't cooperate*, I could hear it say.

I ordered our standard pitcher of wheat beer.

Abhimanyu feigned shock, 'Aren't you guys waiting for trivia to start before you start loading up on the alcohol? You'll need to stay sober to win,' he teased.

I made a face. 'Yeah, yeah, keep mocking me because you've beaten us a few times. Tonight's our turn,' I said, with more bravado than I felt.

'I hear that until I arrived, you had a good track record of beating our team, so I wouldn't be too surprised if that happened,' he said.

He paused for a beat before adding, 'Except if you decide to needle George, that is.'

I blushed. I hoped everyone had forgotten about the brawl, but it was going to haunt me for a few more weeks. Until someone else picked a fight with George anyway.

'You were right, by the way,' he said. 'George should've given you the point.'

I looked up, my eyes widening. He'd actually checked the answer and was admitting I was right? Before I could say anything, the bartender plonked our pitcher on to the bar.

'Enjoy your beer,' Abhimanyu said, flashing that killer smile yet again. 'I'm getting herbal tea so our team can focus on beating the pants off your team.'

'Really?' I got very flustered. Shit, were they beating us because they weren't drinking, while we were getting sloshed? I wondered if I could give away the beer and get my team a pot of herbal tea instead.

He laughed out loud seeing the confusion on my face.

I blushed beet red. After all that time spent at the Circle of Success workshops, I should've known not to take everything he said so seriously.

'I'm also getting a pitcher. Of the Amber Ale,' he said. 'And peanut masala.'

'I love peanut masala!'

'I know, you took some home in your hair last time,' he grinned. I covered my face with my hands. It was time to head back to our table. I picked up my pitcher and turned to go.

'All the best,' I said.

'I look forward to beating you,' he replied.

Before I could frame a comeback, George's voice filled the room. 'Good evening, quizzers! Looks like all our teams are on time today.' He threw a pointed look at The Sherlock Homies as my team hooted and they looked embarrassed.

I hurried to our table. Tonight, George had decided to go back to the old format because many teams had shown up. I began handing pencils around. Shirin made a big show of pulling out a pencil from her own bag and pretending like she couldn't see the one I was holding out. Kavya and Krish raised their eyebrows, but Upasana shook her head, indicating there was no point trying to talk about this.

'I'm also hoping that today's trivia is less, erm, entertaining than the last time when we had Whiskeypedia here,' George added, looking directly at me. This time, The Sherlock Homies hooted.

'That guy has a smile to die for,' said Krish, breaking into my thoughts.

'Yeah, Oscar definitely wasn't the right nickname for him,' Kavya said.

So I wasn't the only one admiring Abhimanyu's smile. I could feel my cheeks getting hot so I started to look down at my pencil, willing George to begin.

'First question of the evening: Connect: Malinga Bandara, Jeetan Patel and Shane Bond,' he boomed. My heart sank as I peered at the projector and realized this was a question on international cricket.

Great. We were going to lose yet again. To my surprise, Krish snatched the answer sheet and began writing out, 'The only Super Subs who won Man of the Match awards.' It actually read like a legit answer, so I looked at him in surprise.

'I used to have a crush on Shane Bond,' he grinned.

'Finally! I thought your obsession with cricketers will never be useful,' Shirin quipped. I laughed along with everyone else and tried to catch her eye, but she continued to freeze me out. I sighed. It was going to be a long night. I only hoped it would end better than it began.

The first question turned out to be a harbinger of good luck for us. We were unstoppable that day. The evening ended with us beating Sherlock Homies. I updated my mental tally of our scores to thirty-one–twenty-seven. If this streak continued, we could get ahead of them soon!

'Good game, guys,' said Abhimanyu, walking up to our table.

'That answer on Chandler's dad was brilliant,' he said to Kavya.

She grinned. She was immensely proud of being exceptional with *Friends* trivia. In fact, she spent a lot of time playing Friends Trivia on the Quiz Up app, 'to keep myself sharp'. The two of them began chatting. I tuned out as I tried to catch Shirin's eye. She was steadfastly staring at her phone, seeming absorbed with finding an Uber. She stood up abruptly and went outside without looking at any of us. I wanted to call Shirin, but Kavya tapped me on my shoulder.

'We live down the road, in Paradise Apartments,' she was saying to Abhimanyu.

Down the road from where, I wondered. I had missed quite a bit of this conversation so I wasn't sure why Kavya was telling Abhimanyu where we lived.

'Oh really? How are you getting home?' Abhimanyu asked.

'Uber,' said Kavya. 'Have you tried parking at this place? It's insane!'

'Actually, I have,' he smiled. 'They have a valet. Would you guys like a ride? You're on my way,' he said.

I did *not* want to go on a car ride with Abhimanyu. I wanted to sit in an Uber and tell Kavya all about what was going on with Shirin. Just as I was about to jump into the conversation and refuse, I heard a crack of thunder. My heart sank. I knew that Kavya would accept the ride, and there was no way I could refuse. If there was even the mildest inkling of rain, every cab driver in Bangalore went into hiding. This would actually be our easiest way to get home.

'Oh, that would be great. Thank you,' Kavya said.

We walked out of the pub and waited by the valet station. A big, fat raindrop fell on my nose, assuring me that accepting the ride was the best decision.

'Wait, is *this* your car?' I said incredulously as Abhimanyu stepped out in front of the car the valet had brought out front.

'What's wrong with it?' Abhimanyu asked, eyeing his functional sedan. I had always assumed he would be the kind of person who drove a flashy car.

'Nothing,' I replied. 'I just assumed you'd have a fancier car.'

'Oh you mean something more suited to leadership,' he drawled in the perfect imitation of Ash, as he made air quotes for the word 'leadership'. Kavya giggled, while I struggled to keep a straight face.

'Ah, so Ms Kandasamy is well aware of the goings-on at Glam,' he said, continuing his Ash impression. Kavya quickly let herself into the back seat, ensuring I was forced to sit in the front with Abhimanyu. I sat down, and placed my bag in front of my feet.

When we agreed to ride with Abhimanyu, I was convinced this ride would rival the one with Shirin and Upasana in awkwardness. Surprisingly, that wasn't the case. Abhimanyu didn't try to force conversation for the sake of it and instead focused on playing music. It was helpful that his taste in music seemed to mimic ours. My only complaint was that he was playing the Hindi version of A.R. Rahman's hits, which in my world was tantamount to blasphemy. I spotted Kavya cracking up through the rear-view mirror when the first song, 'Dil hai chhota sa', began. But then, she began singing along and I joined her. I leaned back into the seat and closed my eyes, feeling like Kavya and I were at home by ourselves.

'Time for some music trivia,' Abhimanyu said. 'Roobaroo' from Rang de Basanti was playing.

'What?' I asked. I couldn't recall anything specific about this song, and I was a true-blue Rahman fan. There was no way he knew some trivia about the Mozart of Madras that I didn't know.

'When Rahman first saw the lyrics of this song, he couldn't come up with a good hook. At the time, Rakeysh Omprakash Mehra cleared his throat. That's how the 'unh unh u' tune came about,' he replied.

Kavya and I burst out laughing.

'You made that up! I'm not falling for your jokes twice in the same evening,' I insisted.

'Of course not,' he said in a mock-injured tone. 'Go on, Google it if you don't believe me.'

'Just because the Internet says so, doesn't mean it's true,' I said. 'What if someone just made it up and put it on Wikipedia?'

'So if you don't believe an actual fact, the defence is to blame the Internet?' he said. 'But if you disagree with George, then the Internet is your best friend?'

'There's no way I wouldn't know this about Rahman. I'm a Rahmaniac,' I said.

He threw his head back and burst into laughter. 'A what?'

'You haven't even heard of the term Rahmaniac, and you call yourself a fan,' I challenged.

He kept laughing.

'To be fair, it is an actual term for super fans of Rahman,' Kavya jumped in from the backseat. 'Maybe you should concede on this one.' I was so wrapped up in our mini argument that I'd almost forgotten she was there. Now I turned around and reached out to give her a high five.

'After my gentlemanly move of offering you a ride, I was hoping you would be on my side,' Abhimanyu quipped, as he looked at Kavya in the rear-view mirror. She smiled widely, but refused to change sides.

'Fine,' he conceded. 'You win.'

I grinned and did a mock victory dance with my upper body, in sync to the tunes of *Humma Humma*.

'This time,' he added.

Ah. So his habit of using pauses to deliver a strong rebuttal wasn't just restricted to office debates.

Kavya and Abhimanyu began sharing a new list of Rahman trivia facts. But I wasn't listening any more. He was smiling that 1000-watt smile of his, the one that had everyone from the entire admin posse at work to Krish completely smitten by him. It was almost magnetic. Suddenly, I felt a little fizzy pop in the pit of my stomach. I was also starting to feel a tad light-headed. I wondered if I'd had too much to drink.

As we approached our apartment, I mentally admitted that Kavya had been right earlier that evening.

Abhimanyu was most definitely not an Oscar.

Actually, he was more like . . . an Elmo. A sweet, lovable, doe-eyed muppet.

Not that I would *ever* admit that to Kavya.

13

New Moons Open the Door to New Opportunities

'A senior colleague will recognize the spark in an idea you've been mulling over. Strike now while the iron is hot,' I read Abhimanyu's horoscope out loud as I dunked the crisp dosa into the tomato chutney.

It was one of those mornings when Kavya had decided to go all out with breakfast. Normally, we just grabbed some fruit or made eggs. But once in a while, Kavya decided we needed nutrition and vowed to go on a health kick. This typically involved signing up for a new gym membership and cooking elaborate meals. It usually went on for a few weeks until something big came up at work, at which point she rejoined the rest of us mere mortals in the world of Swiggy-fuelled meals and procrastinating on our gym attendance. Today, we were having piping hot dosas, with drumstick sambhar, home-made gunpowder and tomato chutney. She'd also whipped up some vile-looking green smoothie that she insisted was 'healthy' but I refused to taste it.

'Why are you still nosing around his horoscope,' Kavya said. 'He's such a nice guy, and you're obsessed with this random idea!'

I took another bite of my dosa and stared at her. 'What do you mean random? You know things finally started looking up only when I pitched to him based on the horoscope!'

'That was a coincidence,' she insisted. 'You were so well prepared he would've changed his mind anyway.'

She blew on her chai and took a sip.

'No, I'm certain he was open to the idea only because his horoscope had already primed him,' I insisted. 'And that means that today is the day Ash needs to bring it up with Abhimanyu. So, I have to talk to Ash and plant the idea in his head. Thankfully, he was already sounding interested the other day . . .'

'Didn't Abhimanyu get really upset with you the last time you dragged Ash into a conversation? Wouldn't he be pissed off if you went behind his back?'

'. . . I know, I'll catch Ash during his smoke break and casually talk about this,' I said, not really listening to Kavya. She didn't believe in any of this astrology stuff, but now that I had seen how well it worked as far as Abhimanyu was concerned, I definitely believed in it. And I was going to pursue this till I got promoted.

What other option did I have?

★★

'Hello, Ms Srinivasan,' Ash smiled as I scrambled into the lift.

If only he knew how much trouble I had taken to engineer this seeming coincidence. I had been sitting on a bean bag by the side of his office all morning so I could see when he left for his mid-morning smoke break. Our bean bags were more for show than they were functional, and the semi-deflated bag had given me a terrible backache. I told myself it would all be worth it. I felt a pang of nostalgia for the days when Shirin's vantage point near Ash's office would've helped me track Ash sans breaking my back. But those days were long gone.

Sitara, focus, I told myself sternly.

'Hi Ash, how are you?' I asked.

'Doing well, thanks. Where are you headed?' he asked politely.

'Just going to grab some chai from the tea stall outside,' I smiled. Everyone knew the *tapri* wallah outside our building made better chai than anything you would find inside the office. 'I also wanted to talk to you about the subscription programme we discussed . . .'

'Why don't you join me? I'm getting chai too,' he said while making the 'zip your lips' gesture he made whenever we were in an elevator and started talking about work. Ash was paranoid about eavesdropping. As though the guys from ICICI Bank on the floor below us would steal our ideas and suddenly begin giving away beauty hampers to all their premium customers! I busied myself with staring at my reflection in the mirrored elevator doors.

Once we got downstairs, we walked silently to the tapri. I ordered my usual ginger-elaichi chai. Ash got his chai and a cigarette. He gestured that we should stand by a tree on the side. I didn't say a word until he lit his cigarette and took a sip of his chai.

'So, what did you want to discuss?' he asked as he puffed on his cigarette.

'I've been working on the subscription programme and I now have all the details,' I replied, as I pulled out my phone and handed it to him so he could see the presentation.

'Hmm . . . ' he said, skimming through it. 'Show me the details of the benefits?' I quickly scrolled to the right slide so he could read it. I walked him through each benefit and why it was important to Glam.

'Of course, this has been discussed with Abhimanyu. He's also on board . . . ' I began to pre-empt any questions about Abhimanyu's involvement.

'Perfect timing!' Ash said. I wondered if he was also following a horoscope that said he would hear of a great idea today. Otherwise 'timing' didn't really make much sense. And he hadn't registered a word I'd said about Abhimanyu's involvement.

'Vimala Paul just joined the board at Glam. It's not public news yet, so keep it to yourself,' he said, referring to the ex-CEO of Happy Foods, one of the country's largest food and beverage companies. I knew she was the first female member of the board, but beyond that, this information was basically above my paygrade, and I didn't know how it mattered. I focused on what Ash was saying.

'Cypress Capital has just invested in a new start-up, BeauPlus, which has a loyalty programme for beauty products. We need to counter it before they get the funds to become a strong competitor. If we are able to create this programme, our investors will give us the additional funds we need. And, I can tell Vimala that we have a play in this space. She asked me why we didn't yet have a programme like this just yesterday. We must turn it around at once!'

I tuned out as he went on about how Vimala had identified subscription programmes as the perfect fit for the target customer, and how she really understood the target customer.

Of course, now that she said it, suddenly I had magically figured out how to think like the target customer, I thought darkly.

Barely a week and a half ago, he and Harsh insisted I knew nothing about 'Tania', our fake customer persona. But now that what I was saying matched with something that a hotshot exec had also said, suddenly it was a brilliant concept. I began silently sending up thanks to the entire pantheon of Hindu Gods for Cypress Capital and BeauPlus. Thanks to them, Vimala Paul and all our investors were on my side.

'I've been discussing this with Abhimanyu, and we wanted to bring you the detailed plan next week,' I said.

'The sooner the better! In fact, let's meet first thing Monday,' Ash announced, giving me the meeting slot that he usually reserved only for very important people, like board members or the CEO. 'Make sure Abhimanyu is there as well. I want to see a full execution plan, including a detailed marketing plan. BeauPlus and Cypress won't know what hit them!'

Oh no! If Abhimanyu had to be in the meeting, I needed to make sure it wasn't a bad day as per his horoscope.

'Give me a minute, Ash, I think Abhimanyu mentioned he will be out of office some time next week,' I stammered as I took my phone back and began checking Abhimanyu's horoscope for Monday.

Ash looked a little upset that I was not jumping at this opportunity. Thankfully, AstroZone showed me that Monday was a star day for Abhimanyu. Finally, a sign that my project was meant to be!

'Ash, Monday works,' I said. 'I've sent you an invite. Thank you so much for this,' I smiled.

We headed back upstairs in silence. Ash was busy checking his email and I was lost in thought about my narrow miss. I didn't know what excuse I would've come up with if Monday hadn't been a good day for Abhimanyu horoscope wise. I realized I had to be careful with how I played this horoscope game. As more people got involved, it became more complicated. I had just got back to my seat when my phone pinged.

Glam Office Messenger Group Chat

[#Best-Buds@Glam—12.00 p.m.] Upasana: Sitara, what have you done?

[#Best-Buds@Glam—12.00 p.m.] Sitara: I was drinking chai. What could I have possibly done?

[#Best-Buds@Glam—12.01 p.m.] Upasana: Dhruv told Abhimanyu that you spoke to Ash and there's a presentation due Monday. Mr Singh does NOT look happy.

[#Best-Buds@Glam—12.01 p.m.] Sitara: I just got back to my desk. How did Dhruv hear already?

[#Best-Buds@Glam—12.03 p.m.] Upasana: Oh, he has Ash's new executive assistant, Kanika, wrapped around his little finger. She tells him about Ash's meetings as soon as they are scheduled.

[#Best-Buds@Glam—12.04 p.m.] Sitara: No way!

[#Best-Buds@Glam—12.04 p.m.] Upasana: As if you didn't know he was a bit of a weasel. EVERYONE knows about his Ash-stalking!

[#Best-Buds@Glam—12.05 p.m.] Shirin: When did Sitara have good judgement? Or pay attention to things that don't involve her?

[#Best-Buds@Glam—12.05 p.m.] Sitara: I said I was sorry, Shirin.

Shirin has left the chat.

[#Best-Buds@Glam—12.07 p.m.] Sitara: Shit, what do I do to patch up with her?

Upasana is typing . . .

'Sitara, can I see you in my office please,' I looked up to see Abhimanyu frowning.

Uh oh. This did not bode well. I started thinking of ways to buffer my claim that my conversation with Ash was purely coincidental. Maybe I could say that Ash asked me about the proposal and things escalated?

Dhruv was sitting in Abhimanyu's office, looking like the cat that had got the cream, the milk and some cheese to go. There was no way I could wriggle out of this easily.

'It's come to my notice that Ash has heard about your project,' Abhimanyu said, taking his seat. I continued to stand in a corner awkwardly. 'Ideally, I would've liked to control the scheduling of the presentation to give us enough time to prepare but we don't have that choice now that you've already blocked a meeting on Monday morning. It's short notice, but we have a lot of work to do.'

'We?' Dhruv said, looking aghast.

'Yes, we,' he repeated, much to Dhruv's chagrin. 'This presentation needs to be Ash-ready. Sitara, you already know what I expect in terms of execution plan details. I'm expecting you to coordinate with all the relevant teams. Dhruv will be the point person on marketing.'

I glanced at Dhruv. With every sentence that came out of Abhimanyu's mouth, he looked more and more unhappy. He expected me to get a solid dressing down from Abhimanyu for making us all work on such short notice. Instead, we were in planning mode. Even worse, he was being asked to make an entire section of the presentation deck. I was as surprised as Dhruv was that I was getting away with this.

'Abhimanyu, this is extremely short notice,' Dhruv began, trying to remind his boss of the fact that the short notice was entirely my doing. 'What about my campaign?' He began jiggling his foot impatiently.

'You can move the deadline. This is our top priority now that Ash is thinking of taking this to the board. It's got potential to be our star project this quarter,' he replied.

Dhruv looked supremely upset. The wheels were starting to turn in his head. If the review on Monday went well, my project would be ahead of his. And if this became something the board backed, it was almost certain he would lose that promotion to me.

I held my breath, expecting Abhimanyu to say something to me about going to Ash. To my surprise, he gestured that we could both leave his office. For some reason, he was giving me a pass. I suspected it was because he didn't want to waste time yelling at me when it could be spent on getting work done. As we left Abhimanyu's office, Dhruv's face was mottled red, a mix of anger and frustration. I, on the other hand, could barely hold back my grin.

The stars were aligning in my favour.

14

Don't Spend This Saturday under a Cloud

I've always believed Saturdays should be restricted to three activities: nursing your hangover from a Friday night binge-drinking session; a boozy brunch (which could result in a hangover); or reading on the couch all day. After all, what good was a Saturday if you couldn't waste it? There was all of Sunday left to finish any chores you could effectively put off. And yet, this Saturday found me stone-cold sober, dressed in a pair of yoga pants and an old T-shirt, staring into my laptop screen at work.

In order to get myself into a 'productive' frame of mind, I had gone against all my Saturday morning principles, woken up early and made a rare appearance at the neighbourhood Cult. After grabbing some breakfast that negated all the calories I'd burned by making a fool of myself at the Dance Fitness class, I had made my way to work so I could make the most of the day. I was hoping to finish everything by the evening so I could go home and proceed with the binge drinking. I fully expected the day to be terrible, so I had worn my 'lucky' butterfly earrings.

The earrings seemed to be working. Dhruv had sent me an email titled 'Marketing Inputs—Subscription Programme' at midnight. I had been half-expecting him to not send me anything because Upasana had told me he had spent all day ambling around chatting with people. He was definitely super annoyed with Abhimanyu's directive. But then again, he wouldn't want to annoy his boss. Or Ash. I clicked on the email.

I had every other input I needed for the presentation and Dhruv's email contained the last piece of the puzzle. I knew he was trying to throw me off-guard with the timing on the email. That's why I had planned to spend Saturday morning working on the presentation. I downloaded the slides Dhruv had attached.

At first glance, the marketing plan looked passable. Good, even. But then, I noticed that the smarmy bastard had put in projections that effectively showed that irrespective of any amount of marketing, this programme would not succeed. There was no way I could use this. It negated everything I was trying to prove. I marvelled at Dhruv's ability to follow his boss's instructions, while still making sure he was effectively ruining my chances at getting promoted. Forget a promotion, this 'plan' would get me fired if Ash ever laid eyes on it. I realized I would have to make an entire marketing plan from scratch. One that showed our programme would succeed.

'There goes my Saturday,' I muttered as I began pulling out older presentations to find some marketing plans I could modify and use.

Thank God I bought a venti Starbucks mint-chocolate macchiato and a chocolate croissant, I thought. If I couldn't rely on alcohol to get me through the day, I would rely on an explosive carb and sugar combo to fuel me.

Glam Office Messenger Chat

[9:00 a.m.] Sitara: Hey, do you have good examples of marketing plans that I can use for my presentation to Ash tomorrow?

[9:05 a.m.] Upasana: Wasn't Dhruv working on your marketing plan?

[9:05 a.m.] Sitara: Don't ask! He gave me a 'plan' that proves no amount of marketing will lead to this programme ever succeeding. There's no way I can use it.

[9:07 a.m.] Upasana: Wow. He must be really worried! Abhimanyu was so particular about your project, he'd have Dhruv's hide if he found out . . .

[9:07 a.m.] Sitara: Really? Wouldn't he want Dhruv to get promoted?

[9:08 a.m.] Upasana: He seemed super excited about yours. Anyway, check your email. I've sent you some examples.

If only she knew the 'reason' for Abhimanyu's excitement, I thought.

I was firmly convinced it was entirely because I'd timed my pitch based on his horoscope. I shut the chat window and began downloading the plans Upasana had sent.

'That was one expensive tea you had with Ash!'

My head snapped up in shock. I looked up to see Abhimanyu standing by my seat, smirking. He was dressed for the weekend in a polo neck T-shirt and shorts. I had never seen him wear shorts before, and I had to say, the man was hot. All that cycling had ensured he was extremely fit.

Stop staring, I told myself. It was hard to tear my eyes away.

'How come you're here?' I asked.

'Ash wanted to see our three-year plan for marketing on Monday. I don't work well at home, so I figured I'll come into the office to get it done. I was also expecting to look at the final draft of your presentation.'

'But how did you know I'd be here?'

'I assumed I would get an email,' he laughed. 'You said you'd send me the draft by 4 p.m. I was planning to finish up the three-year plan and then send you my comments. Of course, I did not expect you to be around to take that feedback in person.'

He took the desk near me and began setting up his laptop. I saw that he had also come prepared for a long day, with a travel mug and multiple boxes of snacks and food.

'Apple slice?' he offered.

I felt completely unhealthy sitting with my croissant that was coated in butter and surrounded by a tiny mountain of chocolate bars that I'd got from the vending machine. My table was like the 'before' shot of an impending heart attack.

'No thanks,' I replied. I hadn't put myself through the class from hell only to eat an apple slice. I needed all the sugar and carbs today.

'Wouldn't you rather sit in your office?' I asked. It was so odd to have him sitting right by me. Not to mention how distracting it was, given how hot he looked. I couldn't stop myself from giving him a once-over.

'Actually, I thought I'd sit in Ash's cabin today, but this way, I can also share my snacks,' he quipped.

We worked in companionable silence for the next few hours, punctuated only by Abhimanyu offering me snacks. I was glad to accept most of them, since it saved me the trouble of foraging for food from the vending machine, the Starbucks or the Swiggy app that was busy sending me alerts, reminding me that it was time to order a meal. The only downside was that his supply seemed to be filled with healthy eats only.

Hours later, I was stuffed to the gills with snacks and had remade my entire presentation from scratch. I had created a marketing plan that looked good and also projected good results. I showed it to Abhimanyu without telling him that this wasn't Dhruv's plan. I didn't want to risk showing him the version that claimed the project wouldn't work. Abhimanyu decided we needed to spice up the plan. Instead of trying to coordinate over email, he decided to fill in for Dhruv and suggested that the two of us brainstorm. I wasn't going to refuse an opportunity to get in-person feedback and gratefully accepted. We traded ideas back and forth until we came up with something we knew Ash would love.

'This is great,' he said as I went through the slides one last time. 'I think we have a winner. Good work, Sitara!'

For the first time, I saw that 1000-watt smile within the office. My stomach fizzed and popped. I wondered if the overdose of snacks was giving me heartburn.

'I couldn't have done it without your help,' I replied. 'Thank you for spending your Saturday throwing around ideas with me. I think the presentation really benefited from that!'

PING!

WhatsApp Chat

> **[5:00 p.m.] Inaya:** Chithi, where are you? I've given Amma three sniffs of lavender oil to calm her down already, and the instructions say that any more could be dangerous. When will you get here?

'Oh crap! I forgot,' I yelled. How on earth could I have forgotten? I had got reminders from Sahana all through the week!

'What's going on?' Abhimanyu asked, concern writ over his face, as I frantically pulled up the Uber app. I couldn't see a single car. I was so screwed.

'I forgot my dad's birthday party,' I wailed. 'It's at six and I should've left already!'

I heard a loud crack, and that's when I looked out of the window for the first time all day. It was pouring outside. No wonder there were no cabs. I opened up Ola as well so I could check on both.

'My sister is going to kill me,' I muttered. I began gathering my stuff and haphazardly pushing it into my bag. Sahana had also sent me a bunch of messages, starting off with sounding concerned that I was stuck in the rain, moving on to wondering if I had been abducted, and ending with telling me that I better be dead and lying in a ditch somewhere because if not, she would kill me. I immediately sent her a message to say I was stuck in terrible traffic and would be there soon. She would know I was lying when I would eventually straggle in, but for now, it would buy me time.

'It's pouring out, so many people will be late. I'm sure you'll manage to get there,' Abhimanyu said.

'Except my sister is a master planner and asked everyone to get there early to pre-empt the rains. It's a surprise party for his sixtieth, so I have to be there before he arrives!'

'Listen, you're never going to find a cab right now,' Abhimanyu said.

No shit, Sherlock, I thought.

'I can drive you,' he offered.

That got my attention. I finally looked up from my phone.

'It's at my sister's place in Malleshwaram,' I told him. 'You'd be going completely out of your way and you'll be stuck for hours in traffic trying to get home.'

'So what's your plan?' he asked bluntly. 'Walk? If you think you're late now, you will most definitely be late if you attempt that.'

I had a mental image of me showing up sweaty and drenched, just in time to yell surprise for my dad's next birthday party.

'This is so nice of you, but there's no way I can waste any more of your time. I'm sure you have plans for the evening,' I said, even though I was desperate to take him up on his offer.

'Believe me, all I have planned is to go home, get some ramen and watch TV. I would rather be your substitute driver than spend yet another boring evening at home. Aren't you late?' he pressed. I stared at both the apps on my phone, willing one of them to magically find a driver. But I was completely out of luck.

'Just buy me dinner if that'll make you feel better,' he said. 'Give me a good recommendation in the area and I'll go there after I drop you.'

'If you're sure . . . ' I said.

'Sitara, I wouldn't offer if I wasn't,' he replied. He picked up his things and began walking purposefully towards the door. I followed.

At times like this I wondered if I was better off planning my day by looking at the weather forecast instead of a horoscope!

15

A Day of Surprises and Not All Pleasant

'Which college student did you steal this playlist from?' I asked as I scrolled through Abhimanyu's Spotify playlist on his phone which was connected to the car's Bluetooth system. 'A.R. Rahman, Arijit Singh, Coke Studio are all great choices. I can even understand Shakira, I mean the woman is hot. But why on earth do you have Ellie Goulding?'

'My music taste is perfectly normal,' he insisted, even as the opening bars of 'Call Me Maybe' poured out from the speakers.

I raised my eyebrows.

'Some of the songs remind me of college,' he said, as I resisted the urge to point out that 'Call Me Maybe' definitely didn't come out when he was in college. He smiled nostalgically, showing off the dimple that was otherwise well hidden. 'Until then, I hadn't heard a single English song. I grew up in a small town, and we didn't really know much about English music.'

Now that was surprising. He didn't come across as someone who'd grown up in a small town at all. I could've sworn he was a clueless city child like I was.

'Well, I'll forgive this weird selection as long as I don't stumble upon the Backstreet Boys,' I said.

Immediately, he turned down the volume and began a rendition of 'I Want It That Way'. In Hindi. To say I was stunned was an understatement. Firstly, this guy could sing. And secondly, he seemed to have translated the entire song!

'Oh my God,' I breathed. 'I don't know whether to admire your memory and translation skills or to judge your terrible taste in music!'

'Listen, there are boy bands whose music is actually great for cycling,' he said, with a sheepish smile.

All that healthy food and cycling? No wonder the man looked the way he did, I thought, as I tried hard to ignore the mental image of his abs and those oh-so-toned calves he'd been showing off all day.

'Oh! You're into cycling?' I said, trying to distract myself. 'I'm part of a weekend cycling group. I'm not very regular, but I've gone on a few trips. What about you? Group or solo?'

I had conveniently stretched the truth, and hoped he wouldn't jump at the chance to 'join' me. I had tried to join a weekend cycling group once in a misguided attempt to recreate my childhood nostalgia of cycling around the neighbourhood. I soon realized that whatever calories I burnt were more than replenished by the meals I consumed at pit stops. The final straw came when I went on one of their 'away' trips to Wayanad, where I gave up on cycling by midday and instead rode around in the car that was meant for 'assistance' in case of emergency. I didn't have the guts to show up again after that.

'Well, I used to be in a group,' Abhimanyu began, with a faraway look on his face.

'You can let me know if you want to come on one of our weekend rides. I can add you to the WhatsApp group where they share details . . . ' I offered.

'Maybe,' he said evasively. I sensed that there was more to the cycling story than he was letting on, but he seemed to be reluctant to share. I lapsed into silence, racking my brains to think of a way to change the subject.

'So,' he broke into my thoughts with that familiar smirk. 'Why don't you connect your phone to the Bluetooth and show me what supposedly good music sounds like?'

I busied myself with trying to connect my phone to the car's Bluetooth system when Abhimanyu suddenly jammed on the brakes. I looked up and realized we were stuck in a traffic jam.

'Oh no! I'm going to be so late,' I said, as I stared at the long line of cars ahead of us.

'*Main toh raste se jaa raha tha* . . . ' burst out through the car speakers.

Oh crap!

I was so busy looking at the traffic, I had accidentally played my favourites playlist instead of my carefully curated 'for public eyes' playlist. I blushed furiously as Abhimanyu burst out laughing and mimed eating bhelpuri. I tried to sink lower into my seat and avoided his looks. After all the fuss I'd made about his musical tastes, how terribly embarrassing it was to be caught with a campy 1990s Bollywood number on my playlist. I wondered if I could get away with claiming this was a playlist from someone's sangeet.

'*Tujhko mirchi lagi toh main kya karun,*' Abhimanyu began singing along with full gusto. He moved his head and shoulders to the beat, looking like he was one dance floor away from breaking into a dance. I stared at him with my mouth open. This was so far removed from the serious and staid Abhimanyu we saw at work. Even at the Circle of Success retreat where he was more relaxed, we didn't see this side of him!

'Unlike you, I'm not a music snob. And I will not pretend I don't love 1990s Bollywood songs,' he threw at me as he continued with his impromptu singalong.

There was a red hot warmth spreading from the roots of my hair to the tips of my toes. My arms prickled as he sang, and I noticed that his voice was giving me goosebumps. I needed to distract myself before he noticed that I couldn't stop staring. I looked away and suddenly remembered I was in yoga pants and a ratty T-shirt that proclaimed my love for naps. Sahana would kill me for showing up looking like this.

I pulled out some eyeliner and lipstick from my bag so I could do a quick job of pretending I was somewhat dressed for this party. I would claim I meant to stop at home but got delayed at work, and that my make-up was my attempt at trying to look passable. Besides, trying to put on eyeliner while we were stuck in a standstill was probably my only shot at it. I would probably poke myself in the eye if I tried it at any other time.

If Abhimanyu thought it was odd that I was putting on make-up in the car, he was nice enough to ignore it as he continued to sing along. Soon, he began calling out requests as I played the in-car DJ. At some point of time, the traffic began to move. We spent the drive playing our favourite songs and singing out loud all the way. I hadn't done this with anyone except Kavya before, but oddly enough it didn't feel weird. In fact, I was just as comfortable with Abhimanyu as I was with Kavya. I leaned back into my seat, shut my eyes and sang out loud as song after song played.

'You have arrived,' the voice on Google Maps suddenly broke into my thoughts. I looked out of the window and saw that we were right outside Sahana's house.

'Thank you . . . ' I began as I picked up my bag. It was an awkward moment because I didn't really know what to say now that we had arrived.

'Chithi! There you are,' Inaya materialized by the car, a bottle of some essential oil clutched in her hand. 'Amma is so mad at you. I can't even give her any more whiffs of this calming blend!'

She stuck her hand with the bottle through the window, as though giving me a calming blend was going to help the situation. I busied myself with getting out of the car to avoid replying to her.

'Why are you sitting next to the Uber driver?' she asked, peering suspiciously at Abhimanyu.

'Inaya, this isn't an Uber,' I cut in hurriedly to stop her from embarrassing me. 'This is my colleague.'

'Hi, I'm Abhimanyu,' he said. He stuck his hand out at her and to my surprise she shook it.

'Oh,' she squealed. 'You had a toffee in your hand. But Amma said I'm not allowed toffees today because there's cake . . .'

'It's fine, eat it,' I said. She didn't wait to give either of us a chance to change our minds. Within seconds the toffee disappeared into thin air, much like how it had appeared— seemingly from thin air.

'Well . . .' I began as I looked at Abhimanyu awkwardly, wondering how to end this conversation and leave gracefully.

'You can park over there,' Inaya helpfully jumped in, showing off the caramel sticking to her teeth.

'No, I was just dropping Sitara off,' Abhimanyu began.

'But why? The cake is yummy. I ate the leftover batter!'

'My sister does make amazing cakes,' I offered.

Inaya very rarely warmed up to someone so quickly. I suspected the toffee had something to do with this.

'I couldn't possibly impose . . .'

'Uncle, you have to come. I'm trying to develop my ability to spot kindred spirits. You seem to be one. Come, please,' she grinned.

'Inaya, are you sure you're not identifying kindred spirits based on who gives you toffees,' I grinned.

'Listen, you don't have time. Amma is already mad and we've been standing here for five minutes already,' she said gesturing to her bright purple *My Little Pony* watch.

Abhimanyu looked at me.

'Inaya really wants you here,' I smiled. 'Come in, the food will be great. And there's the cake to look forward to!'

'We also have Dilli-style chhole bhature . . . ' Inaya began.

'You don't have to give uncle the whole menu,' I cut her off.

'Dilli-style,' he mused. 'Really? I haven't had that since I moved . . . '

I could sense he was beginning to waver.

'Come on!' Inaya began pulling at my arm. I gestured at Abhimanyu to follow us. He still looked mildly uncomfortable but parked his car by the side of the road and started walking by me.

'This is weird. I'm not invited, it's a family function,' he said.

'Actually,' Inaya jumped in. 'I was allowed to invite three friends, and only two of them are here. You can be my third friend. Now you're invited.'

'Besides, do you really want to miss the chhole bhature?' I smiled.

He fell silent. We walked up to the door quickly. I knew I was really late and thought it would be a great idea to sneak into the house before my parents showed up.

The front door was slightly open. Ram must have left it that way because the baby was asleep.

I confidently walked up to the door and opened it.

I stepped inside, and—

'SURPRISE!'

I stood at the entryway in shock, as the lights snapped on and I stared at a room full of people who clearly weren't expecting me. A bunch of balloons fell on my head.

'What are you doing here?' Sahana yelled. 'I messaged you to tell you that Amma Appa are almost here and you should come in through the back door. And you, Inaya, didn't I tell you to tell Chithi . . . '

Inaya shrunk behind me. Clearly, in her excitement she had forgotten to pass on the information she had been sent out with.

'I'm sorry, I didn't see your message,' I began. I tried to collect the balloons that were flying about as I stepped in.

'You didn't answer your phone either . . . '

'What's going on here?' my father's voice broke into our argument.

There was stunned silence.

'Surprise!' yelled Inaya, right on cue.

Almost immediately, everyone else gathered their wits and weakly joined in. Someone began singing 'Happy Birthday' in the background as people slowly joined in.

Sahana stared daggers at me.

'Happy birthday, Appa,' I said as I extracted my badly wrapped gift from my bag and handed it to him. I thanked God I had purchased and kept this gift in my bag, anticipating I might forget about the party on the actual day.

'And this is . . .' said my father, staring at Abhimanyu and getting to the crux of the matter very quickly.

Abhimanyu was now looking extremely uncomfortable. I sensed he was trying to evaluate if he could just sprint away and pretend he wasn't here. My father reached out and shook his hand vigorously.

'Thatha, this is Manyu Uncle,' Inaya announced. 'He's a kindred spirit, my new friend and the third friend I invited.'

Manyu? She'd given him a nickname already? I wondered if I should step in, but I didn't know what I could possibly say.

'Happy birthday, Sir. I'm Abhimanyu. I work with Sitara. Don't mind me, I'm just here to drop her. Nice meeting you . . . ' his voice trailed off, as he continued to look hassled.

'Oh, no. You must join us. At least have some cake,' my father said, ushering him inside. 'Tell me, what do you do at Glam?'

Abhimanyu began answering my father as I looked around the room. My heart sank as I realized that everyone was dressed to the nines in formal wear, Kanjeevaram sarees and the like. Meanwhile, I was in my gym wear and even the make-up I'd hurriedly applied in the car wasn't really helping my cause. Almost as soon as I realized it, Sahana materialized by my side and gave me a sharp look.

'You need to change,' she said, glaring at me. Even her temple jewellery seemed to be tinkling in a disapproving tone. 'Come with me.'

That tone brooked no disagreement. I looked back to see that Abhimanyu was still in conversation with my father. I went up to them and told Abhimanyu I would be back in a few minutes. Sahana dragged me away by the arm like a goat being led to slaughter.

She had gone all out for this party. My dad's favourite songs were playing in the background, and there were fairy lights everywhere. She'd even taken the trouble of decorating the rooms upstairs even though nobody would go there. We got to her bedroom and she opened her cupboard, trying to find me something to wear. I wanted to tell her I was OK with what I was wearing, but I knew that wouldn't end well. So I waited as she scrunched her face and analysed a bunch of 'options'.

'Here,' she said handing me a neon-orange anarkali. It was exactly the kind of vibrant colour that she and my mother loved, and I hated.

'Sahana, it's really orange . . . ' I began. She raised her eyebrows at me and gave me a deathly stare. I shut up immediately.

'This is perfect for the occasion,' she announced, like she was a celeb stylist tasked with transforming an unfashionable duckling into a passable swan. 'I'll see you downstairs in five minutes.'

I stared morosely at the bright, shiny outfit. Well, at least there would be cake.

By the time I changed and went back downstairs, I hoped Abhimanyu had left. I was wearing the bright orange anarkali. It was a weird length on me because I was taller than Sahana. She had got her revenge by giving me something she must've purchased post-partum. It dipped dangerously low at the cleavage thanks to the bad fit. I tugged at the neckline hoping I wouldn't accidentally flash my entire family. I entered the living room and stopped in shock. I stared open-mouthed at the scene in front of me.

Abhimanyu was standing at the centre of a group of my relatives, regaling them with some story. The group had my father's sister Vasantha Athai and her daughter Janaki, a duo I tried to avoid with utmost diligence at all family gatherings. Even worse, I spotted Ambi Mama, who had found an unsuspecting victim in Abhimanyu. Ambi Mama was a random uncle who was related to us in some way that nobody remembered. Every Tamilian family has an Ambi Mama, and he attended all our family functions as the token Ambi of ours. I knew I would have to go there and extricate Abhimanyu before Mama latched on to some random story and bored him to death. Inaya had wisely taken stock of the situation and abandoned Abhimanyu. She was now sitting in a corner reading a library copy of *Anne of Green Gables*. That explained her sudden obsession with kindred spirits. Her friends were sitting next to her, trying to put together a complicated jigsaw puzzle.

I took a deep breath and walked up to the group.

'Ah, you changed,' said Abhimanyu with a grin. I tugged at the neckline yet again and then folded my arms across my chest hoping to cover up.

'Hi, *kanna*'! What a lovely kurta,' said Vasantha Athai. 'So bright!'

'It's Sahana's,' I admitted, knowing that Athai didn't mean 'bright' as a compliment. I was sure the outfit looked fantastic on Sahana. But I was really not doing it any justice, given my constant tugging at the neck and the fact that I had visions of myself looking like a giant, fat, shiny orange.

'That explains it,' Janaki said, going on the offensive immediately as was her wont when it came to me. 'It's really not your type of outfit, no? You normally wear those washed out colours! Remember the last time we met, I thought your brand new kurta was a second-hand one!'

She tittered. Janaki had hated me ever since we were kids, because our grandmothers had dedicated their lives to making us compete with each other in everything ranging from our marks at school to who wore the bigger *pottu*.** Unfortunately for her, I regularly won. That hate remained unwavering till this day. We often regressed to

---

* A term of endearment in Tamil
** Tamil for bindi, a small coloured mark worn on the forehead between the eyebrows

our childhood selves the minute we were near each other. I made a mental note to try and be the bigger person today.

'I had to come directly from work and didn't have time to change,' I explained politely. 'All of you are looking so nice!'

'Yes, this is a Sabya,' she said, as she twirled to show off her saree. It may have been a branded saree but unfortunately for her, it was a shade of brownish-green that looked like Chak had thrown up all over her.

'And I loaned her my favourite set,' Vasantha Athai jumped in, ready to show off her extensive jewellery collection. She gestured to the glittering diamond earrings and necklace that Janaki was displaying. At the right angle, the jewellery covering both of them could effectively blind someone.

'Sitara never cares about how she looks,' said Janaki. 'You remember how you spilt paint all over my favourite dress?'

I took a deep breath, trying to channel my adult self, but the five-year-old within me won. I burst out, 'as if you didn't get your revenge by decapitating my Ken doll. Which wasn't an accident, unlike the dress . . .'

'Oh, you never knew how to look after your things. Don't you remember how you fell into the fountain at the amusement park?' she butted in as a red flush rose up her neck. 'You were naked on the ride home!'

'And what about the time when you ate too much cake and threw up on yourself?' I gave back as good as I got. 'My room hasn't smelled the same ever since!'

'What about . . . ' she began, but stopped when Athai pinched her arm.

'Abhimanyu was just telling us about himself before you two rudely interrupted him with this childish argument,' Athai said, shooting me a look as though the entire argument was my fault and her daughter was an innocent bystander.

'Yes, quite an impressive young man,' said Ambi Mama. 'And so nice of you to bring Sitara. She's always alone at family functions, since she refuses to settle down.' I realized that Mama was as inappropriate as ever, not bothered that he was sharing unwanted information with my colleague!

'Speaking of settling down, did you see Arjun's proposal?' Athai said, as I struggled to keep my face neutral. The three of them launched into a full blow-by-blow, as though they were recapping the highlights of a cricket match that Abhimanyu had missed. I wondered how I could gracefully leave and also extricate Abhimanyu who had now heard way too much about my personal life.

'I think Amma is calling me . . . ' I began as Janaki smoothly cut in with a wicked smile.

'Did *you* watch the proposal,' she said, her tone dripping with fake concern. 'Must've been so difficult to see that, no?'

'Oh, Arjun and I were old news,' I said feigning nonchalance. I readjusted my neckline. 'Besides, you know I hate cricket so I didn't watch it.'

'Of course, of course,' she snickered.

'Sitara, Inaya is calling you,' Abhimanyu broke into the conversation.

'No, she's over there reading,' Ambi Mama said, effectively cutting off our exit route.

'Subtlety really isn't your forte, is it?' Abhimanyu twinkled at the group as he held my elbow and steered me away from them.

They stared at him in shock.

I burst into laughter.

'I don't think anyone has ever insulted them that subtly before,' I gasped. 'Thank you!'

'I don't know what came over me,' he said, blushing a deep, dark red. 'But they were attacking you, and you didn't deserve that!'

'You were brilliant,' I insisted even as he scrunched up his face and said, 'Should I go back and apologize?'

'No way,' I insisted. 'You did something I always wished I could do, except I'd never be able to get away with it. You're never going to see them again, so say what you like.'

'So, about this Arjun . . . ' he began, looking quite stricken. 'I won't mention it to anyone at work.' He ran his hand through his hair uncomfortably. Somehow, that just made him look cuter than ever.

'Thank you,' I said. 'We broke up a while ago, but he's been back in the news. He's the one who proposed during the India-England match. But I've moved on now. Except my nosy family doesn't quite get that concept!'

'As long as you're sure you're okay,' he said, staring intently at me.

'I'm more than okay,' I replied, smiling at him. And for the first time in all these years, I finally meant it.

At that, he smiled. His entire face lit up and I watched that deep dimple show up on his cheek. It gave me goosebumps. This smile only came out at certain times, and almost never in the office. It never failed to take my breath away.

He took a step towards me. Almost reflexively, I took a step back.

'Inaya is busy with her book,' I blurted as my stomach churned and I wondered what was going on with me. 'You can leave, if you want to.'

He looked back at Athai and Janaki who were staring at us and gossiping in hushed tones. 'I know it's your father's birthday, but nothing stops you from leaving either,' he said softly.

It was the most insane idea I'd ever heard. And not something I would ever entertain.

'It's time for cake,' Sahana broke into my thoughts. She caught my arm in an iron grip as though she'd sensed I was considering leaving. She dragged me to the dining room where everything was set up for the cake cutting.

Appa cut his cake and we all sang for him.

'Speech,' someone yelled.

'Thank you all for coming,' he said. 'I'm especially thankful to Sahana for putting this together. And to Sitara for showing up,' he said.

I looked up from my mouthful of cake. Wow. He wouldn't let a single opportunity get by when it came to making fun of me.

'The offer to leave is still open,' Abhimanyu whispered.

'No . . . ' I trailed off as we both walked to one side. My mother came up behind us.

'Sitara, when do you find out about that promotion?' she asked.

'It'll take a while, Amma,' I explained. 'First, there's a project I have to complete and then we'll see.'

'OK, good,' she said. 'So you were working late today because of the project?'

'Yes,' I said. 'I told you this when we met for lunch . . .'

'Work is all you ever talk about,' she said dismissively. 'You need to be settled too,' she continued as she stared meaningfully at Sahana, who was standing with Ram and the two kids looking like a picture-perfect happy family from a toothpaste commercial.

'Amma,' I began, but she wasn't listening to me any more. Her friend was gesturing to her, so she walked away, having delivered her lecture.

'I'm going to step out and start the car,' Abhimanyu broke into my thoughts. 'I'll be there for five minutes. You're welcome to join me if you want to leave.'

I watched him walk out and wrestled with my conscience. On the one hand, Sahana would kill me if I left before dinner. But on the other hand, everyone here was obsessed with my single status. Normally, I would hang out with Inaya but she seemed lost in her book. Just as I was mentally convincing myself to stay, Ambi Mama began making his way in my direction.

The thought of a second conversation with him in one evening did it for me.

I ran out.

16

Pluto Is about to Wake

'Sitara!'

'Drive as fast as you can,' I said to Abhimanyu who was putting the car into gear. Sahana was outside the house yelling at the top of her voice.

'You cannot possibly leave right now!'

'Sorry, Sahana,' I said, waving at her as we drove by. 'I'm sorry we're missing dinner, but I have to leave because I'm feeling sick.' Before she could say anything else, we left her standing outside the gate with her hands on her hips. She was shaking her head with that mix of disappointment and frustration I was used to seeing from my family.

'I'm sorry you had to go through that,' I said to Abhimanyu. After this evening, I didn't think I could call him a 'colleague' any more. He had been regaled by my family's quirks in full colour. And, he now knew all about my past. To his credit, he didn't seem fazed by either.

'Well, it was way more entertaining than television,' he laughed.

'Oh my family can beat any TV show when it comes to entertainment,' I said.

'So, what's the next song?' he asked.

I busied myself with setting up the car's Bluetooth. Soon, we went back to blasting his cycling songs and singing out loud. Even though traffic was moving at a snail's pace, we were not bothered because we were having so much fun.

Suddenly, my stomach growled. I pretended to clear my throat and sang the chorus of '*Chaiyya Chaiyya*' even louder, hoping that the beats would divert attention from the fact that my stomach sounded like an angry bear.

'Hey, there's this new Italian restaurant that has just opened by your house. Let's grab dinner before I drop you,' Abhimanyu said.

'Oh, no! You don't have to do that,' I said, completely embarrassed that he felt the need to stop my demon stomach from growling so loudly.

'Come on, it'll give me some time to hear some more embarrassing stories,' he joked. 'Or, I can share a few of mine so we're even?'

I tried to refuse out of politeness, but he insisted. I gave in. After all, I had missed dinner and I didn't have anything else planned. Besides, I had promised to treat him to dinner in exchange for the ride.

'How can anyone like pesto?' I said, wrinkling my nose.

'I love pesto!'

'It's green,' I said, making a face. 'Nothing green tastes good! You must be one of those horrible people who like pineapple on pizza.' Or maybe this was a result of his health kick. Green food. I shuddered at the thought of it.

'I'm not. Pineapple on pizza is blasphemy. However, I think you're the weirdo who eats cold pizza taken directly out of the fridge the next morning!'

'Guilty,' I laughed. 'It tastes much better, you know.' And while I wouldn't admit it, I was too lazy to spend the few seconds microwaving food when I was hungry.

I took a sip of water.

'OK! Favourite movie?'

'*Ratatouille*,' he said without missing a beat. 'I rewatched it last night, that's why I felt like ordering it today . . .'

'You expect me to believe your favourite movie is an animation? Seriously?'

'Why not? I love animated movies, especially the old 2D ones. I even considered becoming an animator, but it didn't pay enough.'

'You're kidding! I love animated movies too! Who's your favourite Disney prince?' I asked cheekily, expecting him to say he hadn't watched the princess-y ones.

'Prince Eric from *The Little Mermaid*. He can sing and he loves dogs. Also, he doesn't care that Ariel can't talk, he accepts her for who she is,' he said, with a smile that rivalled Eric's swoon-worthy one.

My mouth was hanging open in shock.

He laughed.

'I have two sisters,' he explained. 'I have seen every princess movie multiple times. I know all about Barbie's extended family as well as the plots of *The Baby-Sitters Club* and the *Sweet Valley High* series.'

'So you're used to this reaction when you subtly throw out trivia on these topics,' I said.

'Haha, your turn. Who's your favourite prince?' he asked.

'Well, not really a prince,' I said, as the server placed our food on the table. 'But my favourite is Peter Pan.'

'That means you know why Peter Pan flies all the time,' he said, taking a bite of his ratatouille. I racked my brains but couldn't think of a reason. I wondered if he would notice if I sneakily pulled out my phone and tried googling the answer.

'Give up?' he challenged, as he picked up a piece of garlic bread.

'Fine!'

'Peter Pan flies all the time because he Neverlands,' he announced, looking extremely pleased with himself.

I glared at him. 'Clearly, you stayed in Neverland mentally! Have you been telling this joke since you were ten?'

'You're just mad you didn't get it,' he said. 'It's obvious you hate to lose.'

'Who told you that?' I asked indignantly.

'It's evident from the way you've been trying to push your project forward. Also, a little birdie told me how you were so focused on winning the team Quidditch race at the office picnic that you tripped someone with your broom.'

Oh God. I wondered who told him that story. Possibly someone from the admin and HR posse while trying to hit on him. They were always the source of all gossip.

'Inaya also told me some entertaining stories,' he said, as though he could read my mind. 'Something about a lemon and spoon race . . . '

'I didn't trip anyone,' I defended myself hotly. 'It was an accident. She just happened to be in the way of my broom. Not all of us are super coordinated athletes who cycle every day!'

He stopped laughing abruptly. I'd hit a nerve yet again. *What is it with him and cycling*, I wondered.

'It's not my finest moment,' he said softly. Yet again, I'd said that out loud by accident. I started to say he didn't have to confide in me, but for some reason, he decided to speak.

'I used to be in a cycling group when I was in Delhi,' he said. 'We went on trips to nearby places . . . '

'Do you miss it?' I asked.

'Actually, no. That's where I met my fiancée.'

For the second time that night my mouth dropped open. I didn't know he was engaged. It felt like a punch to my gut. The air whooshed out of my lungs. I wondered if the wine I was drinking was getting to me.

'Ex-fiancée,' he corrected himself. 'We broke off the engagement. That's why I moved. I wanted to move immediately after the break-up, but my horoscope kept indicating it wasn't the right time. I had to wait until my move would be most fruitful.'

I couldn't hold back any longer.

'You're one of the smartest people I know, and yet you insist on believing in this horoscope, "right time" type stuff! Why?'

He sighed.

'Come on, it makes no sense. You stayed in a place with terrible memories all because you were waiting for the right time?'

The wine was definitely getting to me. I was saying way more than I would otherwise.

'Firstly, this entire conversation is off the record. And by that, I mean don't share this with anyone on the team. I really don't want to be the newest hot topic of gossip. Especially on your group chat,' he said.

He was well informed on what we were up to in our private groups. I wondered how he'd heard of it. None of the other bosses knew of their existence.

'I'm not going to tell anyone,' I replied. 'After all you've done for me today, you're a friend and I don't gossip about my friends.'

He smiled.

'I didn't believe in astrology or horoscopes and all that,' he began, taking a deep breath. 'A year and a half ago, I met Pooja . . .'

Pooja.

I had visions of a tall, athletic looking girl, wearing stylish athleisure clothes and looking like she had stepped out of the pages of *Vogue*. I bet she had silky straight hair and was always perfectly made up. I tried not to roll my eyes.

'It was love at first sight. Within months, we knew we wanted to be together and so we decided to get engaged. Except, my family astrologer insisted it was a bad time. He told me to wait. At the time, even a few months sounded like eternity. I refused,' he said, a dark shadow falling over his face.

He seemed to be struggling to get the words out.

I reached out and held his hand, hoping to offer him some comfort. I had never seen him look so vulnerable.

'Listen, you don't have to tell me the rest of this story,' I said.

He took a deep breath.

'No, it's fine,' he said, composing himself. 'On the day of my engagement, my grandmother passed away.'

My heart stopped for a second. Was he carrying the burden of that guilt upon himself? I squeezed his hand and wondered if it would be terribly inappropriate to give him a hug. We were friends, but he was still a colleague.

'I'm sure that was a coincidence,' I said, opting to stay seated. I didn't want to freak him out with any sudden moves.

'I wish,' he sniffed. 'Weeks after that, I discovered that Pooja was cheating on me. With the guy who ran the cycling group.'

He buried his head in his hands. I moved mine back, wondering what to do with it now. It was tingling all over.

'I was so stupid. It had been happening all the while, and I just didn't see it.'

'I still think it was a coincidence,' I began.

'Maybe it was,' he said. 'But the timing was exactly based on what the astrologer had said. You think I would risk taking a chance after that?'

His voice was muffled, so I reached out and held his hand again.

'Abhimanyu, how can you be sure this works?' I pressed. 'The other day, you said you were using the AstroZone app, but this happened because you didn't listen to your family astrologer.'

'I couldn't really go back to the family astrologer because I'd argued with him. There's no way I could admit I was wrong. So I tried out many different things before I discovered this one works best. Whenever I've followed it, things have gone perfectly!'

Of course. Even when it came to something as unscientific as astrology, he still went about identifying his preferred source in the most scientific way possible. I was about to point out the irony of what he'd said, but I didn't want him to think I was making fun of him. I sensed it took him a lot to confide in me. And so, I did what I would do for any friend. I got up and gave him a hug.

For a second, he was still, almost statue-like in shock. And then he hugged me back with a muffled thanks. My stomach exploded with butterflies. The blood rushed to my cheeks. Slowly, I went back to my seat, wondering if he could hear my heart pounding.

'Thank you,' he said again. 'You're a good friend.'

I smiled and looked away quickly as my heart began hammering in my chest. I busied myself with taking a bite of my pasta so I didn't have to look at him.

During the drive back, he insisted we listen to my playlist. In the spirit of our newfound friendship, I played the list that had all my favourites. Whenever an A.R. Rahman song came up, he sang along in Hindi even though I only had the Tamil versions. It was quite impressive to see how he managed to keep track of the lyrics.

It wasn't until he turned off the ignition that I realized I was home.

'Thanks for the dinner and the ride,' I said. 'And for putting up with my family. And of course, your help with that presentation.'

'*Friendship main no sorry, no thank you*,' he said, doing a perfect Salman Khan impression. I laughed.

'Seriously, you would have done a great job even without my help. I'm fairly certain Ash will green-light this, and I'm excited for you.'

'I needed a lot of help and I appreciate the time you took out for brainstorming,' I said. I wondered why I was suddenly sounding so formal. It was time for me to go home, but somehow, I couldn't bring myself to step out of the car and end the night.

'See you on Monday,' he said, effectively breaking the spell. 'Thanks for dinner, it was. . . fun,' he finished.

'Somehow, you're not convincing me,' I replied with a wry smile. 'I hope you have a fun Sunday! Thanks for rescuing me twice today!'

I got out and walked into the house thinking of what an odd day it had been. It had started out terribly, with Dhruv's attempt to botch up my project. I lost my entire Saturday to work, and I was worried about presenting to Ash on Monday despite Abhimanyu's confidence. I also couldn't believe that Abhimanyu had walked into that disaster of a party and survived it.

And yet, I hadn't had such a fun evening in a long time.

Maybe the butterfly earrings had brought me some luck after all.

17

Spend a Quiet Day with Your Loved Ones

'Where were you?' Kavya asked as I walked out of my room the next morning, bleary eyed and half asleep. I blinked and rubbed my eyes. She was a little too awake and put together for a Sunday morning. I stared at her bright blue yoga pants and fitted white T-shirt.

How did she manage to go to the gym this early, I wondered.

I looked down at my comfy and well-worn Snoopy pyjamas. They were so old, they had a hole in one knee but I loved them and didn't ever plan to get rid of them. Kavya was still looking at me expectantly, but I didn't say anything. I needed caffeine before I could formulate any sort of response.

'Well,' she pressed. 'Where were you? Don't tell me you worked all night?'

'I had to go to Appa's surprise party,' I said. 'But we got stuck in traffic on the way home so we decided to stop for dinner. Sorry, I forgot to message you that I would be home late,' I yawned as I busied myself with making a cup of filter coffee.

'We?' she asked, giving me a pass for bailing on our plans for a late-night catch-up session the minute she heard there was a 'we' involved in this story.

'Tell me about your date,' I said, stifling a yawn. Kavya had gone on a Tinder date the previous night and I knew this would divert her from the questions around 'we' and who it constituted. I took a sip of the coffee, made a face and added two heaped spoons of sugar.

'So, we were supposed to meet at that new place, The Permit Room,' she began.

'Ooh! The one that makes those south Indian fusion cocktails?'

'Yes,' she replied, as she walked into the living room and settled on the couch. She hugged her legs to her chest.

'He spent the first fifteen minutes asking whether I drink or smoke. It was so weird.'

'Maybe he was looking for a girl to take home to his mom,' I quipped.

'But that wasn't how he was asking the questions. It was more like what's the farthest you've gone. Oh get your mind out of the gutter,' she said as I waggled my eyebrows.

'Anyway, we moved on to other topics and I thought that was it. Until our drinks came. Then, he tells me he has something to show me.'

'Please tell me he didn't show you a dick pic,' I said.

'Ugh, you really do need to get your mind out of the gutter,' she shuddered. 'No. He tells me he has his own business, and wants to show me his website. And guess what this business was?'

'What?' I asked, as I picked up the giant bag of cream and onion chips lying on our coffee table. This would work as breakfast until we got around to going out for brunch.

'POT,' she burst out.

'Pots? Like ceramics?' I wondered whether he had tried selling her a bowl or a water jug or maybe a ceramic replica of her face.

'No! POT as in weed! The dude's a dealer. He uses Tinder to find new customers!'

I almost fell off the couch laughing. I had to place my coffee cup on the coffee table, otherwise I would've definitely scalded myself by spilling it right down the front of my shirt.

'It's not funny,' she insisted, as she struggled to stop her own giggles.

'When I told him I'm not interested, he asked me to change my profile pic because I apparently looked the type . . .'

'He thought you looked like a pothead?' I didn't risk taking another sip of my coffee for fear I'd snort it out of my nose.

'Apparently. I mean, I've had guys hit on me saying that I have "*nasheeli aankhein*", but this guy went a little too far!'

I wiped the tears of laughter from my eyes. Kavya had some truly entertaining Tinder dates, including one extreme do-gooder who lived on his parents' couch and made no money, who called her 'Lucifer in the flesh' for being a corporate stooge, but this one was definitely the worst of the lot!

'So, who were you with?' she asked, staring at me.

I squirmed as I wondered how I could change the subject again. I had hoped that she would forget my use of the word 'we' as she talked about her date, but Kavya knew me too well. I reached out for a clutch to tie my hair as I attempted to evade her questions. I kept clutches in every room because I kept breaking them. Mostly because I couldn't find the large ones that could hold all my hair. So I ended up breaking them as I tried to force every last curl into them. Sometimes because I dropped my clutches and broke them. Ok, most of it was because of dropping them. I owned so many clutches, that even if Rapunzel wanted to tie up her hair, I'd be able to lend her some and still have a few left over.

'Abhimanyu was in the office, and he offered to give me a ride home,' I said nonchalantly.

Kavya stared at me. 'So he dropped you home, and then you went to your dad's party?'

I didn't answer.

'Wait, what are you saying . . . ' she looked at me like I had grown a second head.

'I was really late and I had to get to Malleshwaram as soon as possible . . . '

She took a chip from the bag and chewed on it thoughtfully.

'So he drove you all the way to Malleshwaram?' she asked, as her eyes widened in surprise.

'It was raining and there were no cabs,' I tried to defend myself.

But Kavya had now realized something else. Damn her sharp mind that never failed to miss a trick!

'You said you had dinner on the way back. Oh my God! You took him to your dad's party,' she said, covering her open mouth with her hands.

'It wasn't like that,' I said. 'Once we got there, Inaya invited him . . . '

'I suppose Inaya also invited him to take you for dinner,' she said.

'No, we left early because my family was being, well, you know, their usual judgemental selves. But then we got hungry, so we thought . . . '

I couldn't continue because Kavya was looking at me as though I had confessed to committing a murder.

'And here I thought I had the most entertaining date yesterday,' she said. 'But your date escalated quickly!'

'It wasn't a date,' I insisted. 'We got stuck in a jam, so he suggested we stop for dinner before we get home. Perfectly innocent.'

'Yeah, really innocent. You seem to be in a lot of car rides with him these days. Are you sure there's nothing going on?' she asked. 'Especially now that he's met the parents!'

She waggled her eyebrows at me, and then reached out and grabbed the packet of chips.

'Some of us don't want to go out with people we work with,' I said, as if she didn't know about my now non-existent crush on Dhruv.

'Anyway, I can't go out with him, he's not really my type, what with his astrology obsession.'

'I'm sure there's a reasonable explanation for that,' she said, cramming a fistful of chips into her mouth.

'We-ell, he does have a reason,' I admitted.

She stared me down until I gave in and gave her the gist of what Abhimanyu had told me the previous night, skipping the parts about Pooja cheating on him.

'Listen, don't say anything to Upasana or Shirin,' I added.

'Ooh! A secret office romance,' she replied.

'Ugh! No. There is no romance. He shared some things with me as a friend and I don't want to leak his personal story to the world . . . '

'Of course, it's just friends sharing personal stories. There's no romance whatsoever,' she replied sarcastically.

'There's no romance,' I insisted.

'Uh huh. He makes big revelations about his personal life, and you still think you're just friends,' she said, making air quotes around the word friends. I felt like I was a Bollywood celeb being grilled by a journalist.

'We're friends,' I repeated like a broken record. I now felt even more like those celebs as they insisted every relationship was nothing more than a friendship.

'There's nothing going on between us,' I said again as I took another sip of coffee.

Nothing.

Except that I'd stayed up till 4 a.m. going through his sparse Facebook profile after he'd accepted my friend request.

Except that I went through every last photo on his Instagram, trying to find one of Pooja to see how I compared.

Except that I was also pathetic enough to stalk his LinkedIn activities to come up with things to talk to him about.

Except I then shut off my phone, and tossed and turned while thinking about the look on his face when I hugged him in the restaurant.

Except that I couldn't fall asleep thinking about how that hug made me feel.

Except . . .

'Where do you want to go for brunch?' I asked, wanting to stop thinking about Abhimanyu.

Kavya gave me a dirty look and harrumphed. She wasn't letting me off the hook so easily.

'You worked together all day?' she asked.

'Marketing is super important for my presentation, you know that,' I said.

'Did he make any other life-altering revelations to you?' she asked. 'Or is he introducing you to his parents next?'

'We do share a love of 1990s Bollywood music, but so do you and I,' I said weakly.

'Sitara!' She leaned forward and clapped in front of my face.

'Good morning! Smell that coffee!' She pushed the mug closer to my nose. 'I don't think he's being nice, it sounds like he really likes you.'

'Of course not,' I insisted. 'He's still hung up on his ex-fiancée. And I have a crush on someone else.'

I mentally thanked God I hadn't got a chance to tell Kavya yet about my disastrous evening with Dhruv and how his sliminess had completely turned me off. I could hide behind a pretend crush on him.

'Meh, that guy's a weasel and you know it,' she dismissed Dhruv entirely, as though she always knew it wouldn't last. 'Are you *sure* you don't like Abhimanyu?'

'Of course I like him,' I said. 'But I don't like him, like him. He has this terrible habit of acting like he's always right, he likes healthy green food, he's sarcastic and he listens to Ellie Goulding!'

Kavya raised her eyebrows and walked out into our balcony.

'If you say so,' she called out as she picked up the watering can. 'Eats healthy food! What a turn-off.'

'I say so. Now, what about brunch?'

'You're being very quick to change the subject. What will I do with you?' she gave me a broad grin.

'What?'

'You don't even realize what you've got yourself into.' She shook her head and started watering our hibiscus plant. 'You may want to think about this horoscope game you're playing. When you realize the truth, it will come back to haunt you. I'm sure you'll get promoted even without this obsessive horoscope checking.'

'Just because you're focused on your Tinder escapades doesn't mean everyone else is also in that frame of mind,' I insisted as my cheeks heated up. 'Can we please just pick a place for brunch? I could do with a mimosa.'

'How about the new Italian place down the road?' she winked.

Yet again, I remembered why it was a terrible idea to share an apartment with your best friend. Your monthly budget forced you to abandon your plans every time you wanted to murder them.

18

Behold Your (Un) Lucky Moon
in Pisces

'Will this work? I'm not convinced that people will pay to get these freebies,' Ash said. He took a sip from his coffee cup as I tried not to look at the 'ASS' that the Starbucks barista had helpfully scrawled on it.

Across the table, Upasana was stifling her smile as she pretended to take notes. I knew she was busy doodling.

'Ash, our customers are extremely value conscious,' I began. 'This programme charges a yearly fee and provides them with a host of benefits through the year. They get free samples, makeovers . . .'

'But why do we need to sell subscriptions? Instead, we can create a loyalty programme, the kind where people have to spend a lot of money to get a membership. That will drive more repeat purchases on Glam,' he interrupted. He leaned forward and stared at me.

I glanced at Harsh. This was one of the most gruelling meetings I'd ever attended. Ash had been firing questions at me, and so far, I had to field them all. Tranquillity had well and truly left the building. I wondered if Ash had stopped drinking the custom blend herbal tea the programme had recommended. Or maybe the effects were wearing off.

I took a deep breath, collecting my thoughts before I responded.

'Actually, Ash, others have done this. The exact same concerns came up at my previous organization, but now we can all see just how well a similar programme has worked for them. We need to communicate and offer great benefits, and people will sign up,' Abhimanyu jumped in.

Ash nodded as I struggled to keep a straight face. My boss was busy avoiding my eyes, while Abhimanyu was busy helping me out.

Must be because his horoscope said that helping the team achieve a big goal will reap rich career rewards, I thought.

'Also, we are planning features like a savings calculator that will show customers how much they have saved. It'll become fairly clear to them that the benefits we are offering far outweigh the subscription fee,' I added. I was hoping this would convince Ash.

He took another sip of coffee.

'On the one hand, you want to create aspirational benefits that are not easily pegged to a rupee value. On the other hand, you want to put a savings calculator. This is not adding up.'

I had a sinking feeling that I was losing my grip on the presentation.

I looked at Harsh again. He appeared to be lost in thought. I hoped not stepping into the conversation was his misplaced way of trying to show I was in complete control. If so, he was doing a terrible job because it felt like he didn't care about this project, or me.

Harsh took a deep breath and looked up. I perked up. Maybe he had finally decided to step in. Then he reached out for the bottle kept in the middle of the table, poured himself a glass of water and leaned back in his chair. He took a long sip, while I ground my teeth in frustration.

'Actually, the vision is that we have one category of benefits that are linked to things like discounts and cashbacks that we can value very clearly. But we are also proposing things like expert makeovers, access to a personal stylist and so on, which can't be valued. They're things that will make people want to sign-up,' I replied to Ash.

'Let's take a step back,' Harsh began. I held my breath for a helpful comment. 'I feel like we are rushing into a marriage with this list of initiatives, without dating first.'

Um, what?

'I mean, I wouldn't marry someone on the first date,' he continued. 'I have to know her . . . '

There was an awkward pause as every single person in the room stared at him, wondering where he was going with this.

' . . . and she has to like me,' he finished with a grin.

At that moment, I wished that Harsh had stuck with his original plan of not speaking. Anything would've been better than that ridiculous analogy.

Ash stood up. I held my breath, hoping he wasn't about to storm out of the room.

'Harsh has a point,' Ash said, as he leaned against the wall. 'This concept sounds interesting, but I don't think we've identified how this project will get us our next round of funding.'

He looked directly at his reports Harsh, Abhimanyu and Abhijit. Now would be the perfect moment for Harsh to give a concrete solution. But he was busy staring at the ceiling as though the answers would magically appear there. Or maybe he was thinking about dating and marriage. I was furious. I had given Harsh a cheat sheet before this meeting, and it had included the answer to this question. I would have to answer this myself.

'Ash, you've always said the best way to prove whether something works is through an experiment. We can offer a version of this programme to a small, targeted group of customers and measure the impact on all our metrics. It'll help us prove the concept with no questions, and make an effective pitch to the board.'

Ash continued to sip his coffee and stare at his leadership team. It was almost as if he hadn't heard a word I had said. I wondered if I should jump in again.

'Sitara is right,' Abhimanyu's baritone broke into my thoughts. 'From a marketing standpoint, we can identify the right target group to test this concept. We will need some product changes to effectively measure the results, and, of course, sales will have to crack the first set of deals, but this is doable . . . '

Abhijit immediately jumped in.

'Boss, the sales team is stretched thin. We're struggling with the margins as it is, and now you also want me to go out and get freebies for an experiment with low volumes,' he whined in that nasal voice of his.

My heart sank. If Abhijit wasn't willing to get deals, there was no way we could run an experiment. And he was tough to argue with because he would keep whining until the other person gave up. He always made it seem as though anything we suggested would lead to an apocalyptic end.

'In that case, I will fund the deals for the experiment from my marketing budget,' said Abhimanyu immediately.

Abhijit opened his mouth but shut it as soon as he saw Ash nod and smile at Abhimanyu. Ash tossed his now-empty coffee cup into the dustbin kept in the corner of the room. He walked back to the table and sat down.

'Now we're getting somewhere. Sitara, do you have any resourcing asks?' he asked.

I thanked God for the brainstorming session with Abhimanyu over the weekend. I hadn't even considered that Ash would ask about resourcing, but Abhimanyu had specifically asked me to put a slide on this. I quickly pulled it up so everyone could read it.

'We will have to deprioritize some other project if we need to do this,' Harsh burst out immediately. He scowled at Abhimanyu.

'Harsh, we can relook at our roadmap to figure out prioritization . . . ' I began, wondering why he was even saying this to Ash. I had shown him this slide earlier and he hadn't said a word. Besides, even if we needed to bump something off the roadmap, that was a call Harsh could take.

'Abhimanyu,' Harsh cut me off, 'this is the third request from your team. You need to prioritize between this, the changes needed for Dhruv's campaign and the new analysis tool you wanted by the end of this month.'

He looked very pleased at having pushed Abhimanyu into this situation. I wondered if Harsh was angling to get Dhruv's project deprioritized to make it easier for me to get a promotion. Thankfully, Dhruv wasn't in this meeting. He'd finally managed to convince Abhimanyu that he was really busy on his campaign and now Upasana was working with me instead.

'Ash, BeauPlus just raised $50 million in funding for their beauty box. We have the beauty customers, we need to invest in them,' I said, hoping this would tip the scales and get Dhruv's project deprioritized.

Before Ash responded, Abhimanyu leaned forward. He took a sip of his coffee before he began speaking. 'If we were to run an experiment, I expect we will need about two weeks of data to prove our results. We should deprioritize the work on the new tool and pick it up after this has launched.'

Harsh did not look pleased. And neither did Upasana. She put away her notebook and looked at Abhimanyu.

'I've been working on this tool for two months,' she burst out. 'We can't deprioritize it!'

'We need to prioritize projects that will bring in funding,' Ash interjected. 'Whatever does not contribute to that goal is not critical.'

He effectively ended any debate with this pronouncement.

'Upasana, we can discuss alternatives to unblock you offline,' Abhimanyu added, in a tone that brooked no argument. She looked extremely annoyed, but didn't say anything now that Ash had weighed in. She opened her notebook and went back to doodling. I suspected Abhimanyu would soon feature as a dragon in her next comic. Or a vampire. Or Dracula. Basically, something that she could kill on the pages of her sketchbook, if not in real life.

Harsh smiled widely, looking as though he had won an award. Of course, now that Ash was on board, he would immediately act as though he was responsible for making this happen.

'OK folks, get to work. I look forward to seeing the results,' Ash announced and swept out of the room.

Abhijit immediately pulled Abhimanyu to the side and began a heated conversation on how he was supposed to hit the monthly targets and also have 'his guys' find partners for this experiment. I walked over to them, hoping to add my two cents, but Harsh got there before me. He gestured to indicate I should leave them alone.

So now Harsh decided to get involved, I thought bitterly.

★★
★

Glam Office Messenger Group Chat

[#Glaminions—11 a.m.] Bhargavi: I cracked it! Ash's name is Ashwem.

[#Glaminions—11.01 a.m.] Aakash: Um, what?

[#Glaminions—11.01 a.m.] Bhargavi: He was talking about his sister today, and he said her name is Kabini. Like the river!

[#Glaminions—11.02 a.m.] Dhruv: So?

[#Glaminions—11.04 a.m.] Bhargavi: Arey, his parents are following that trend of naming their children after the places they were conceived in! You know, like Dakota or Sydney or whatever.

[#Glaminions—11.07 a.m.] Dhruv: So you think Ash was conceived on a beach in Goa?

[#Glaminions—11.10 a.m.] Bhargavi: Why not? As if you have a better idea!

I stifled a laugh and began typing a response when Upasana suddenly grabbed my arm. I was still standing outside the meeting room and I looked up expectantly, thinking she would suggest grabbing a coffee.

She was glaring at me.

I was confused.

'What was that?' she burst out.

'What?' I blinked at her in surprise, as I tucked a stubborn curl back behind my ear.

'Some friend you are,' she muttered. 'Bringing up that funding story so Ash would deprioritize my project! And this, after I help you. Thanks a lot.'

'Upasana . . .' I began.

'I know. You need your promotion, so your work trumps all. Never mind that the rest of us also have targets. Who cares as long as you get your way!'

'That's not fair,' I burst out. 'I wasn't trying to get your project deprioritized! I was only trying to make sure that my experiment got the green light . . .' I reached out to grab her arm, so I could stop her from walking away.

'It's not about whether or not Ash, or Harsh, or even Abhimanyu would listen,' she spat out. 'The point is, you didn't even try to interject! I cannot believe you would do that to me.' She blinked hard, and I knew she was fighting to hold back her tears.

'Upasana . . .' I tried again. She shrugged and turned away. She began walking toward the exit. I saw Shirin get up from her seat and run behind her.

I began walking towards them, but didn't know what to say now that they both were mad at me. I stopped and sighed.

If Shirin, who was generally quick to forgive, still hadn't forgiven me for refusing to swap meeting slots with her, I didn't know what to expect from Upasana who was known for maintaining a running hit list of all those who'd wronged her. I guessed I would be the one featuring as Dracula or a vampire in her sketchbook today. Or maybe even a female Judas.

I felt the beginnings of a headache. I pressed at my temples.

As I walked back to my desk, I spotted Dhruv, Aakash, Bhargavi and a few others huddled in a corner. The looks I got when I passed them suggested I was the hot topic of discussion. I overheard some words like 'selfish', 'aggressive', 'cut-throat', 'anything for a promotion', and so on. Not one of them had been in the meeting, so I wondered how the office grapevine already had all the updates. Especially since they were busy discussing Ash's conception while the meeting was going on.

That's when I remembered—the meeting room we were using had thin walls and was adjacent to Abhimanyu's office. Dhruv must've parked himself in the office as we often did when the bosses weren't there. He had probably overheard the entire conversation.

What a slimy bastard, I thought.

He was definitely relaying the blow-by-blow, and adding as much extra masala he could to fan the flames. I wondered if he had created a separate Instant Messenger group just to relay this information, because there was no mention of it on the regular group. I couldn't believe I once had a crush on this guy. Just looking at him now made my skin crawl.

'This is how you get ahead in the corporate world! Every rung in the ladder is someone you're stepping on and that's exactly what she's doing,' I overheard someone say, as everyone giggled.

The comment was timed and said in a sotto voce loud enough to get a rise out of me. I bit my lip to stop myself from responding.

At that moment I hated Dhruv. He was just as smarmy as Aakash, but did a much better job at covering his ickiness. I pulled out my phone, pretending to be completely absorbed in it, so it seemed like I wasn't bothered by what they were saying.

And that's when I spotted the notification.

Best-Buds@Glam has been archived.

19

Forget Work and Go for Sheer Unadulterated Pleasure

Sub: Mandatory fun event!

Hello Team,

It's been a while since we let our hair down! The Good Times@Glam Club cordially invites you to our mid-week karaoke night.

RSVP: This is a mandatory team event. Let me know if you have a pressing reason that prevents your attendance.

We look forward to singing away the blues with all of you!

On behalf of the Good Times@Glam Club,

Mallika M.

Head, HR

PS: Request that you do not bring your families/significant others.

I stared at the email that had come in last week. As always, I had ignored it because it came from HR. I rarely read their emails, especially not when I was busy. However, there was no way I could skip this inane event short of faking a heart attack. HR took Good Times@Glam events very seriously. A few months ago, a group of us left the team cricket match they had arranged within a couple of hours. They expected us to give up our entire Saturday baking in the hot sun and playing a terrible game of cricket with mostly uncoordinated colleagues. I shuddered at the thought of spending my free time with people like slimy Aakash, smarmy Dhruv, the giggly HR and admin posse, the stand-offish sales guys and other such annoying characters. The minute Upasana, Shirin, Bhargavi and I got our beers at the pub across the street from the field, our phones simultaneously pinged. We all got personalized screaming texts from Ash, reminiscent of the Howler from *Harry Potter*, about how irresponsible we were, how we didn't appreciate the hard work HR put in to improve 'employee morale'. The worst shot was where he called us 'arrogant' for thinking we were above such events. That was enough to force us to abandon our beer and head back to the match.

I scrunched my nose as I considered really faking a heart attack to get out of the mandatory fun event tonight. I would've done it, except I was terrible at acting. There was no escape. I would be forced to endure an evening of screechy voices, drunk colleagues and general cacophony.

WhatsApp Chat

[6.00 p.m.] Kavya: When are you getting home tonight?

[6.00 p.m.] Sitara: Soon. I hope.

[6.01 p.m.] Kavya: You hope?

[6.02 p.m.] Sitara: I'm stuck at a table filled with the HR and Admin posse. Every single one of them is sipping on white wine sangrias with muskmelon. Ew!

[6.02 p.m.] Kavya: You LOVE sangrias.

[6.03 p.m.] Sitara: I do, and I'm having one too. But it's not fun when you're bored out of your mind!

Kavya is typing

. . .

Last seen today at 6.05 p.m.

Kavya was probably wondering why I was sitting with the HR and Admin posse, wanting to spear myself with a cocktail stirrer. Normally these work parties were made bearable by the fact that Upasana, Shirin and I stood in a corner, making fun of everyone. But tonight, the two of them were studiously ignoring me. I would have to wait till I got home to explain what had happened to Kavya. I sighed and pushed my phone into my bag.

I looked around the table, wishing I was anywhere but here. My phone felt like the life raft to take me away from this sinking ship of an evening, and I'd given up my place for someone else. So far, they had discussed the benefits of waxing your upper lip instead of threading it ("Ranjani told me about it, and it has been a life changer"), the best contouring videos, whether or not Abhijit was playing hard to get with Mallika (it sounded more like she had an unrequited crush and was reading 'signs' into everything), and the most effective class at Cult (close competition between Dance Fitness and HIIT).

They all were tittering and preening, the kind of group I wouldn't normally be caught dead in. I felt like the crow that had accidentally stumbled into a party of parrots. I looked around to see if I could escape, but everyone else was busy avoiding my eye.

'He's so hot no yaaa?' Meghna, one of Mallika's numerous minions, said. She pulled out a small, glittery fuchsia compact and checked her reflection. Yet again, I wondered just how much time these women put into getting ready. Every single one of them had changed out of their work outfit into a short, glittery party dress. They had also found the time to redo their make-up, looking like they'd jointly watched endless YouTube videos on creating 'evening looks'. Meanwhile, I looked like something the cat had dragged home in my rumpled Zara striped blue top and jeans. I took a long sip.

A wave of giggles broke into my thoughts.

'I vote for Abhimanyu,' said Anila. Immediately a bunch of people raised their hands to second her. I blinked, wondering what was going on.

'Who gets your vote?' Mallika asked me.

'Huh?'

'We're doing a poll,' Meghna whispered. 'Hottest guy in the office. Your vote?'

I sipped my drink pretending to think it over. I wasn't interested in contributing to this ridiculous poll.

'I'm going to corner him on the dance floor,' Anila slurred.

'You wish,' said Meghna.

An argument broke out on which one of them was going to stealthily corner Abhimanyu on the dance floor. I began wondering how I could get away from this table and this completely banal conversation.

'Oh God! He's headed here. Quick! Do I look OK?' said Meghna breathlessly, as she continued to pout at the mirror on her compact. Her friends didn't reply. They were all equally busy with checking their appearance. I looked up to find the reason behind this burst in activity and locked eyes with Abhimanyu.

Oh.

He smiled. I felt my cheeks grow warm. There was that fizzy feeling in my stomach again. I took another sip. As he approached our table, I opened my mouth to say hello. But before I could get a word out, the rest of the women surrounded him. It was like bees swarming around a honeycomb. They were soon joined by a few more women from the office. Quickly, the group launched into a stream of never-ending questions, all directed at Abhimanyu.

'Too bad this isn't one of our family events,' said Meghna, sounding completely insincere. 'Would be great to meet your wife.'

There she was, desperately fishing for details. I wondered if she knew just how unsubtle she seemed.

'No wife,' Abhimanyu said.

She flashed a blindingly white smile. I wondered if she'd also snuck in a dentist visit in addition to the outfit change and make-up refresh. Her teeth didn't look this white during the day. They seemed almost predatory now.

'We also allow girlfriends,' said a giggling Parul as she leaned forward, almost as though she wanted him to get a full view into her low-cut top. He averted his eyes.

'No girlfriend either,' Abhimanyu replied. 'So, when do we actually begin with the karaoke?'

Good segue, I thought. Those nosey women were about to launch into their investigative mode and wouldn't have let him be until they got every little detail out of him.

'Oh, we need to be properly sloshed before we sing,' said Meghna, her words already beginning to get that blurry, drunken edge. She moved forward and pushed Parul to the side so she could stand next to Abhimanyu.

'Hey Sitara,' said Dhruv, sidling up to me. I ignored him. He was the last person I wanted to speak with right now. Or ever.

'Hi,' I said and pulled out my phone as if there was something very important I needed to do right away.

'Your drink is almost over. Let's get another,' he said.

'No thanks, there's still some left,' I said.

'Come on. It'll give us a chance to talk,' he smiled.

Once upon a time that smile would've given me butterflies. But now, he just seemed smarmy and desperate.

'Please,' he said, when I didn't reply.

I gave in. I didn't have anyone else to talk to, and it would be good for me to stop eavesdropping on the HR posse's conversation with Abhimanyu. I probably lost ten IQ points with every new comment I overheard. I decided I would get one last drink, pretend I had developed a migraine and then leave. I walked with Dhruv towards the bar.

'You look really pretty tonight,' Dhruv said as soon as we were alone. 'What are you planning to do this weekend?'

Lose myself in the latest Sophie Kinsella and surface only on Monday morning.

'Oh, I have exciting plans,' I replied, without adding any details.

We each got another drink at the bar. I picked up my glass and walked out from the stuffy room towards the outdoor area. Dhruv followed me. I leaned on the balcony and took a sip.

'So, what are these exciting plans?'

I didn't respond, just took another sip of my drink. He decided to continue the conversation even though I hadn't said anything.

'I have to work all weekend,' he pouted. I was certain this was his attempt at looking like a cute, little lost boy. Unfortunately, it wasn't working any more.

'Abhimanyu moved up the deadlines for my campaign. I have a lot to do now,' he complained.

'Last weekend was my turn, so this one's yours,' I replied, unable to resist the impulse to make a sly dig. I waited to see if he would defend his marketing plan.

'I had to be honest with my evaluation,' he said, attempting to sound apologetic but coming off as insincere. 'I still don't think your idea will work.'

I resisted the impulse to roll my eyes at him.

'We'll soon find out,' I replied, not wanting to engage with him further. 'I hope you get some free time this weekend. I had to spend all of the last one working on a new marketing plan.'

'Yes, I need a break. Sometimes, I dream I don't have to check my emails before I fall asleep. That I'll get out of bed and maybe even have breakfast before I check them again the next morning,' he said, side-stepping the conversation around his failed attempt to sabotage me.

I didn't reply. He raised his beer to his mouth and looked out at the Bangalore skyline, or what we could see of it from the terrace. The lights in the distance created a halo around his head. I squinted so it looked more like the devil's horns that should emanate from his head.

'Speaking of projects,' he said, 'how's yours going? All set?'

As though you don't already know what happened today, I thought. I shrugged and took a sip so I didn't have to answer. The speed at which I was drinking to avoid speaking to him, it was like a bad drinking game.

'OK, OK, you don't have to give away your secrets,' he said, raising his hands in submission.

I raised an eyebrow. I'd never seen Dhruv back away so easily. There was something weird going on here. I shivered slightly and rubbed my arms.

'Tell me this though,' he said and leaned forward. He was now standing really close to me. It was no longer an acceptable distance for two colleagues. I took a step to the side. I wondered what he was trying to pull. I did not want a repeat of his cold, clammy hands holding on to mine.

'What will it take to convince you to go out with me?' he whispered.

I nearly spit out the mouthful of alcohol I had glugged. 'What?' I coughed out.

'Last week, you called our drinks conversation a date. But then you left before I could properly ask you out. I want to date you,' he smiled again and moved closer to me, as though it was perfectly natural to declare that you liked someone you had deliberately torpedoed.

I took another step to the side. 'Firstly, that wasn't a date. And secondly, we work together. This is weird and inappropriate.'

'There's no rule that we can't date,' he grinned wolfishly. I felt like Little Red Riding Hood. Except being eaten by the Big Bad Wolf seemed like a preferable alternative when compared to being pursued by Dhruv.

'We are competing for the same promotion . . .' I began, trying to think of more reasons to turn him down.

A few hours ago, this guy had been gossiping about me, and now he was claiming he liked me? It made no sense. He was definitely up to something, and I didn't want to get involved.

'If the promotion thing bothers you, we can date unofficially until they announce that I am getting the promotion,' he cut in smoothly.

His arrogance was no longer attractive. I clenched my fists. At that moment, I desperately wanted to punch the smile off his smug face.

'I'm sorry, Dhruv, but I don't like you that way,' I said.

Past Sitara was probably staring at me with her mouth open in shock, and yelling at me that I'd lost my mind. But I knew what I was doing.

'You're kidding,' he said as he finally took a step back.

'No, I'm not.'

'But . . . but . . .' he stuttered, looking a little shaken for the first time in all the time I'd known him.

'Well, I have to get going,' I said, wondering what else I could say to end this conversation. Years of reading *Cosmopolitan* hadn't really prepared me for this. How did you tell someone that there was a time you may have liked them but now you actually hated their guts? Or that you didn't trust their motives one bit?

'Fine, no hard feelings then,' he replied. His voice was calm, but his face betrayed the fact that he was very pissed off. 'Let's keep things professional. It'll help when you lose the promotion to me.'

There was nothing left to say.

He walked away and I stood at the balcony looking out at the city. A few minutes later, I walked back inside. It was time to claim the pretend migraine and leave.

I walked into the bar and blinked as my eyes adjusted to the light and smoke inside. Someone was doing a killer performance of '*Raabta*'. Whoever was singing was drawing crowds like a rock star. Every woman from office and a few of the pub's other patrons were all crowded in front of the stage like groupies. Some people were doing the wave, others were holding up lighters. Had Arijit Singh himself decided to attend our office karaoke night? I had never heard such a good performance at a work event before. Typically, we always sought refuge in the balcony once our colleagues began singing because none of them could hold a tune.

'*Tera nazaara mila*,' the voice rang out as clear as a bell, and I finally looked at the stage to realize that the singer was Abhimanyu.

'*Roshan sitara mila* . . . ' My heart began hammering in my chest. I wanted to look away, but our gazes were now locked and I couldn't tear my eyes off him.

Oh, shit.

I'd been judging everyone else, but in a span of a few seconds, I had also transformed into a groupie. Who knew that the man could sing like that? Screeching out 1990s Bollywood numbers in the car had not prepared me for this level of talent. Goosebumps erupted on my arms. Much as I tried, I couldn't look away. I was drowning in those soulful eyes as he kept singing. He looked like a perfect rock star with his floppy hair, faint stubble and that killer build. As he finished the song, people began asking for an encore.

I took a step forward, wanting to speak with him. It felt like there was an invisible string that was drawing me towards him.

But then, Meghna jumped on stage and grabbed his hand. I watched as she dragged him on to the dance floor and began grinding against him as the next singer began a screechy rendition of *Shut up and Dance*. He looked extremely uncomfortable but didn't extricate himself from her grip. The posse had definitely planned its attack. One by one, each of the women tried to, not so subtly, push away whoever was dancing with him and take her place. When Parul finally managed to wrangle her way up to him, she was rewarded with the track changing to a slow, romantic rendition of *Wonderful Tonight*, albeit one being sung by someone so drunk that the words were all blending into one another. She was hanging off his neck, without leaving an inch of space between them. She had definitely strategized her moves before tonight.

As I watched her whisper into his ear, I couldn't take it any more.

I ran out of the pub, stopping only to collect my things from the corner I'd dumped them in. As I stood outside waiting for my Uber, I pulled out my phone to text Kavya. And then realized I didn't know how to explain what I was feeling. To distract myself, I called my sister instead.

'It's Chak's bedtime, what do you want,' Sahana said as she answered the phone. As if on cue, Chak wailed in the background, showing off his lungs' power.

'I . . . I . . . ' I gulped, not knowing how to explain my emotions. 'I'm confused . . . '

Sahana sighed and then called out to Ram.

'Can you put Chak to bed?' I heard her say. 'The other baby seems to be in the middle of a crisis.'

'Hi, Sitara,' Ram called out.

I huffed. Wasn't Inaya their other baby?

'What's going on?' Sahana said. I heard her walking towards the balcony and settling into her favourite swing.

'I don't know . . .' I began.

'Sitara, I've had a long day. My plan was to put the kids to bed, break out my new bar of Lindt orange chocolate and catch up on *Made in Heaven*. Instead, I'm talking to you. What's going on?'

'Ooh, is the show good?' I asked. 'I've been hearing about it, but I haven't had the time to begin watching it.'

'If you want to discuss OTT shows, we can do that when we meet,' she said pointedly. 'What's confusing you? Something at work or something to do with a man?'

I pouted as I checked to see if the Uber was anywhere nearby. It wasn't.

'Why can't it be something else?'

'It's always one of the two,' she said. 'Going by how you are avoiding the subject, I think it's something to do with a man.'

'Somewhat.'

'Does it have to do with Inaya's new friend Manyu?' she asked. I cursed my niece and her newfound obsession with kindred spirits. She'd trained my sister's eagle eye right on to him by drawing attention to him.

'Kind of . . .'

'Finally,' she said in a tone that indicated she had been waiting for me to bring this up. 'What's going on?'

'I don't know,' I wailed as the words came out in a rush. 'I had a crush on Dhruv but he's a bastard and he got everyone at work to hate me, and tonight he claims he likes me but I turned him down. And Abhimanyu has been really nice and we're supposed to be colleagues, but I feel so weird when I'm with him. Like he's being nicer than he should be . . .'

'So, you like him,' she pronounced.

'No, I don't,' I said. 'We're friends. We hang out after trivia sometimes and he's nice . . .'

'That wasn't a question,' she said. 'You like him. I could see it from the way you were looking at him at Appa's party.'

A strange feeling washed over me.

'You're available. It sounds like he is too. You're just too scared to ask him out because you don't want to be rejected.'

'No,' I muttered. 'We're just friends.'

'You can lie to me, and you can lie to Kavya,' she said, making me wonder when she'd spoken to Kavya. That traitor!

'But you're wasting your time lying to yourself. Anyway, don't say anything to him. It doesn't sound like you're ready for a relationship, and I don't want you to get hurt.'

'I don't like him,' I insisted, sounding completely unconvincing even to myself.

'Hello Cleopatra, Queen of Denial,' she said and yawned. 'I'm going now. Call me when you've stopped being delusional!'

With that, she hung up on me.

20

Mars Brings Conflict to Projects

Ten pairs of eyes were boring into me. I felt like I had fallen into a pit of poisonous snakes hissing at me. Or into a cage of hungry hyenas. Or a well of crocodiles biding their time. Irrespective of how I chose to look at it, I was cornered. And not in a good way. I had set up an 'Execution Workshop' to bring everyone on the team together and ensure they were committed to finish their parts of the project on time. I had also invited Abhimanyu, so I'd have leadership support. Plus, his horoscope said *'put more time into long-term projects, they will be game-changers.'*

I looked around the room, trying to find one sympathetic face and found none. I wondered if I should've tried a different approach, maybe one that involved rebuilding bridges before I dragged everyone into the meeting. One by one, I had somehow managed to alienate the entire team. Upasana had managed to drop off the project so I was stuck with Dhruv, the founder of the 'We Hate Sitara' club, who had been taking great joy in spreading rumours about me. Shirin, who avoided my eyes even when I directly addressed her, was still holding a grudge. Without her and Upasana, I didn't even attend trivia last week. The sales team was always anti new projects, so they were never going to be on my side. The engineering team didn't hate me, but calling any of them into a long meeting was enough to get on their hit list.

And now, I'd forced this group of disgruntled people into a two-hour long meeting. There was nothing the team hated more than an extended meeting. I had also ordered snacks and chai from Chai Point, a team favourite, as an incentive for putting them through this. Unfortunately, it wasn't helping, and I suspected it had less to do with the length of the meeting and more to do with the fact that they hated me.

'Basit, this list of partners isn't good enough,' I said. Basit was on Abhijit's team and had been tasked to find partner offers. 'We need bigger brands and more exciting offers.'

'Let's be realistic,' he said, almost rolling his eyes at me. He took a bite of the banana cake in front of him. 'Why will a big brand offer freebies? What are we giving them in return? You haven't given me anything worthy of a pitch!'

Oh please, I thought. I knew Basit's problem was that this wasn't adding to his revenue targets. He would probably refuse to sleep with his wife if it wasn't linked to a sales incentive!

'They're getting a base of new customers,' I argued. 'We can work on a revenue-share in the initial phase, and once we've proved that they're getting new customers through this, we can work on a barter deal.'

'As if money grows on trees,' Dhruv cut in.

Now that Abhimanyu had brought Dhruv back on the project, Dhruv was being most unhelpful and had spent the entire meeting jumping in to give his opinion on things that had nothing to do with marketing. He was convincing every single person in the room not to do their job. Either he was extra miffed by my rejection earlier this week or he was making sure he put in all efforts to sabotage my project, so he would get the promotion. Or both. I stared at him balefully as I began putting up my hair into a bun. This meeting room, normally a replica of the Tundra, was feeling exceptionally warm.

'Sitara has a point,' Abhimanyu jumped in. He took a sip of his chai and leaned forward. 'We cannot start with this list, Basit. I'm happy to get involved in partnership conversations with the bigger brands. I think we can offer them marketing exposure, which they'll appreciate.'

'But, Abhimanyu, we've already committed our best marketing slots for the month,' Dhruv began, grasping at yet another reason to shut down my project.

'Our current inventory doesn't match the scale of our ambitions,' Abhimanyu said. 'We need to be more creative. As a senior member of the marketing team, I'd like to see you come up with solutions, not problems!'

Dhruv shut up. He glared at me, as though it was my fault that Abhimanyu had yelled at him. He began typing furiously, giving the impression he was sincerely taking notes. But I knew he was sending updates on the Glaminions group. Or whatever new group the team had created that didn't include me. I hadn't seen a single message since the day we presented to Ash. I looked around the room, spotting telltale signs of their chat. Shirin was biting her lip, a sure shot sign she was trying to hide her smile. Bhargavi was twirling her hair, something she did when she was throwing out one of her zinger lines. And Dhruv couldn't keep the smarmy look off his face.

'Sitara, we need to update the marketing plan,' Abhimanyu broke into my thoughts.

Great. I'd be stuck with Dhruv again. I stifled a groan. I loved my job, but on days like this, I hated the fact that it required me to work with people I couldn't stand.

'I'll work with you,' Abhimanyu continued and I looked up in surprise.

'Boss, I can do it,' Dhruv looked up from his laptop, looking equally surprised at being excluded. It was as though the past hour had never happened. He was the one who had insisted it would be impossible for us to launch this programme in a month. And now, he wanted to be a wet blanket through every stage of the process!

Abhimanyu glared at him. He leaned forward and poured himself more chai as Dhruv looked at him expectantly. The longer Abhimanyu took to respond, the more rattled Dhruv got. Just as he opened his mouth to say something, Ash suddenly entered.

'Why so serious, team?' he drawled as he walked in and headed straight towards the container filled with banana cake. It was his favourite, and one of the few things that he indulged in. I realized he must have spotted the delivery bags and had come in to grab a slice. I wondered why he was taking the trouble. Everyone knew it was Ranjani's job to make sure he didn't miss out on banana cake.

'We're hashing out the execution details to launch the subscription programme,' Harsh jumped in. Now that Ash was here, he was pretending he was super involved in the conversation. Up until now, he had been staring at his phone as though he was busy saving the world one tap at a time. Knowing him, he was probably playing Candy Crush. Or ogling at the lingerie section on Glam under the guise of 'testing new features'.

'Ready to go live on the twenty-fifth?' Ash said.

The colour drained from my face. The entire room grew ominously silent. He wanted us to launch in two weeks? I'd just spent the past hour trying to convince everyone we needed to launch in a month, and they'd acted like we needed to bring in Tom Cruise as this was the latest instalment of *Mission Impossible*. How on earth would we get this done in two weeks? Before I could argue, Ash walked up to the whiteboard. He scrawled out '25 September and 4 October' on the board in bold.

'These are the dates we need to hit. We will launch the experiment on 25 September. This group will present the final findings on 4 October. If all looks good, I will take it to the board meeting on 9 October,' he announced. He looked around with a big smile, as though he was expecting a standing ovation for his impeccable planning skills.

'Definitely, Ash! We will absolutely make those dates. Team, let's hustle. Let's list out all the conflicting projects so we can make sure folks in this room have enough bandwidth to execute,' said Harsh, immediately taking the role of the leader who was in charge. He was puffing his chest out, looking like a proud peacock in heat. To make it clear that he was in charge, he walked up to the whiteboard and began writing random interim milestones on it.

If he had paid one smidge of attention, he would know he had missed out at least five steps, I thought angrily.

'Ugh, I can't believe we're stuck working on this,' I overheard Basit whisper to Dhruv.

Bhargavi rolled her eyes, as she muttered '*roz hi kuch naya aa jata hai yahan*'.* Meanwhile, Shirin was biting her lip so hard I was worried she was going to draw blood.

'Team, this is our most critical project so let's double down,' said Ash. He stared at Basit and Bhargavi to make it clear he had overheard their whispers. With that, he sashayed out, leaving the rest of us to figure out how we were going to make these magical dates come true.

'Launching a project at this scale is like giving birth,' Harsh began, as if he were intimately acquainted with labour and all that it entailed. Everyone in the room was waiting for him to finish his monologue so that we could begin to work. I stopped listening and began surreptitiously checking Abhimanyu's horoscope to

---

* Something new comes up every day!

verify whether Ash's dates were 'good' or if I needed to prepare for damage control.

I placed a Starbucks coffee cup and a paper bag with an almond croissant on Shirin's desk. She ignored me. I turned it around so she could see 'SARI SIREN' was written on it in block letters.

'You can keep your apologies to yourself,' she said. Upasana walked by, and I silently handed her a cookie and a coffee cup that said 'SARI WHOOPSNA'.

'Listen, I'm really sorry . . .' I began, addressing them both.

'You're not,' Upasana said coldly. 'You just want our help. You think we don't know what you said?'

'What?'

'We're not falling for that innocent look!' Shirin jumped in. 'We know *exactly* what you think of us.'

I was at a loss for words for a few seconds. I opened and shut my mouth a few times, like a gaping goldfish, as I racked my brains for the right response.

'We've been friends for years. I don't know what you heard, but let's talk. Maybe I can explain,' I begged.

'It's not just about what we've heard. You're selfish,' Shirin burst out. 'You couldn't even swap a meeting! And that wasn't a one-time thing.'

'Yeah, it's not just meeting slots, it's also meeting rooms,' Upasana added.

Shit, shit, shit.

I had been pretty anal about swapping meeting slots and rooms, but I had a reasonable explanation. Except, it wasn't one I could share. I mean, how could I tell them that there were very few meeting rooms on our floor that were 'lucky' for Abhimanyu. Or that I had to fiercely protect the dates I scheduled meetings on because they were 'good' dates per Abhimanyu's horoscope. I wondered if it was time to finally confess. I really didn't want to lose my friendships over this.

'I can explain . . . .' I began.

'Never mind. I'm not ready to talk to you,' Upasana said and walked away, leaving the coffee cup and cookie untouched. I looked at Shirin, hoping I could salvage at least one friendship.

She picked up both the Starbucks cups and the paper bags, and pointedly tossed them all into the dustbin.

There was nothing I could do.

21

Saturn Opposes Mars to Increase Your Workload

There were only ten days left to launch the experiment.

Ten days to close out partnerships with a belligerent sales team who was insistent that this was a fool's endeavour.

Ten days to come up with the final designs for our landing page, while the entire design team had decided to take time off to attend a colleague's wedding, necessitating me to coordinate with people over the phone while they were half drunk.

Ten days to put our marketing plan into action without having to run to Abhimanyu for every question since the rest of his team was going out its way to avoid me.

Ten days to launch the most important experiment of my entire professional career when the entire team seemed to be rooting for me to fail.

Ten days that were giving me a lifetime's worth of stress.

Things were moving forward, but every last person on the team would have to burn the midnight oil to get them completed in time. I convinced Binoy, one of our best designers, to work on the project from the resort the design team was holed up in in the backwaters of Kerala. He agreed, but that meant Aakash's upcoming launch was stuck, and he was fuming.

I cajoled Basit into convincing partners to sign up even though he spent all his time whining about how I was asking for the moon. I even worked on the marketing plans myself, just so I didn't have to get in either Dhruv or Upasana's way. And yet, I was worried that we hadn't done enough.

'How dare you guys bring this half-baked presentation to me?' Ash yelled as everyone in the room squirmed uncomfortably.

Clearly, the Triangle of Tranquillity had washed away and instead left us with the ever-explosive Fountain of Frustration. No one had the guts to point out that we hadn't actually invited Ash to this meeting. That morning, Ash had waltzed up to my desk and insisted he reviewed the execution plan. I explained to him that many things were pending, and, at the time, he acted as if he understood that things wouldn't look ready but were still under control. Now, it seemed as though his memory had been modified and we never had that conversation. He was pacing the room, yelling, looking every bit like a fire-breathing dragon with smoke coming out of its ears.

'What is this?' he yelled at Shirin, as he pointed at a printout of the estimations she had been working on night and day.

'Ash, this is still a work in progress . . .' she began. She tapped her fingers nervously on the table, and then reached out to grab a puff pastry.

Ever since Ash had accelerated all our deadlines, we had been working around the clock. The team had food coming in all day, every day—idli-vada combos from Sri Krishna Cafe, doughnuts from Krispy Kreme, Meghna biryani, the list was endless. Stress eating had become the new team activity.

'This is nowhere close to what we need,' Ash exclaimed, staring at Shirin as though she was a tiny creature that had crawled out of a hole. 'You've been here two years and you think this analysis qualifies to be shown in public?'

I chewed at my cuticles. At this point, I had no fingernails left and was dangerously close to injuring myself if I bit off too much.

'Ash . . .' I began, and immediately shut up when he shot me a thunderous look.

'This is a work in progress,' Abhimanyu jumped in. He ran his fingers through his hair, which now stood on edge. Even when the man resembled a porcupine, he was still heartbreakingly cute. 'We'll follow-up with you when this is ready.'

But Ash was not ready to listen. He insisted on looking at every slide and yelled at every single person. He had put his extensive vocabulary to use, managing to find a new way to call a person incompetent each time.

'Inept . . .'

'Unskilled . . .'

'Amateur hour . . .'

'Blundering nincompoop . . .'

The insults were endless. Five minutes later, and halfway through the presentation, he stopped.

I held my breath wondering what could possibly come next.

'This presentation is so incomplete, I cannot waste a second more. Get out! All of you!'

My eyes widened. Ash had had some pretty large meltdowns but he had never thrown so many people out of the room before. I sat frozen in my spot. Everyone else seemed equally shocked because nobody moved. They were all staring at him.

'What are you waiting for? Go!'

We filed out of the room in silence.

I got to my seat, trying to fight back tears. This was one of the worst meetings I'd ever been in. I began wondering if it was time to find a new job as I took a few deep breaths. I walked over to the water cooler to fill my bottle. I took a sip and closed my eyes to clear my head.

PING!

Glam Office Messenger Chat

[3 p.m.] Abhimanyu: Don't worry about Ash. I've spoken to him. He'll talk to everyone and smooth things over.

[3.00 p.m.] Sitara: Thank you. You're quite the miracle worker to have got him to cool down.

> **[3.02 p.m.] Abhimanyu:** My sources tell me it's been termed the Thursday Thunderstorm. Care to confirm?
>
> **[3.02 p.m.] Sitara:** I have no sources. Everyone hates me.
>
> **[3.05 p.m.] Abhimanyu:** I'm sure they don't hate you, they're stressed.
>
> *Abhimanyu has left the chat.*

I hadn't considered going to trivia, but with all the stress at work, I decided it would clear my head. I didn't have the guts to approach Upasana and Shirin at work but I hoped they would show up to blow off steam too. As I was on the way to Last Call, Kavya messaged to tell me that she was stuck in a work crisis and wouldn't be able to make it. I felt a mild sense of foreboding, but I clung to the hope that the need to relax would outweigh any resentment the others had against me.

As soon as I walked into Last Call, I realized how wrong I was. Our team's usual table was empty. Even Krish wasn't there, despite his gigantic crush on George. Krish had attempted to come to trivia even while he was sick because he didn't want to miss a chance to flirt. But now, it looked like Upasana had told him all about our argument and he was taking her side. Sometimes, hatred can far outweigh love or friendship. It would be really awkward to participate in trivia by myself. I wondered if I should abandon this and head home. I could get back to reading *Every Last Word* and lose myself in Richard's problems, instead of my own.

'Sitara, over here,' I heard a voice yell out.

I was surprised to see Satish from The Sherlock Homies waving at me shyly. I walked over, wondering why he was bothering to talk to me. Over the years, we had been cordial if we ever ran into each other outside of trivia, but we weren't friends and there wasn't much for us to say to one another.

'George said that you guys weren't going to be here tonight,' he said when I reached their table.

'I must've missed the memo,' I said lightly, pulling my cardigan. I was feeling cold. The Sherlock Homies had picked a table that was directly under the AC vents whereas we normally sat in a warmer corner.

'If you're by yourself, you may as well join us,' said Namrata as she took a sip of her drink. 'You could help us get a leg up on the literature questions!'

'Um . . .' I began, feeling extremely awkward about the entire situation. I couldn't even begin to imagine playing with a different team. And that too one that was our arch-enemy! This would completely mess up my mental tally of wins and losses.

'Come on,' she said. 'I know we haven't spent time together, but Abhimanyu will be here soon so it's not like we're all strangers!'

'And you can get to know the rest of us too,' Arnav twinkled.

I wondered if Abhimanyu had said something about me to them. I couldn't understand why his friends suddenly wanted to rescue me from being that loser who sat by herself at trivia night. As I considered whether I should make up an excuse and leave, each of them kept insisting until they wore me down.

'Well, OK,' I said and sat down. Arnav immediately poured out a glass of beer and handed it over. I had barely been here a few minutes and already my supposed trivia nemeses were being nicer to me than my own so-called friends.

'So, where is Abhi? I never really understood why you guys don't all carpool from work,' asked Namrata. She grinned knowingly when she said the word 'carpool'. I wondered if she knew about the other times we had carpooled, and what exactly she had heard about them. My stomach fluttered unhelpfully at the thought of my car rides with Abhimanyu.

'Well, it's hard to coordinate,' I said, as I grabbed a plate and served myself some peanut masala. 'What with last-minute meetings and other such things. I didn't spot him while I was leaving today, otherwise I would've asked him if he wanted to carpool.'

'Ah, still the ever-elusive ISI agent,' Arnav said as the rest of the group erupted with laughter. He saw my puzzled look and explained.

'Abhi was known for disappearing slyly at b-school. Once we were having chai. I swear, one minute he was right there, the next we realized he had jumped into an auto and left. The next we heard from him, he had gone to his then-girlfriend's college. Which by the way, was in a different city!'

My eyes boggled. Who would've thought that the staid Abhimanyu had such an adventurous streak?

'The things he does for the women in his life,' said Satish, looking at me in a meaningful way.

The way he said it made my stomach flip. I was starting to feel uncomfortable. I wondered if it would be terribly rude to check my phone until Abhimanyu arrived. I suddenly felt like I had been called over to this table with the express purpose of grilling me. If only Kavya were here, she would have been so excited to see a table full of people to give her company with her conspiracy theories.

'So, I only know that you work with Abhi, but I don't know what each of you does,' said Namrata.

I shot her a grateful look. I began telling her about my job, and what it was like being a product manager. She turned out to be a regular customer, and was thrilled to give me various suggestions on how the app could work better for her.

'Are you guys going to talk about lipstick all night?' Satish groaned.

'It's important,' Namrata shot back. 'Besides, who knew I could tell Sitara all my complaints? I've been wasting my time giving Abhi my list when I should've been befriending her!'

I smiled.

'So, how do you all know Abhimanyu?' I asked politely. I didn't want to seem like I was monopolizing the entire conversation by talking about Glam, especially since the rest of the table, with the exception of Namrata, was clearly bored with the topic. Besides, I really wanted to know more about Abhimanyu.

'I have known Abhi since he was six and moved next door,' Namrata immediately began. 'So I'm the keeper of all his secrets.' She winked at me. I wondered what kind of secrets she knew, and what it would take her to spill some of them.

'Zaina went to school with us,' she continued. 'The three of us were inseparable through our childhood.'

'And, he was kind enough to set me up with Namrata once we met at b-school,' Arnav jumped in with a grin. He draped an arm around Namrata's shoulders and smiled down at her. Wow, a couple that quizzed together. That was rare.

'I joined the group because we all shared an apartment when we first began working in Delhi,' said Satish. 'Our group is very *Friends*-like in some ways.'

'Except, we're not that incestuous,' Namrata jumped in as they all burst into laughter.

'Well, I wouldn't really know about that,' I quipped.

They stared at me for a second and then began laughing.

'This one will keep Abhi on his toes,' Arnav said, as he downed the rest of his beer in one gulp. Namrata threw a coaster at him.

'We're just friends,' I said, wondering just how many more times I would have to set the record straight on this. It was bad enough that my sister and my friends were on my case about Abhimanyu. I was now getting the sense that The Sherlock Homies also thought there was more to our friendship. Even as I insisted we were friends, I could see that each person at the table was looking unconvinced.

Suddenly, I wondered if this was a good idea. I felt cornered and didn't want to justify myself to a bunch of strangers. I decided I would finish my beer and make up an excuse to leave.

'Sorry,' Arnav said, as Namrata shot him a look. 'I've forgotten how to behave in polite company. I didn't really mean anything, I was just going by . . . '

But I never really found out how that sentence ended. The door opened and in walked Abhimanyu.

Except, he wasn't alone.

He was with a woman who was a dead ringer for a supermodel. She had straight, shiny hair with blonde streaks and was wearing a bodycon dress. I wondered if she really was a supermodel, since she looked familiar. She was hanging off his arm and was staring at him all moon-eyed. Meanwhile, every guy in the bar was surreptitiously staring at her.

'Abhi,' yelled Satish. 'And Pooja! What a surprise.'

Oh. *Oh.*

They came over as Satish continued, 'We just invited Sitara to join us because her team isn't here tonight.'

Abhimanyu stared at me, his eyes widening in shock.

'This is Pooja,' he began, as she glared daggers at me. 'She's here to . . . '

But I had no interest in hearing about what she was here to do.

'It was great meeting you all, but I feel a migraine coming on,' I said, as I collected my bag and phone. 'I'll be pretty useless at trivia tonight, so let me just get home. Bye!'

I sprinted through the pub at a speed that would've made Usain Bolt proud and grabbed the door. I pushed and pushed, but the door just wouldn't open. I was about to throw my entire weight at the door to force it open, when someone interrupted.

'Ma'am, it says pull,' a helpful server said as he passed by. I nearly died of embarrassment. I had been here so many times and still had forgotten how the door worked. I pulled and ran out into the street.

I couldn't hold back the wave of emotions washing over me. My mind was exploding with thoughts. All this while, I had been thinking we were becoming friends, and good friends at that. And yes, my stomach seemed to be in a perpetual state of butterflies when he was around and my heart was often hammering in my chest. So maybe, just maybe, my sister and Kavya were right.

But how did it matter if I liked him, I thought as I rubbed my fists against my eyes to stop the wave of tears threatening to engulf me.

It was clear he wasn't completely over his cheating ex. And she was here, in Bangalore. So they were most definitely getting back together. Yet again, I had managed to fall for a guy who didn't seem to reciprocate my feelings.

I kept running down the street, putting as much distance as I could between myself and the bar. I would hide out somewhere before getting an Uber. By the time I got to the end of the road, tears were streaming down my cheeks. My mind replayed the moment when they walked in over and over. He knew I'd be there, so it was his way of sending out a message.

Well, now I knew what I'd told Sahana was right. It didn't matter what I felt. It didn't matter if I was in denial.

As far as he was concerned, we were just friends.

And maybe not even that.

We were just colleagues.

22

Don't Let Self-Doubt Stop You

Some people can wake up the morning after a drunken binge all bright-eyed and bushy-tailed. I'm not one of them. The next morning, I woke up with no memory of what had happened after I got home. I felt the beginnings of a massive headache pounding behind my eyes. I shuffled out of my room and sat down on the couch, pressing my temples, hoping that it would somehow help the pain.

'Good morning,' Kavya said as she plonked a tray on the coffee table in front of me. She'd thoughtfully placed a Crocin, a glass of water and a mug of steaming chai. There was also a plate of biscuits and a bowl of curd. While the very sight of curd turned my stomach, Kavya strongly believed in its curative properties for hangovers. I knew she would eventually force a few spoonfuls down my throat. The very thought made me gag, so I stopped thinking about the curd and focused on the other items instead.

'What happened?' I croaked as I picked up the Crocin. I popped it in my mouth, took a sip of water and shuddered as I tried to stop myself from throwing up.

'You couldn't really put together coherent sentences, but I guess you've *finally* realized just how much you like a certain marketing head, given you polished off an entire bottle of gin after seeing him with his ex,' she speculated.

I groaned and covered my face with one of our cushions. It smelled musty, reminding me that neither of us had bothered to change the covers recently, even though we had promised our landlady that we would wash them regularly. I kept the cushion back on the couch because it wasn't helping my attempt to avoid hurling.

'I don't know what you're talking about,' I said.

I looked around for my phone. It hadn't been in its usual place on my nightstand and I didn't know where I had put it. Until now, I had assumed I had left it on the coffee table, right by the empty bottle of gin that was still glinting at me this morning, but it wasn't there. Kavya just watched me in silence as I frantically began searching for my phone. I was throwing cushions off the couch, and attempting to look underneath the chairs as well.

'I last remember having my phone with me while I was sitting here,' I said. 'Did you see where I put it?'

'All I remember is that you were busy stalking Abhimanyu on LinkedIn because apparently that's the only form of social media you can rely on to keep tabs on him,' she rolled her eyes at me. 'And then you whined about how life is unfair, how it's idiotic to trust cheats because once a cheater always a cheater, how you're the only one who really knows the real Abhimanyu . . . ' She picked up a biscuit and chewed on it thoughtfully. 'If I remember correctly, your exact words were: If he wants to be fooled by a cheater again, then fuck him.'

'I'm certain I didn't say fuck him,' I said, even though I knew I was highly capable of saying it. I'd said way worse for far lesser transgressions in the past.

I continued to look for my phone. By now, I had looked in every corner of the living room. I upended my bag and rifled through it but it was nowhere to be seen. If only I had any memory of what I'd done after polishing off the gin, I would've known how to retrace my steps and find that damned phone. I was starting to mildly panic as my head throbbed.

'OK, maybe you didn't swear,' said Kavya, noticing my obvious distress and trying to go easy on me. 'But I cannot watch you fall down that rabbit hole again and whine about Abhimanyu and Pooja. I listened to it for hours last night.'

She walked over to the fridge and pulled out a bottle of water. She poured herself a glass and began drinking. Suddenly, a flash of memory came back and I remembered. I ran into the kitchen like a woman possessed. I picked up the fruit bowl from the counter and brought it into the living room. I began tossing the fruit out one by one as Kavya watched me with a bemused look on her face. At the bottom of the bowl, I found my phone. I gleefully pulled it out.

'You put your phone into the fruit bowl?'

'I was hiding it so I wouldn't drunk text,' I said.

Kavya was well aware of my track record with drunk texting. I had the habit of sending effusive messages to all my friends when I was drunk and sad, or drunk and angry. I had damaged quite a few friendships by giving unsolicited advice, ruined some brand new relationships by professing my undying love to a near stranger, and even made the mistake of having an extensive conversation with my mother about her flawed approach to child-rearing. I had learnt the hard way to hide my phone while I was still on the brink of sobriety to make sure that I didn't become a danger to myself.

As I unlocked my phone, pieces of last night started coming back to me. I'd stood on a random street corner for half an hour sobbing uncontrollably while I waited for an Uber. I had come home in a blinding rage and insisted that Kavya join me for a night of drinking. She'd had one glass out of politeness, while I had lost count. I had spent hours sleuthing around on the Internet until I finally found Pooja's Instagram profile. Unfortunately for me, she had set it to public so I'd spiralled into a wave of self-loathing and judgement as I had tortured myself by looking at her picture-perfect, posed photos. I had lost all control when I spotted her most recent photo. An extremely lovey-dovey picture of her and Abhimanyu at trivia. It didn't help that she had captioned it as: 'I'm bae's lucky charm. Look who won trivia with me by his side.' I had promptly decided to make a drinking game out of every like that picture got and kept refreshing the page.

Kavya had tried talking me out of it but that's when I had launched into my lecture about how the entire world was unfair and how cheaters didn't deserve a second chance. I distinctly remembered I had said 'fuck him' more than once and had followed it up with some more very colourful phrases as well. Clearly, the drinking game got terribly out of hand given that the picture was super popular and it single-handedly led me down the path of polishing off the bottle in entirety. I looked up and spotted the bottle again. I really needed to get it out of my sight, else it would keep reminding me of my self-destructive binge.

Thank God I had remembered to hide my phone at some point. I shuddered to think of what I may have done or who I may have messaged if I'd had my phone. I wondered if Abhimanyu even knew that his latest life update was all the rage on social media. Or maybe his so-called social media detox was only limited for as long as he wasn't with her. Now that they were together, maybe he wanted the world to know. Ugh. I had shut Instagram after that because the picture was making me want to throw up. Besides, I'd spotted new likes and I didn't want to begin the drinking game afresh.

'I don't want to be the one to say I told you so . . .' Kavya began.

I shot her a dirty look and she shut up. She picked up the mug of tea and handed it to me. I began taking slow sips.

At least I still had one person on my side.

Even if she was insisting on exercising her right to say 'I told you so' in the most annoying, self-satisfied, smug manner.

I pressed my temples wishing I could will this hangover headache away.

I stumbled into work bleary eyed, with a continued headache. I realized a little too late that I should have taken the day off. Especially since today also happened to be the tenth anniversary of Glam's launch, because of which a havan had been organized outside our building. It turned out I wasn't the only one with a hangover. I overheard from the whispered murmurs that the rest of the team had gone out for drinks after work too. Almost everyone was either clutching their head or nursing a water bottle in their arms as they stared sleepily at the huge bonfire-like pooja flame in front of us.

I was standing in a corner by myself, yet again. Abhimanyu had walked up to me to say hello, but I hadn't encouraged conversation so he'd gone back to stand with the senior management, all of whom were crowded directly behind Ash. Ash was looking particularly devout this morning, with a large *teeka* on his forehead. He was also wearing kurta and pyjama instead of his usual attire of formal wear. He looked different in this avatar. He was sitting next to the pandit who was busy chanting. I rubbed my eyes, wondering how much longer this pooja would go on.

Suddenly, I realized everyone was starting to pay attention to the pooja. The pandit was a stickler for the norms. He had already yelled at Ranjani for not having the right pooja thali and other paraphernalia ready. And now, he was making all the senior management sit next to Ash and quizzing them on their antecedents for pooja reasons. He appeared to have gone around the circle and had finally settled on Ash.

'Gotra?' he said.

'Bharadwaj'. The pandit began his chant by yelling out the gotra.

'Village?'

'Jhunj'. He continued by yelling out the village name.

'Father's name?'

'G.D. Bakshi.'

'*Poora naam bataiye*,*" the pandit said in all seriousness.

'Gagan Deep Bakshi.' He was mollified, and now yelled out Ash's father's name.

'Name?'

There was silence.

The pandit frowned disapprovingly. And then repeated the question.

Ash mumbled something.

'What?'

He mumbled again. The pandit glared.

Ash took a deep breath and mumbled something that we were all straining to hear.

---

* What's your full name in Hindi

Phones began pinging. I wished I was still on the team's group chat. I was definitely missing some major entertainment. I was disappointed that Ash had managed to share the information really quietly. I looked around and realized nobody had been able to overhear the conversation over the din of the pandit's entourage who had been continuing the chants while this exchange was going on. I was about to tune out of the chanting again, when the pandit picked it up with renewed vigour.

And that's when the pandit and his entire entourage loudly chanted in chorus:

'Bharadwaj gotra, Jhunj gaanv, Shri Gagan Deep Bakshi putrey, Shri Asaram Bakshi . . . '

Every whisper was instantly silenced. The team looked at each other in shock. I looked up and met Upasana's eyes. Even though she and Shirin were still mad at me, in this moment, we were all united in our glee at having found out the answer to the mystery. There was a smile tugging at the corner of her mouth, and as we looked at each other, we allowed ourselves a tiny giggle. The giggle set off a ripple of other smothered laughs, and soon the entire team was trying to hide the smiles and laughter that threatened to burst out of us.

Asaram. I made a mental note to apologize to Sahana for telling her she was terrible at picking names. Poor Ash had a much tougher time. No wonder the man had officially changed his name on every single piece of paperwork.

As I giggled yet again, Ash finally raised his head. His face was mottled red with rage. He glared at every single person until they were as poker faced as they were at the start of the pooja. We knew we couldn't risk his wrath, not when appraisals were around the corner.

PING!

Glam Office Messenger Group Chat

> **[#Glaminions—11.45 a.m.] Bhargavi:** And you guys thought I was being ridiculous when I suggested Ashwem!
>
> **[#Glaminions—11.45 a.m.] Aakash:** Who could've imagined THIS?
>
> **[#Glaminions—11.45 a.m.] Dhruv:** Asaram! How do we keep a straight face while addressing him as 'Ash'?!
>
> **[#Glaminions—11.46 a.m.] Upasana:** Doodle in progress of Ash-as-Asaram. Check it out this evening, at my desk!
>
> **[#Glaminions—11.46 a.m.] Shirin:** So we're splitting the money we had pooled for the winner on drinks? Nobody won . . .
>
> **[#Glaminions—11.48 a.m.] Bhargavi:** Done. I will figure out a time and place. Everyone be there or be square!

I smiled. They still hated me, but when it came to the mystery of Ash's name, it seemed to trump all other misunderstandings. I hoped that once my project was launched and complete, they would eventually forgive me.

Sometimes, all it took to improve a terrible relationship was interesting gossip!

23

The Winds Bring with Them
a Windfall

Was my work stressful? Yes.

Was it even more stressful when I was trying to coordinate a launch? Definitely.

Was it the most stressful when I was trying to coordinate a launch where people were avoiding me? Absolutely.

After the havan on Friday, I spent the entire weekend working. I then spent the week pushing everyone else to complete their parts so nothing would be delayed or could go wrong. I was already the most hated person in the office, so I had nothing to lose by being pushy. By now, there wasn't a single person who wanted to speak to me. And so, I sent my directives over email. I didn't receive any responses, but I wasn't expecting any. Thanks to Ash, they were forced to do what I asked, otherwise they would've left me to my own devices.

The only person who seemed to genuinely want to help me was Abhimanyu. I was curious to know how he'd got back together with Pooja, but I made sure our conversations were restricted to work to protect my feelings. I didn't want to cross over into anything that seemed like friendship again. Especially since the trivia night debacle had taught me that we were colleagues and nothing more, as far as he was concerned. He had tried joking around with me a few times, but I had shut him down promptly. He was now being very guarded, taking his cues from my behaviour.

It was almost midnight and the two of us were sitting bleary-eyed in the 'War Room' with the rest of the launch team—Harsh, Dhruv, Shirin, Basit, Abhijit, Sridhar and the engineers on the project, Heena and Shivam. I didn't understand why all corporates pretended that launches were so life-altering that they needed to be compared to a war. It was as though the outcomes of our work were life-and-death situations, when all we did was drive the wheel of consumerism.

The War Room was all set up to facilitate a launch. There was a table along the wall piled with coffee and snacks. It was also covered with empty cartons and leftovers of lunch and dinner, giving the room a musty smell of stale food mixed with sweaty bodies. The trash can in the corner was overflowing, with paper cups spilling out over on to the carpet.

At the front of the room was a large TV screen which was set up to monitor important numbers like the number of people signing up for the subscription, the number of deals they claimed, the revenue Glam earned and so on as soon as the launch was complete. This screen would stay in the War Room over the next few weeks to allow us to track our progress. I knew from previous launches that people loved seeing the numbers climb. The room would become a favourite hangout place post a big launch as people would stop by to look at the screen while taking a coffee break. All the senior management would stop by at least once every hour, thus making it a great place to showcase how dedicated you were to the company's cause.

I'd set up a slide on the projector with our launch checklist so that each person in the room could call out when their steps were complete. I checked off the confirmed items. The list also had time for each item on the checklist, so we knew if a step was taking too long. We had to ensure that we went live at midnight, so everything needed to go like clockwork. As I surveyed the room, I felt good and prayed that things would go according to plan. There was nothing worse than when a big launch went off track, and Ash had pinned all his funding hopes on this one, so I couldn't afford to make any mistakes. I smiled as I saw everyone peering into their laptops, completing the last-minute checks.

'There's something wrong with the targeting,' Abhimanyu suddenly said.

I held my breath, hoping Abhimanyu had made a mistake. This couldn't be happening.

'I tested it yesterday, it was working correctly,' Dhruv replied, as he leaned to look into Abhimanyu's screen.

They were both looking concerned, which was the last expression I wanted to see on anyone's face. I took a deep breath to collect my thoughts and then moved into damage control mode.

'Heena, please take a look,' I said, gesturing towards Abhimanyu's laptop.

I poured myself a glass of water. I started nibbling at my cuticle as I looked at the clock. It was 11.50 p.m.

Shit, shit, shit!

We needed to go live in ten minutes. A hiccup at this stage would derail everything I'd worked so hard for all these days. I began chanting all the prayers I knew, in the hope that divine intervention would save the day.

Heena walked over to Abhimanyu. Mentally, I was urging her to sprint so she got to the other side of the table faster. I got up and walked quickly over there as well to see if I could help in any way.

'See here,' he pointed at his screen as Heena peered into it. 'I don't see any users within this segment. This isn't working!'

I felt the blood rushing towards my head as my pulse quickened. If Abhimanyu was right, and the targeting wasn't working, we couldn't launch the experiment. Even if we did launch it, nobody would see it because there were no users in the target segment. This was a disaster! A problem like this could take days to fix, and we were on a deadline. Ash's scrawl with the dates was still there on the whiteboard—25 September— and it seemed to be mocking me.

Heena immediately began looking into the code. With every second that she stared at her screen my blood pressure rose. I was racking my brains trying to think of what could have happened.

'Guys, this should've been caught in the bug bash we did yesterday,' Harsh jumped in. Until now, he'd been sitting in a corner with his eyes half-closed as he scrolled endlessly. It was almost as though he had been waiting for something to happen before he jumped in.

He stared balefully at Abhimanyu, making it clear that there was only one person to be blamed if something went wrong with the launch. Trust Harsh to make sure that his ass was covered well in advance. He was a genius when it came to prioritizing himself over anything else. I now realized he had decided to attend this meeting to divert the blame for any mistakes from himself to other teams. Everyone in the room was now looking at Abhimanyu. He ran his fingers through his hair, making it stand on end.

I poured out a cup of chai and handed it to Heena. I was still thinking of all the changes we'd made since yesterday and trying to figure out if I could come up with something that might help us figure out what went wrong. Suddenly, a thought struck me.

'Heena, you remember that fix we made yesterday evening after Dhruv did his testing?' I said, hoping I was on the right track. I continued to chew at my cuticles. At this point, I didn't care if I drew blood. Maybe the pain would distract me from my skyrocketing stress levels.

'Yeah . . .' she said, as she continued to peer at her screen. She began furiously switching between the numerous tabs, trying to locate what I was talking about.

'Can you check if we moved it from the staging environment to the production site?' The staging environment was our testing playground and changes made there wouldn't reflect on the actual app. Moving a change once it had been tested from staging to production was a super obvious step and pretty much coding 101, but I knew the stress of launches sometimes resulted in people forgetting the basics.

Heena began looking to see whether she had done everything that needed to be done. I held my breath. I looked up at the clock.

11.57 p.m.

We had exactly three minutes. I prayed to all the Gods I had ever heard of and hoped I wasn't sending Heena on a wild goose chase.

'Abhimanyu, can you check the segment now?' she asked, finally looking up from her computer. I held my breath and crossed my fingers. At that moment, I would've crossed every possible body part if I could to give myself as much luck as possible.

We stared at him with bated breath. The room was dead silent. Slowly, he looked up from this screen, smiled and gave her a thumbs up sign.

I let out my breath in a long whoosh.

11.59 p.m.

We'd made it.

'You were right, Sitara,' Heena said.

'OK, we're ready to begin dialling up our launch,' I said, as everyone in the room sat up straighter.

We were a couple of minutes late, but thankfully we were going to complete the launch. I began going over the checklist one by one. After we had finalized everything, the experiment went live. I looked at the clock one last time.

12.10 a.m.

We had done it. We were ten minutes late, but we had pulled off the biggest launch Glam had seen in recent times.

I let out the breath I'd been holding in a long whoosh.

'Congrats, everybody,' I said as the room broke out into whoops and cheers.

Everyone began congratulating one another and there were a lot of high fives in the room. One by one, people began picking up their stuff and getting ready to leave. I went into my drafts folder and clicked 'send' on the launch email I had written earlier in the day. I knew Ash would call me if he didn't see it as soon as the launch was completed. I did not want to have a conversation with him at this hour.

The rest of the group packed up and left within half an hour, but I didn't want to leave any loose ends, so I stayed back. I checked and re-checked each step multiple times. Abhimanyu offered to stay with me and give me a ride back since it was really late and he was the one closest to my place, but I refused. I didn't want to spend any time alone with him. I told him I had arranged for an office cab and that I was OK with going home alone. At one in the morning, I sent out my last email. I was finally done.

I looked at the large TV screen. Even though it was the middle of the night, we had already managed to get 100 subscribers. I cheered silently. It was time to go home. PING!

Glam Office Messenger Chat

[1.00 a.m.] Harsh: Good work on the launch.

[1.00 a.m.] Sitara: Thanks, Harsh.

[1.02 a.m.] Harsh: Just one thing. This marketing hiccup should've been identified sooner.

[1.02 a.m.] Sitara: Agreed, Harsh. I'll update our testing process to include checks so we don't run into such problems in the future.

[1.03 a.m.] Harsh: OK. But make sure marketing owns up to this.

[1.04 a.m.] Sitara: Actually, in this case, it wasn't entirely on marketing. It was a miss on the engineering side, and I also should've verified this sooner.

[1.04 a.m.] Harsh: Everything is a team effort. But every item on the checklist has one owner. In this case, the owner was marketing. Remember that.

Harsh has signed out.

I rubbed my eyes and yawned. It was too late to process the political angle that Harsh was trying to bring in here. I decided it was time to go home.

This could wait until tomorrow.

24

Daggers Are Drawn

'So, what was the hiccup?' Ash asked, as he looked at Abhimanyu pointedly in the team meeting.

Like everyone involved with the launch, I had come in late that morning. As soon as I entered, Kanika told me Ash wanted to meet the entire launch team. At the time, I thought Ash wanted to congratulate us for a successful launch. When I walked in and saw how the counter for new subscribers was climbing on the screen, I was even more convinced it was a congratulatory meeting. And so I had settled into my seat without thinking too much. But now, I realized there was a different agenda. I may have got too complacent too quickly. I started to feel a sense of foreboding.

'When we were five minutes away from the launch, the targeting didn't work. It could have been a launch blocker, but we were able to fix the issue,' Abhimanyu replied. 'The team is updating our processes so it doesn't happen again.'

I wondered why this glitch required a meeting. A post-mortem would've been understandable if the glitch had actually stopped the launch or delayed it significantly. Since it had been fixed in all of ten minutes, it didn't really warrant a meeting. And yet, there was something on Ash's mind. I watched as Ash continued to stare at Abhimanyu without saying a word. I had a slight pang as I remembered Abhimanyu's horoscope—'Uranus in opposition to the sun will cause tensions in your work relationships.' I still didn't believe in living life by a horoscope, but I knew Abhimanyu would link this meeting to it. Even though I wasn't talking to him right now, I had an inexplicable urge to tell him not to interpret the events of the day as a sign from the stars.

'We should do a detailed post-mortem. This is marketing 101 and we messed up,' Harsh jumped in. He looked around the room at each person, before finally settling on Abhimanyu, making it evident that the buck stopped there.

The penny started to drop. Harsh was up to something. I wondered what he was getting at, and what he had planned for Abhimanyu in this meeting.

'That targeting mistake could have stopped the launch,' Ash said. 'If it wasn't for Sitara and Heena, we would be having an entirely different conversation today.'

That's when I realized I wasn't the only one that Harsh had pinged last night.

Shit, shit, shit.

This meeting was a well-planned attack on Abhimanyu. And it had been cleverly orchestrated by Harsh. I suspected he wasn't happy he hadn't been able to claim credit for this project, and this was his way of discrediting Abhimanyu so that he could hog the limelight.

'Ash, we're already making sure this never happens again . . . ' Abhimanyu began, but Ash was in no mood to listen. He launched into a lecture on the importance of testing protocols, mechanisms, responsibility and what not. He wouldn't let Abhimanyu get a word in edgewise. I saw Abhimanyu get flustered for the first time in all the time I had known him. He was raking his fingers through his hair repeatedly, and his face was flushed.

As Ash began talking about the worst case scenarios, I couldn't hold back. I knew this was one of those times when I needed to keep quiet, especially since it was evident Harsh had something up his sleeve, but something within me urged me to do the right thing.

'Ash, it's my fault,' I burst out as ten pairs of eyes turned to bore holes into my skull.

There was stunned silence.

Even the AC stopped humming. Every single person was staring at me slack-jawed and open-mouthed. Harsh looked like he wanted to kill me or worse. I could almost see the smoke emanating from his ears.

Ash especially looked shocked I had jumped into the conversation. For the first time ever, he had lost his train of thought and was staring at me with his mouth hanging open. I mustered up all my courage to speak.

'Once Dhruv had finished testing and we had completed the bug fixes, Heena and I should have checked to confirm that all the fixes had moved to production. We missed that. And analytics also didn't pick up on this when they did a round of monitoring . . .'

I looked around the room. Every single person was watching this exchange, waiting to see how this would end. As always, Basit and Abhijit were leaning in their chairs, making it clear that sales had nothing to do with this. Shirin was looking me straight in the eye for the first time in weeks. She had an inscrutable expression. Harsh looked like he was about to have a fit; a vein was pulsing angrily in his forehead and his fists were clenched.

'I think everyone will agree we each missed picking up a cue that could've helped us address this sooner,' I finished.

There was an ominous silence.

'We cannot have multiple owners for every step, things will fall apart,' Harsh jumped in. He shot me a venomous look. I knew I would pay for this transgression soon. 'In this case, the single owner and point of failure was marketing.'

He looked at Abhimanyu. Dhruv slowly edged his chair away from Abhimanyu and closer to the sales team, acting as though he had nothing to do with marketing. If he could've, he would've probably sat on Basit's lap and pretended they were one person with two heads. I had already set myself up for an earful from Harsh, but somehow, I just couldn't keep quiet. Maybe it was the lack of sleep. Or maybe it was the guilt.

I couldn't stop myself from adding, 'Harsh, I will put together a new checklist for future launches and ensure that a single person is responsible for every step, including checks to make sure fixes have been moved. However, this time, we didn't have this step and so we can't blame a single team.'

I held my breath, waiting for the axe to fall. Every single person was now looking at Ash to gauge his reaction. I began chewing on my cuticle.

As Ash looked around the room thoughtfully, my heart began hammering and I could hear the blood pounding in my ears.

'Fine,' said Ash. 'No harm done. Just make sure you put a process in place so this doesn't happen again.'

I held back a sigh of relief. Obviously, none of us would dare point out that the very first thing Abhimanyu had said was that we had put a process in place already. Like most meetings in the corporate world, this could've been an email.

Ash swept out of the room grandly, followed closely by Harsh who was angrily whispering something to him. I was convinced this entire situation had been orchestrated by Harsh just to make Abhimanyu look bad. I wondered what kind of larger political game he was trying to play here. I knew Harsh, and this was likely the first step in a well-planned effort to cause Abhimanyu's downfall.

Slowly, everyone else began shuffling. I was the last to leave, because I sat back and drank three full glasses of water to bring my heart rate back to normal. I couldn't believe what I had just done. More importantly, I couldn't stop thinking of what Harsh would do to me for getting in the way of his best laid plans. He wasn't going to let this go easily. Even the increasing tally of subscriber numbers on the screen weren't calming me one bit.

I slowly walked out of the room and went to my desk. My cheeks were flushed and I was sure my blood pressure was through the roof. Almost immediately, Shirin materialized by my side. It was the first time in days she was anywhere near my desk.

'What were you thinking!' I thought her eyes would fall out of her head.

I didn't say anything.

'You didn't have to say a word,' she continued. 'Ash would've yelled at marketing, and Abhimanyu would've sorted it out. Why did you defend them when Harsh wanted them to get into trouble? Didn't you see his face?'

She placed her laptop on my desk and looked directly at me.

I took a deep breath. 'It wasn't their fault,' I said softly.

'Sitara, you committed career suicide,' she said, looking at me with a weird expression on her face. 'What if Harsh doesn't clear your promotion because you went against him so publicly?'

At that, the guilt came back. But it was also mixed with the knowledge that I had effectively skewered my own promotion. The one thing that I had worked so hard for.

'I had no choice,' I said hotly as Shirin gaped at me. 'I'm not the promotion hungry, back-stabbing bitch you think I am. Besides, no matter how badly I want it, I cannot let it come at the cost of someone's reputation. Especially when he's been my only friend this past month!'

I suddenly realized what had driven my outburst in that meeting room. I no longer wanted the promotion at the cost of everything else. For the first time in my life, I realized what Sahana kept trying to tell me. Winning was important, but there were some things that were more important than winning. Like friendship and loyalty. Or even . . . but I couldn't, I wouldn't, bring myself to complete that thought. My cheeks grew warmer as my heart desperately tried to send a message that my brain was working overtime to reject.

'Oh God,' said Shirin, her eyes widening in realization. She had sensed the unsaid in my rant. She waved at Upasana who slowly walked over to where we were standing.

I took a deep breath.

'Before we talk about anything else, let me just say I'm sorry. I've been a self-obsessed jerk. I was so focused on my promotion, I forgot to be a friend . . . '

'Yes, you were a terrible friend,' Shirin said bluntly. 'There was a lot of shit going on with both of us too but you didn't even try to find out!'

'I'm so sorry,' I said, appalled at how thoughtless I'd been.

'You haven't been there for any of us,' Upasana chimed in. 'You didn't once think of how your actions would affect either of us.'

'I know,' I said, distraught at how hurt they seemed. 'But I have learnt what's most important to me.'

'You mean who,' said Shirin with a wicked grin, as she proceeded to tell Upasana just what I'd done in the meeting.

Upasana's expression softened. 'Wow,' she let out a soft whistle. 'So the old Sitara is finally back?'

'She is. I don't know if I deserve it, but will you two forgive me?' I held my breath, waiting to see what they'd say. They were my best friends and I didn't know what I'd do without them.

They smiled.

'We've been waiting for you to re-emerge,' said Shirin. 'And what I just saw was an improved version of the Sitara we love!'

Upasana held out her arms, her eyes shimmering. Shirin grabbed my arms and drew me into a three-way group hug. I didn't know until that very moment just how badly I had needed that hug.

'Thank you for being there for me,' I said, my voice muffled with my face buried into Shirin's hair.

We stepped back, and I was gratified to see them both smiling at me.

'Of course we're there for you,' said Upasana in a tone that brooked no argument. 'You're there for us too!'

'And now, it's time for coffee,' said Shirin. 'I think there was something in that rant about Abhimanyu being your only friend that we need to talk about.' She made sure to use air quotes for the word 'friend'.

Abhimanyu. I stood there mutely as all the emotions from the meeting washed over me.

What had I got myself into?

25

The Tide Turns in Your Favour

WhatsApp Chat

[9:00 a.m.] Inaya: Can you ask Manyu if he needs help KonMari-ing his house?

[9:00 a.m.] Sitara: You told him to KonMari his house?

[9:02 a.m.] Inaya: Of course. At the party, he said he was working on many things at the same time, so I told him that decluttering his house will help him declutter his mind. Do you know if he's done it?

[9:02 a.m.] Sitara: You can't just show up at someone's house and KonMari it.

[9:03 a.m.] Inaya: That's what Amma said too :(When I grow up, I am going to be a professional KonMari person. And I will clean people's houses. OK, can you give him the lavender oil I gave you? I'll give you another one.

Inaya is offline.

I placed my phone on the desk and looked at my laptop. My office messenger was lighting up again now that my friends had started speaking to me. I opened the window.

Glam Office Messenger Group Chat

[#Best-Buds@Glam—9:05 a.m.] **Upasana:** Aakash said Harsh yelled at you this morning?

[#Best-Buds@Glam—9:05 a.m.] **Shirin:** In front of the entire team? He's still really ticked off!

[#Best-Buds@Glam—9:06 a.m.] **Sitara:** You don't know the half of it. He refuses to talk to me except to yell at me. It's terrible.

[#Best-Buds@Glam—9:06 a.m.] **Shirin:** Also known as career suicide. You ruined his plan to get Abhimanyu fired . . .

[#Best-Buds@Glam—9:07 a.m.] **Sitara**: I told you, I couldn't let the marketing team take the heat for something that wasn't their fault. Anyway, at least you guys started talking to me again.

[#Best-Buds@Glam—9:08 a.m.] **Upasana:** It was the first time in months you were regular Sitara and not toxic Sitara. We missed you!

[#Best-Buds@Glam—9:08 a.m.] **Shirin:** Too bad Dhruv is still as toxic as ever!

[#Best-Buds@Glam—9:09 a.m.] **Sitara:** And yet, you believed him when he said I purposely moved up review dates. You didn't even think to check with me!

[#Best-Buds@Glam—9:10 a.m.] **Shirin:** You know we're sorry. I even got you coffee.

[#Best-Buds@Glam—9:11 a.m.] **Upasana:** And I swear, we gave the barista the right spelling. We didn't know he'd write 'Shitara'!

[#Best-Buds@Glam—9:12 a.m.] **Sitara:** LOL! @Shirin, we have to run for the review with Ash!

Sitara has left the chat.

'Why're all our reviews in this freezing room,' Shirin grumbled as she rubbed her bare arms.

It was a bad day to wear a sleeveless top. I was dressed in jeans and a shirt with a butterfly print on it. I had already unfolded the sleeves from elbow-length to knuckle-length so they covered my arms fully. I also had a spare cardigan in case I got too cold. Now, I handed it to Shirin who took it with a grateful smile. She busied herself by pulling a chair to the corner of the table where there was a beam of sunlight streaming in, in an attempt to get the most warmth. I started setting up the presentation.

'Ah, we're back to scaling Everest,' Abhimanyu quipped as he walked in. He sat down in the seat next to me as I struggled to angle my chair in a way that I didn't have to look at him. One by one, everyone else walked in and took their seats. There was some quiet murmuring as people chatted among themselves. The room fell silent as Ash walked in and took a seat at the head of the table.

The next hour flew by.

'Based on the data from the past two weeks, it's evident that the new programme will bring in 1 million customers when we expand it,' I concluded. I looked around the room, as everyone nodded and waited for Ash's response. He squinted at the slide for a few seconds.

And then, he got up and smiled.

'This is fantastic work,' he said, drawling on the 'fan' and rolling his 'r's.

My heart beat faster. Ash never used words like 'fantastic'. He always said only superlative projects deserved superlative praise.

'This project will almost certainly get us funding. Folks, we need to prepare to present this to the investors,' he added.

I tried to control my grin. With this kind of feedback, it would be hard for Harsh to justify not giving me a promotion, even if he hated me.

'Thanks, Ash,' Harsh immediately jumped into the conversation, true to form. He was attempting to grab every bit of the credit. 'We couldn't have done it without the assistance of the entire team, including Sitara and the others in this room.'

Ugh. He was giving me the barest credit possible. I was glad Ash had been in enough presentations to know I had done a lot of the work on this project, irrespective of the credit Harsh may try to claim. For someone who had done the barest minimum, Harsh spent a lot of his time projecting to Ash he was the one mentoring me to get these results.

What an ass, I thought.

'Yes, you've all worked hard and deserve a break,' Ash said. 'Let's go out for drinks this evening. My treat.'

The entire room whooped and cheered.

Upasana, Shirin and I walked into the private room that Ranjani had reserved at the bar and made a beeline to the table. There was an array of dips, different kinds of chips, hummus and finger food set up.

'Sour cream, garlic and onion dip,' said Upasana, wrinkling her nose. 'Only a sociopath would eat that at a work event. Or someone who doesn't want to talk to anyone.'

I laughed and served myself some hummus and pita bread. As we moved further ahead to check out the stunning array of pastries, Harsh walked by. He went directly to the sour cream, garlic and onion dip and served himself a large spoonful. Soon he was dunking chips into it and chewing them noisily.

'I'm not surprised he went for the dip,' Shirin said, as we giggled.

I was so glad they'd finally forgiven me. This party would've been hell if we were still fighting.

'Oh, hi, Abhimanyu,' said Upasana loudly over my shoulder. I tried to silently communicate to my friends that

I did not want to be left alone with him, but they were not in a mood to take the hint.

'I was hoping to speak with Sitara,' his voice came from behind me.

'We were just chatting, she's all yours,' said Shirin with a wide grin. She threaded her arm through Upasana's and left, leaving me with no choice but to speak with Abhimanyu.

Some people have no loyalty. And to think they call themselves my 'friends'.

I turned and saw Abhimanyu standing with two drinks in his hand.

'You've been avoiding me for a while . . . ' he said matter-of-factly.

'Yes,' I said, too tired to come up with an excuse. 'Sorry.'

'Why?' he said, taking a sip of his drink.

I looked around to see if there was a way for me to gracefully exit this situation. Yet again, I evaluated whether my acting abilities would pass muster if I faked a heart attack. Now that the project was done, maybe I should spend my weekends practising my fake heart attack. It would help me at work parties.

'Well, it wasn't intentional,' I said, holding the plate in front of me like a shield and backtracking like crazy. 'I've been busy with the experiment. In fact, I was considering heading back to work after one drink to make sure everything is on track.'

'I have to tell you something,' he said shyly. 'About trivia last week . . . '

'Oh, that's old news,' I said flippantly. I didn't want to be treated to the story of how he was getting back together with his cheating ex. I would rather jump off the top of this roof.

'No, I have to explain,' he insisted. 'Pooja showed up out of the blue and was waiting outside Last Call. I didn't know she was coming. We aren't together!'

Oh. *Oh*.

My gullible heart skipped a beat, while my brain frantically tried to control it from taking over. I wondered why he was telling me this. It wasn't any of my business. I had already made my peace with the fact that we were just colleagues. But maybe, he was trying to be friends again? Or maybe, he was trying to tell me he really didn't have anything to do with her any more?

'Good,' I said. And then, because I couldn't help myself, I added, 'I don't think you should be with someone who treated you that badly.'

I started walking away. I didn't want to continue this conversation and I was starting to feel claustrophobic. I stepped away from the bar and went to the open terrace, gulping in the cold, evening air.

'Wait . . . ' Abhimanyu said as he followed me. 'I got you a drink,' he continued and handed me the second glass that he'd been clutching all this while.

'How did you know what to get?' I asked, staring at the melon sangria. It was exactly what I would've got myself.

'I'm observant when I like someone,' he said seriously.

I felt a flutter in my stomach, but I chalked it up to some early hunger pangs. Why had I abandoned the plate of hummus on my way out? I was clearly getting dizzy from low blood sugar.

'I really must check on the experiment . . . ' I began, hoping to get away from here.

'Do you ever stop thinking about work?' He looked at me with a serious expression in his eyes. My heart was now beating so hard I could hear it throb.

He took a sip of his drink.

Suddenly, I felt like this could be my moment. Some people, like Prianca, got a fancy proposal at a cricket match. Others, like me, had to grab our moments wherever we got them. Even if it ended up being in the dingy corner of a terrace, near a dustbin surrounded by abandoned cigarette butts.

'Sitara, I've been meaning to tell you this, but the moment never seemed right,' he said. He took a deep breath before continuing, 'I really, really like you.'

I was completely overwhelmed. I had worked myself to the bone, it had taken me weeks to get my friends to talk to me again, and now, I was no longer able to deny I was completely and undoubtedly in love with this man who was supposed to be nothing but a colleague. It was too much. And so, I did what I always do when I'm flustered. I deflected in the worst possible way.

'I assume you've finished matching our *kundlis*,' I joked. I shivered and in the process also managed to awkwardly spill some of the sangria on myself.

Great. Now I would reek of alcohol.

'In the spirit of honesty, I have to admit that my horoscope says you're the one for me . . . ' he admitted, bursting my happy bubble almost instantly.

I blinked at him.

For one insane, heart-stopping moment, I had thought my time had finally come. I believed he liked me, maybe even loved me, like I did him. With no strings attached and above all else.

Stupid, stupid Sitara. Falling for a man who couldn't be trusted, yet again. Here he was professing his feelings for me, but it was because a horoscope had said so? How could I trust that his feelings would last if they were based on a horoscope?

He misread the expression on my face and took a step forward. Immediately, I took a few steps back. I needed space to process what was happening.

'What are you saying?' I said, hoping he would stop harping about the horoscope and tell me he liked me even if it said I was a vampire in disguise who would cause his immediate demise.

'Yeah, there have been signs for the past month and a half,' he said, adding yet another nail to the coffin of our non-existent relationship.

He forged ahead, taking my silence as licence to share more, without realizing that he was making things worse with every word that came out of his mouth.

'You remember the day we spoke after the Circle of Success session? That day, my horoscope said a chance encounter could result in a budding relationship . . .'

All I remembered was that the damned horoscope had said he would get an idea from unexpected quarters in a few days, and I had been preparing for that.

'And the day you went to Ash without telling me? The horoscope said I shouldn't ignore the sparks flying between me and a woman who knows what she wants . . .'

All I had wanted was to 'strike when the iron was hot' and get a senior colleague to push a project forward.

Why on earth had I not read the rest of that horoscope? Who knew what other incorrect 'signals' it had called out?

'It even said if I found a woman who stood up for me, I should never let her go. On the day you fought with Ash . . .' he said, stepping forward yet again.

Shit, shit, shit.

I fought with Ash because of my feelings for him, and he had chalked it up to a horoscope? I threw my career under a bus because of this man, and he believed I did it because some app said so?

I was now fuming.

'Every single thing that's happened so far . . .' he began, but I couldn't take it any longer.

I held up my hand to signal him to stop talking. The fluttering in my stomach had been replaced by an ominous, sinking feeling. All this while, I had read the 'work' section of his horoscope and shut the app. But it seemed I should've also been reading the 'personal' section. That way, I could've made sure he didn't think I was this mysterious 'one' the horoscope was hinting at. I didn't want to be the shitty consolation prize he settled for just because his horoscope said so.

'Abhimanyu, not every life decision needs to be guided by a horoscope,' I said. 'Sometimes you can think with your heart, instead of basing your decisions on someone else's predictions!'

He stepped closer to me and tried to reach out for my hand. I stepped back again.

I couldn't go any further behind than this because I was now directly in front of the dustbins. Another step and I'd be sitting inside one. I scrunched up my nose as I got a strong whiff of the rot emanating. 'Just because your horoscope said I'm the one doesn't mean that I am the one for you.'

Not in the way that you're the one for me, I thought as tears pricked my eyes. There had never been any terms and conditions attached to my feelings.

'No, that's not what I meant,' he stuttered. 'I like you for you, Sitara. The horoscope just confirmed what I already knew. I swear, my feelings would've stayed the same even if the horoscope had said you were the last woman that I should be with!'

'I wish it had,' I said sadly. 'Then I would know you liked me for me, and not because of all these cosmic coincidences.'

Something that had been rooting inside the dustbin now brushed past my ankle and I stifled a shriek. Don't be a rat, don't be a rat!

'Sitara . . . ' he began, and I held up my hand to stop him from talking again.

'Abhimanyu, if a horoscope can convince you that you're in love with me today, it will convince you that you no longer love me tomorrow. I don't want to break-up just because AstroZone decided that all Ariens will have relationship troubles!'

A relationship is primarily made of two people, and in this one, there would always be three. Abhimanyu, me and AstroZone!

I had been through a relationship where the person was not ready to fully commit to me, and I had been through that heartbreak. I was not signing up for that shit a second time. Even if it meant that my heart felt like it was shattering right now and piercing through every nerve ending on my skin.

'I would never do that,' he insisted. He ran his hands through his hair, looking even more stressed than he had on the day Ash went after him. 'Sitara, I like you. Forget what I said about the horoscope.'

'I wish I could forget it,' I said sadly. 'After everything you've told me about horoscopes, you can't claim it doesn't matter to you. You won't even book a meeting room without considering it!'

'It's not like that . . .' he began with gritted teeth, but didn't know how to end his sentence.

How could the man who followed his horoscope for every move in his life now claim he wouldn't just because he liked me?

'I'm sure your horoscope said that today is a good day to tell someone special in your life that you like them,' I said softly.

He smiled, thinking I was finally giving in.

I rolled my eyes and pushed him out of the way, almost knocking the drink out of his hands.

'Your horoscope was wrong. It's a terrible day to have made this confession.'

I didn't know if he replied.

I didn't wait to hear it.

26

Mars and Aries Pair Up to Bring Fireworks

I had now left two office parties in a row without telling anyone. Yet again, I found myself crossing the street and running as far away from the pub as I could. I didn't want anyone from work spotting me while I was waiting for the Uber. I found a street that was tucked away from the main road and lurked there while I called my cab.

The next morning, I did something that was completely out of character for me. I texted Harsh that I was unwell and wouldn't be in office. I prided myself on a near-perfect attendance record, and I'd even won many of those perfect attendance certificates at school so it felt really odd to randomly take a day off. I knew there would be others straggling into work or taking 'sick' leave since people tended to have massive hangovers after office parties, thanks to the free flowing booze. But it was a mark of pride for me to be the person who still showed up. Nobody cared

I wasn't in office, but that didn't mean I didn't feel guilty, almost as though someone would blame me for taking time off. But I couldn't face the alternative—seeing Abhimanyu. Or worse, having to continue the conversation about his feelings for me. Even though I knew that hiding out at home wasn't a permanent solution, it was enough for today.

And so, I curled up on the couch in our living room, dressed in a pair of old striped pyjama shorts and a tank top. I was halfway through re-reading *The Princess Diaries* when Kavya emerged. She went straight to the kitchen and didn't say a word until she emerged fifteen minutes later to plonk a bottle of water and a plate of Maggi in front of me.

I ignored the food and turned the page.

'Come on, you have to admit this is funny,' she said.

I placed my favourite bookmark to mark my spot, shut the book and stared at her.

'What's so funny,' I wailed. 'I thought we were falling for each other, but it turns out he was just falling for that bloody horoscope!'

She pushed the bowl of noodles towards me and the smell wafted into my nose. I grabbed the bowl as she moved the pile of cushions near me so she could sit on it. I made sure to move my phone under the pile where I couldn't see it. If the phone was anywhere near my hand, I was unable to help myself.

Last night, I'd been on a torturous roller-coaster ride of flipping from Abhimanyu's Facebook, Pooja's Instagram, YouTube videos of Arjun's proposal, and endlessly tracking the performance stats for the experiment. I did not want to deal with the Internet any more. Burying myself in the pages of a book was the perfect excuse. After all, Meg Cabot wouldn't interrupt every few pages with a notification.

'Come on . . .' Kavya began as I took my first spoonful. 'Think about it. There you were, sitting in a meeting room thinking today is a great day to get your project approved. Meanwhile, Abhimanyu was sitting there wondering if *this* was the chance encounter that would lead to love.'

I smiled weakly.

'You were busy thinking he wanted to help you achieve your project goals to reap career rewards. Meanwhile, as you're busy brainstorming and arguing, he was thinking, "sparks of the romantic kind are in the air at work today".'

'Yeah, right,' I said. I took another spoonful of the noodles.

She stretched out her hand. In it, was my phone. The wily woman had managed to dig it out from behind the cushions while I had been distracted by the noodles. And, she had managed to open up the AstroZone app.

I looked at the page she had pulled up and my heart plummeted.

She was right.

'Well, that's only one day . . .'

'Spend more time on longer-term projects, she thought, on the day he was discovering that a long-term love will make itself clearly known,' she giggled.

I couldn't believe my ears.

I moved my chair closer to her so I could see this. For the first time this morning, I peered into my phone. Every single time I assumed that he behaved a certain way because the horoscope had told him it was good for his career, the personal section of the same horoscope had also been hinting that he'd found his soulmate.

Every. Single. Time.

It was uncanny.

'How is it possible that every day that's good for his career is also good for romance,' I muttered as I skimmed through the app.

'Maybe some things really are written in the stars,' Kavya offered.

I couldn't hold back a smile.

'But this also says I can't trust he'll be with me for me. It's all just the horoscope,' I said, my argument sounding hollow to my own ears.

'But you don't believe in horoscopes,' Kavya argued. 'This is just a coincidence. Your idea was good, and so your project came this far. And through the project you got to know each other, and he really likes you.'

It was tempting to believe the horoscope had nothing to do with anything that had happened. For a second, I really wanted to believe it. But I stopped myself.

I knew better.

Kavya stood up and walked to the balcony.

'Aren't you going to work?' she asked, as I placed the empty bowl on the coffee table. I went back to lying on the couch.

'I'm sick,' I replied, as I threw in a fake cough for effect.

She raised an eyebrow and busied herself with filling the watering can.

'Well, look at it this way. At least your project is going well,' she said.

'We still don't know if I'm getting the promotion,' I said. 'After all that's happened, if that slimy Dhruv gets it, I might have to quit immediately.'

'It's lovely to see you're not as competitive as you were,' Kavya said seriously. 'How's the Calm app working for you?'

I had deleted the app about five minutes after I had installed it, but hadn't told anyone that. I picked up my book. Reading about Mia discovering her alternate reality was infinitely better than contemplating the future of my own.

'Listen,' Kavya said, pulling the book out of my hands. 'I think you need some cheering up. Go water the plants,' she said, handing me the watering can.

Normally, I would've argued, but I was too tired. Maybe staring at some greenery would be good for me. After all, the Japanese swear by forest bathing to reduce stress levels. Not that our balcony garden would qualify as a forest, even though we had some plants that were trying to burst out of their pots and take over the entire space. I stepped out into the balcony and began listlessly watering our hibiscus plant.

'Did you see how much the dragon fruit has grown?' Kavya asked. Our dragon fruit was slightly wild. It had grown well out of its pot and was perpetually trying to create a bridge between our apartment and the one opposite. Sometimes, I wondered if it was attempting to meet a friend on the other side.

I looked at the thorny stalk and gasped.

I blinked a few times to make sure I wasn't seeing things.

I wasn't.

Someone was standing right below our balcony with a giant sign in their hand.

Abhimanyu.

The sign said, simply, 'Sitara, let's talk.'

My heart was hammering so hard in my chest that I thought I was having a heart attack. But I didn't trust myself to speak to him.

He moved the sign out of sight to show me the next one.

'I love everything about you.'

That got my goat.

'What do you even know about me,' I yelled, throwing caution to the winds. I couldn't fall for this cutesy move, straight out of a romcom playbook.

'I know you scrunch up your nose when you think. I know you love dark chocolate and hate nuts in your chocolate. I know you'd never admit it, but you're probably re-reading *The Princess Diaries* right now. I know you are the most competitive person I've ever met and also the most loyal . . .'

I stared at him in shock. He was right about every one of those things.

He moved on to the next sign.

'With some luck, we will be together before the end of this year'

'I will give up astrology for you. And *vaastu*, too'

'I like you for you, and the things you do'

'I love you!'

I felt like my face would split into two, from how widely I was smiling.

'Come up,' I yelled. Some of my neighbours seemed to be enjoying this show a little too much, and I didn't want to have any more of this conversation in public.

I had also spotted Kavya walking out towards the gate just as Abhimanyu was finishing up with his signs. She'd winked and waved at me from a distance, so I suspected the suggestion I water the plants wasn't as innocent as it seemed.

'Does that mean I'm forgiven?' he yelled.

'Well, I can't forgive you for that terrible attempt at poetry . . . ' I winked.

'Sitara!'

'YES! Yes, you're forgiven.' Some smart alec decided to start clapping. This was definitely a far more interesting morning than most in our society. I waved at Abhimanyu to come upstairs. As he moved out of sight, there was a loud groan.

'Go watch TV,' I yelled, before I headed back into the house.

A few minutes later my doorbell rang. I opened the door, and there he was, clutching his signs to his chest. Now that he was here, I felt almost shy. He stepped in and closed the door.

'You're terrible at rhymes,' I said again, weakly attempting to make a joke.

He stepped closer to me, ignoring the nonsense coming out of my mouth, and gently moved a stray curl behind my ear.

I shivered.

'There's something I've been wanting to do since the first time I saw you,' he said.

My heart did flip-flops. Before I could ask him why anyone would want to do anything with a person who called them a dick, he pulled me close.

I had goosebumps all over and my neck began to grow warm. The tips of my ears and the back of my neck were on fire.

Gently, he tipped my chin, bent down and kissed me.

It was the perfect kiss—not too pushy, but full of intent. My legs turned to jelly. Initially, I was shy and awkward, and a bit stiff. Within seconds, I found myself responding. And how. If I were Mia, one leg would be up in the air right now signifying just how perfect the kiss was.

He pulled back a little, looked into my eyes and moved in to kiss me again, unhurriedly, as if we had been kissing for ages. I had been kissed before, but never like this.

This felt different, and yet so comfortable.

It felt so . . . right.

He broke off again. We stared at each other, our chests rising and falling, breathing heavily.

'And now you know,' he grinned.

I blushed.

With that, I could no longer insist that Abhimanyu was just a colleague or even a friend. With this kiss, I had given in to a longing I didn't know I could feel. I hadn't felt this way ever—as though we were expressing something deep within that had built over the past days, weeks and months. I reached for him again, but he stopped me by placing a finger on my lips.

'There's one more thing I have to tell you,' he said.

I was breathing so hard that I couldn't reply, so I just looked at him questioningly.

'You and me, we fit. It isn't about a horoscope, it isn't about anything in the stars. There *is* one thing though . . . '

He put his arms around my waist, pulled me close, looked into my eyes and said, 'I don't know if you believe in soulmates, but I do. You're mine.'

27

Good Understanding Makes for a Pleasurable Relationship

The next morning, I woke up in a happy daze even though I had forgotten to remove my contacts and they were now sticking to my eyeballs. I went into the dining area and saw Abhimanyu pottering about in the kitchen. I blinked to make sure I wasn't seeing things.

'Good morning,' he said, in a voice which was too cheerful for the morning.

I wondered how to tell him I wasn't a good conversationalist until I'd had my first jolt of caffeine. Even the glow of the morning after hadn't transformed me into someone who was ready to talk so early in the day. He silently held out a cup of chai. It looked like it had been exactly tailored to my over-milky specifications, and he'd even managed to locate my favourite *Alice in Wonderland* mug.

So this was what it felt like to meet the perfect man. I took a sip and closed my eyes. If heaven existed, I had stumbled into it.

'By the way, we have breakfast too,' he said. 'I went out and got some croissants and I've also made omelettes.'

'Would you mind staying forever?' I said. It had been a while since I started my weekend with anything except a packet of chips as breakfast.

He laughed and leaned forward to kiss me.

'I think we still have some unfinished business,' I said when the kiss ended.

And with that, all thoughts of breakfast were abandoned for a while.

Later that morning, we finally dragged ourselves out of the apartment. It took us a while as we kept getting distracted. I had planned to check out an exhibition that was happening nearby, and I talked Abhimanyu into accompanying me. I figured we could use some fresh air and sunlight.

The exhibition was in an open-air stadium and was focused on handicrafts from around the country. It was lined with dozens of stalls, displaying everything from kitchenware to home accessories to clothes. The entire place was very festive and filled with the typical Bangalore crowd that attended such events. Ladies in handloom and chunky jewellery, teenagers who were there for the evening music and food, all carrying their own bags for their purchases so they could avoid using plastic.

'So, should we get something to eat?' Abhimanyu asked as soon as we entered. He gestured toward the corner at the back where there was a cluster of food stalls, next to an open-air dining area.

'We just got here,' I laughed. 'Don't you want to see the stalls?'

'I'm not really into shopping,' he said. 'But I am willing to watch you shop if you promise to feed me at regular intervals.'

'In that case, let's start with some chaat,' I said and began walking towards the food stalls.

'Bangalore is obsessed with putting carrots into its chaat and that does not qualify,' he insisted. He pointed at a stall advertising millet-based delicacies ranging from biryanis to halwa. 'This looks like something I haven't tried!'

I scrunched my nose in mock disgust.

Of course, the man zeroed in on the most healthy food stall there was in the entire place. Why bother with chaat, rolls or ice cream when one could eat millet biryani. Sometimes, I wondered if he ever ate anything unhealthy.

I asked him about it as we stood in the surprisingly long line in front of the stall. He insisted he did eat unhealthy food and that I just wasn't around to see it. I had my doubts, especially since I've never seen him eat anything that was even mildly unhealthy. However, he insisted he did indulge 'on occasion'.

'Life is too short to waste it on eating millets,' I insisted, as I attempted to convince him this was an 'occasion' that warranted a cheat day.

'You're the weirdest and cutest person I've ever met,' he declared as he put his arm around me.

'I try,' I grinned as we got to the front of the line. I ordered a millet dosa. Of all the options, it looked like the most interesting. I planned to follow it up with an ice-cream sundae for dessert. In order to prove he did eat 'unhealthy', Abhimanyu ordered the millet sweet pongal. We looked around for a bit and managed to snag a table. We ate our food in companionable silence as I people-watched in that happy daze that came from spending time with someone you wanted to be with for a long time and discovering that the real deal was better than anything you imagined.

'So, how come you're named Sitara,' he broke into my thoughts. 'It's not a common name in the south, is it?'

'You have my sister to thank,' I laughed. 'She insisted on naming me and at the time, her favourite rhyme was . . . '

'Twinkle, twinkle little star,' he guessed.

'Yes. She actually wanted to name me Twinkle,' I said as his eyes widened. 'Thankfully, my parents intervened and convinced her they would find a word that meant star instead.'

'Twinkle Srinivasan,' he mused. 'You would've created quite a stir with that name!'

'It's a good thing she wasn't given free rein with my name, given what she's done to her kids . . . ' I stopped mid-sentence as I saw Abhimanyu staring at me with a completely dazed expression on his face.

I wondered if he was still listening to me.

He blushed.

'I'm sorry, I was distracted and lost track of what you were saying,' he said, as he continued to stare at my mouth.

'I guess you didn't want such a long explanation for my name . . .'

'No! The problem is, you start talking and then I start looking into your eyes, but your mouth starts to distract me,' he said. He leaned forward and grabbed my hand. 'Do you think you can abandon shopping? I'll make it up to you.'

I laughed and stood up.

'Yes,' I said.

'No way! You can't stop by saying we kissed, fade to black, end credits. We need details!'

After our attempt at going outside on Saturday morning, we hadn't tried stepping out again that weekend. Abhimanyu finally left at noon on Sunday because we agreed we needed to get our chores done. Kavya came waltzing home almost as soon as he left, further driving up my suspicions that the two were in cahoots. She then convinced me to go for an evening walk at Agara Lake Park with her, Upasana and Shirin.

Of course, it took all of five minutes before she blurted out to the others that 'Sitara has been, ahem, busy with Abhimanyu all weekend'.

I went blue in the face insisting we hadn't spent all our time in the apartment but they refused to believe me. I was told that 'pics or it didn't happen', and since I stupidly didn't click even a single selfie with Abhimanyu at the exhibition, it didn't help. I showed them one that I had clicked just before we left for the exhibition, but they insisted getting dressed didn't mean we had actually stepped out of the apartment.

When I insisted yet again we had gone out, Shirin spat her coffee back into the cup as she laughed out loud.

Upasana straightened her stole, trying to look as calm and collected as always, but struggling to keep the smirk off her face.

'Details, Sitara,' Kavya insisted.

'It was . . . good,' I said, wondering how I could change the subject. It didn't matter what I said, my face was flushed, and I knew I had that faraway, love-struck look in my eyes. 'Actually, it was better than good . . .'

'Ooh . . . ' said Shirin, doing a little hop and skip.

'He looked really tired when he left. Probably from the exertion,' said Kavya.

The cheek!

The three of them stared at me and then burst out laughing. I covered my face with my hands. It had been an intense combination of something that was completely overwhelming but also really straightforward. I hadn't expected just how I would end up feeling. I couldn't keep the dazed smile off my face.

'Oh my God, you've really fallen for him,' Kavya broke into my thoughts.

'Didn't you see that photo?' Upasana said. 'They both look completely love-struck!'

'He did say he's fallen for me too . . .'

'Well, of course. You're irresistible,' Kavya smiled. 'But remember, don't go too fast. I don't want you to show up home one fine day saying you're eloping Madhavan and Shalini style and need me for witness signatures.'

On cue, Upasana and Shirin began humming *Mangalyam Tantunanena.*

'As if!'

When we got home after the walk, Kavya cornered me as I was making some lemonade to rehydrate. 'You have to delete the app.'

I was only partially listening, so I didn't register what she was saying. I was too preoccupied with thoughts of my upcoming presentation. Tomorrow was our final meeting with Ash, and I had a bunch of things to fix. I had decided to spend Sunday evening working on it, and had told Abhimanyu we couldn't meet that night. He had agreed, and said he would take me to dinner tomorrow.

'You can cheer me up if the meeting sucks, and we'll celebrate if it all works out,' I'd teased.

'Well, I don't think it will suck. So it's going to be a celebration,' he insisted.

Kavya poked me in my arm.

'Ouch!' I rubbed my arm. She was clearly mad at me because I'd been lost in thought and hadn't been paying attention to whatever she was saying. I handed her a glass of the juice and then poured myself one. I took my glass and walked over to the couch, so I could open my laptop and begin to work.

She followed me, and perched on the chair opposite the couch.

'Sitara, you have to delete it,' she repeated. She took a sip of the lemonade and then bent down to fish out the container of sugar she kept on the bottom shelf of our coffee table. She added two heaped spoonfuls to her drink.

'What are you talking about,' I said. I was having trouble focusing. My mind was a jumble of work-related anxiety and some not-safe-for-work thoughts about Abhimanyu.

'That horoscope app. You can't keep using it, you know it isn't really responsible for things going well with your project. Or your relationship, for that matter!'

'I'm not completely convinced my project would've got this far if I hadn't followed Abhimanyu's horoscope,' I said. 'But you're right. The project is almost over and I no longer need it.'

She glared at me.

'OK fine. I no longer need it because I don't care about the promotion. For now, I don't want to jeopardize my relationship with him,' I admitted.

She took a long sip of the lemonade and then looked around for a clutch. She put up her hair and then looked at me.

'Man, you really hate it when I'm right,' she said. 'Anyway, I had reserved the right to say I told you so, so . . .'

Ugh.

Sometimes, I wanted to create a roommate agreement a la Sheldon and include a clause to ban 'I told you so'.

28

Beware of the Slithering Snake in the Grass

I felt like I was walking on air on Monday. I bounced into work as though I was walking on clouds, but made sure to look like it was just a regular day. Abhimanyu and I didn't want people at work to know we were dating, and I had already told Upasana and Shirin that.

'All set?' Shirin said as she brought over a Starbucks cup with 'SITARA' written on it. I wondered if it was a sign that everything else would go right today too. I smiled. I had really missed my friends, and I was glad for these moments. I would never again take any of them for granted.

'I think so,' I replied.

I took a sip of the coffee; it had been so long since the Starbucks had mint syrup, so I'd been having to make do with caramel macchiatos. Shirin had somehow managed to find our original drink this morning. It was truly shaping up to be a good day.

'Well, Ash looks to be in a good mood, so you're probably ready for your promotion,' she joked.

'I'm not bothered about the promotion,' I replied.

'I never thought this day would come,' she said, making a mischievous face. 'I did, however, overhear Ash saying he's going to send out promotion updates next week, so you're almost there.'

'I won't lie, getting promoted would be fantastic,' I admitted. 'But I no longer think it is the be-all and end-all. In fact, it's the relationships I've discovered and re-discovered along the way that matter.'

She rolled her eyes at my sentimental statement, but it didn't stop her from reaching over and giving me a quick hug. We went back to sipping our coffees in companionable silence. We had ten minutes before the final presentation to Ash, and I started going over my slides one last time to make sure I was prepared.

My presentation went by as though I was operating on autopilot. As I showed Ash we would definitely be able to get to 1 million customers with this project, it felt like I had achieved the unachievable. One month ago, Harsh had thrown a near-impossible challenge at me. Despite all odds, I had pulled it all off, and I was already proud of myself for coming this far. I stopped talking, took a deep breath and looked at Ash.

For a few minutes, he didn't say anything. Then he leaned forward and looked each person in the eye. There was a mix of expressions—they were impressed with my presentation, excited that the bigger project would be coming our way, but also nervous about what Ash would say. As Ash met someone's eyes, the person sat up straighter and leaned forward. I took a deep breath and tried to curb the impulse to chew on my cuticle.

'Amazing work,' he drawled and . . .

. . . and *smiled*.

I let out a whoosh of relief. People relaxed and began smiling. Ash calling any project 'amazing' was high praise.

'The investors will lap this up,' he continued. 'I can assure you that every single person in this room can expect a bonus.'

I couldn't believe my ears. This was better than anything I could've dreamed of. Shirin mouthed 'congratulations' when I looked at her. If Ash was promising bonuses, it meant he was convinced we would get a fresh round of funding.

'Sitara and Abhimanyu, you have steered this project exceptionally,' Ash announced as he picked up a slice of the banana cake and regally swept out of the room.

The room erupted into a round of cheers.

'You did it, you did it, you did it,' Shirin said excitedly, sounding a little like Professor Doolittle congratulating Henry Higgins.

'Thank you all for all the work you've put in,' I said, still a little dazed.

Abhimanyu, Basit, Abhijit, Shirin, Heena and Sridhar were all excitedly discussing the meeting and how we'd all got to that point.

There were whoops and cheers and 'remember when . . .' I could barely process what was going on.

I pinched myself hard to make sure I wasn't dreaming. It hurt. We had really, really done it. I shut my laptop and looked up, and my eyes met Abhimanyu's. I smiled and he grinned back.

Abhimanyu. The most important thing I'd gained out of everything this past month and a half. I felt an incredible pull towards him but controlled myself because we were still in office.

'Congrats, Sitara,' Dhruv piped in from my side. 'Great work on the project.' His expression and tone suggested he definitely did not think that the work was great, or even good. He sounded extremely jealous. Before I could reply, he walked over to Harsh who was yet to say anything, and who was busy staring at Abhimanyu as if a single look could make him split into smithereens.

But at that moment, everything was too perfect for me to care.

PING!

I ignored the sound of the app notification, thinking I had disconnected my phone from the projector when I turned off the Do Not Disturb setting on the phone.

'Sitara, your phone is still projecting,' Abhimanyu said, coming up to my side. He spoke in a low tone that only I could hear.

My head snapped up.

I looked at the projector and my heart stopped.

Shit, shit, shit.

My phone, still connected to the projector, was now broadcasting a notification from the AstroZone app.

Today's Aries Horoscope: A project initiated today will have long-term success.

I looked to my side to see Abhimanyu looking quizzically at me. So far, he didn't seem to suspect anything. I quickly walked over to pull the phone off the projector, but I was so nervous that I accidentally clicked on the notification. It helpfully opened up the calendar within the app, which made it very clear just whose horoscope I'd been tracking.

Up there on the big screen were my calendar notes. Every last incriminating one of them. 'Catch A after the workshop,' 'D-Day', 'Schedule a one on one on THURSDAY', 'Best Day for A'. It was like looking at the calendar of a deranged serial killer. Or maybe a hopeless stalker.

Before I could say or do anything, Abhimanyu swiftly disconnected the phone from the projector and was now glaring at it.

I began chewing on my cuticles, and this time, I did draw blood but I didn't care. My heart was hammering so hard, I thought it would fall out of my chest. I didn't know what to do. Abhimanyu would think I was a manipulative bitch who was using the horoscope to get him to do what I wanted. Which was true at one point, but wasn't any more. A wave of emotions rushed over me—worry, fear, guilt. I looked up at him trying to figure out what I could possibly say to make things better.

'OK, the thing is . . . ' I began but when he looked directly at me, I kept opening and shutting my mouth, doing a terrific impression of a guppy as I tried to think of what I could say. By now, everyone in the room had figured out that something was going on between the two of us. They had all gathered in a corner and were watching us. Nobody was saying a word.

I continued to gape at Abhimanyu for a while, my mouth opening and shutting noiselessly.

'You seem to have chalked out my entire horoscope. Was this your sick way of getting me to fall in love with you?' he choked out. He was still speaking very softly, and I could see that everyone else was straining to hear better.

I closed my eyes, wishing we could have this conversation in private and not become the centre of office gossip. But it was too late for that now.

'I can't believe you claimed you couldn't trust me because I saw the signs that we were meant to be in my horoscope. Was that a giant act so I'd never find out?' he asked, sounding angrier with every word that came out of his mouth.

'No!' I burst out.

Now everyone was looking at us even more intently. Out of the corner of my eye, I spotted Shirin trying to shepherd people out of the room. But obviously, no one in their right mind would miss the biggest office drama of the decade when they had stumbled upon ringside seats! They weren't even pretending to be busy with their own conversations, that's how shameless they were about their eavesdropping.

My brain finally fired up and I began defending myself.

'It wasn't about getting you to like me. I was trying to get you to approve my project so I could get my promotion. At first. And then I got carried away. But I swear, I've stopped doing it . . .'

There was an audible gasp from the peanut gallery. I ignored them all.

'So, what is this exactly?' Abhimanyu said, coldly, pointing at the two of us. 'Is this even real?'

'Yes,' I insisted, wondering how I could possibly explain that I genuinely liked him and this had nothing to do with the promotion in a way that didn't make me look like a complete dick. I couldn't stand the look of hurt on his face. 'I admit, this entire thing started because of the promotion, but I fell in love with you. I don't care about the promotion any more . . .'

He didn't look convinced. His face was a mixture of disgust, disappointment and anger. I had never seen him this angry before. Not even when I had called him a dick in front of the entire pub.

My heart sank.

'I cannot believe this, Sitara. This whole thing was nothing but your path to a promotion!'

I felt like the world had stopped. My heart was seizing up in my chest. And still, I couldn't get the words out easily. I stepped closer to him but he moved back.

'No,' I said, grabbing his hands, desperately trying to make him understand. 'I stopped doing it a while ago, I just forgot to delete the app. You're more important than that promotion.'

He paused for a minute, and stared deep into my eyes. I searched for the right words, the words that would somehow convince him to smile, to forgive me, to stay. A notification pinged on my phone.

We both looked down at the screen to see that Harsh had invited me to a meeting the next day to discuss 'my new role'.

It looked like I'd got the promotion. But I no longer cared.

'You're the best thing that ever happened to me,' I said.

But it didn't seem to matter. He tossed the phone at me as though it was a hot brick scalding his palms.

'To think all the horoscopes in the world couldn't alert me to the fact that I was falling for a fraud. *Again*,' he said.

With that, he stormed out of the room.

Slowly, the rest of the team shuffled out, ready to spread the latest gossip to the rest of the office. Shirin came over to me and hugged me as I struggled not to burst into tears.

What had started as the best day of my life had just ended as the absolute worst.

★★
★

Upasana and Shirin took me to the Starbucks so I could calm down. I had just spent an hour locked in the ladies' room at work, crying. Abhimanyu had disappeared into his office. Dhruv had gleefully gone around relaying the events of the day to everyone on the floor, after which I had attracted a lot of stares. People were torn between wanting to forgive me because of the generous bonuses Ash had promised and hating my guts because they all knew that something had been brewing between me and Abhimanyu, and that I had fucked it up. Thankfully, they didn't know the details, because our hushed conversation had been almost inaudible, but that didn't stop them from coming up with conspiracy theories. After my crying jag in the bathroom, I had been walking around pretending I didn't care to avoid feeding the gossip frenzy. That's when Upasana and Shirin cornered me.

The first twenty minutes at the Starbucks were spent finally admitting what I'd been up to. Surprisingly, they weren't mad at me. They were glad they could finally understand what had been behind my crazy behaviour, and were really upset that Abhimanyu and I had had such a public fight.

'By the way, Dhruv's campaign tanked,' Upasana announced, once we were done discussing my life.

'Is this your way of cheering me up? Didn't he say something about how it's doing amazingly well in the last team meeting?' I said. I took a bite of the cream-filled cronut, hoping that the sugar rush would improve my mood a little.

'Nope. You know that make-up artiste he had partnered with as the main influencer? He got caught in a row of molestation charges. There's no way we can be associated with that artiste any more. I heard the investors gave Ash an earful for ever partnering with him in the first place.'

'He should've tagged on to your campaign when he could,' Shirin said, taking a bite of her ham and egg croissant.

'As if,' Upasana dismissed her, and pushed her bangs away from her face. 'He told everyone you were playing power games when you moved up the meetings. That's why they were mad at you . . .'

'And he told Aakash you moved Binoy to your project to make sure his would get stuck . . .' Shirin added.

'He tried to make sure that Everest was permanently booked so you couldn't get the room . . .'

'He told Ranjani you said she's the dumbest admin you've ever met . . .'

Suddenly, I was beginning to understand why so many people had stopped speaking to me. After today's fireworks, I didn't see them forgiving me. So far, only Upasana and Shirin had forgiven me and unconditionally at that. But I couldn't care about what the others thought when Abhimanyu was angry with me. He was the only one whose opinion mattered.

'Dhruv is so toxic,' Shirin said. I nodded. All the sugar that I'd consumed couldn't mask the bitter taste in my mouth that came from hearing about his disgusting exploits.

'To be fair, he wouldn't have got away with it if you hadn't been so aggressive,' Upasana said.

'Fine! Yes, I was an ass,' I admitted. 'But that promotion was important to me!'

'Be careful,' Upasana said. 'Dhruv was already mad at you, and with his campaign tanking he's going to be even more angry. I wouldn't expect him to take this defeat lying low.'

'Well, today's meeting would've provided him with a ton of ammunition,' I said glumly. I knew I should care about this, but I just couldn't bring myself to even think about work politics when my heart was breaking.

'You cannot afford to underestimate Dhruv,' Upasana said. 'He has all kinds of tricks up his sleeve.' She was right. Dhruv was a formidable opponent even while he was playing fair, and when it came to playing dirty politics he was a master.

And yet, I couldn't bring myself to care. Even if Dhruv got the entire office to hate me, it still wouldn't matter if only I could somehow convince Abhimanyu that I hadn't meant to be such a manipulative bitch.

I stared glumly into my coffee wishing I could somehow figure out how to get Abhimanyu to forgive me.

29

Mercury in Retrograde Causes Confusion

Ever since Abhimanyu stormed out of the meeting room, I had been staring at my phone as though sheer willpower would convince him to reply to my texts, call me back or speak to me. I did everything I could think of to get in touch, to apologize, to make this nightmare go away. I called and called but he didn't answer. Eventually, after what may have been my hundredth call, my number was blocked. Every WhatsApp message I sent remained unread. I even tried to contact him through Facebook messenger, which was when I realized he had unfriended me. He had even removed me from LinkedIn. It was fairly clear that he didn't want anything to do with me.

It had barely been twenty-four hours since the entire blow up and I couldn't think of anything else other than what I could've done differently as guilt gnawed at my insides. What if I had told him about what I'd been doing when he first told me he liked me? What if I had deleted the app when Kavya reminded me? What if I had never used the app in the first place? The what ifs were endless and I wasn't coming up with any good answers to any of the scenarios. Each and every what if seemed to lead back to the same heartbreaking conclusion—Abhimanyu would hate me forever. Kavya tried to cheer me up by keeping me stocked with tissues, my favourite books, and fed me my own weight in chocolate but nothing helped.

I considered taking another sick day because I was too upset to be productive, but I knew it was pointless. I couldn't be sick forever. Besides, I also had the meeting with Harsh for the 'new role', a thought that no longer gave me any joy. I walked into work that day looking and feeling like a complete mess. My curls were all over the place and I had no make-up on, because when I attempted to put eyeliner and kajal, the tears smudged it, giving me raccoon eyes. The end result was that I looked unwell and had dark circles, which were partly due to sleeplessness and partly due to the smudged make-up that I hadn't been able to completely get rid of. My sole objective of coming to work was to apologize to Abhimanyu, but he wasn't there. I was sitting at my desk, staring blankly out of the window when Harsh called me into his office for the meeting that I had almost forgotten about.

'Congratulations, Sitara,' he said, handing me my promotion letter. I stared at it dully. After all the time, effort and energy I had put into becoming a senior manager, finally seeing the words in black and white did nothing for me. But I had to appear professional, so I began skimming through it.

'Thanks, Harsh,' I said.

'Any questions on the compensation or the designation?'

I was about to say no, but then I spotted something. Something that wasn't quite right.

The designation was right, 'senior manager', and the compensation was also in line with the title, but it said that my reporting manager would be . . . Anirban.

Anirban?

That made no sense. Anirban's team of product managers worked on building tools that Glam used for managing sellers. It was a backend role with very little visibility. It was not the type of role I had ever aspired to, given I had been working on something that was consumer facing.

'There's a typo, Harsh,' I said. 'It says Anirban is the reporting manager.'

He picked up his coffee cup and took a sip. 'No, that's not a typo. We took this performance evaluation cycle as an opportunity to restructure the team. And given the concerns with how you handled things, I thought it best to move you off my team.'

Wait. What did he just say?

My head was spinning.

I had done everything right and yet, somehow, they'd found a new curveball to throw at me. Harsh really was a masterful politician; he'd managed to find a role that was on a team that didn't do much and yet could be passed off as a 'good' role because it was led by Anirban, who happened to be Ash's brother-in-law and was never going to get fired, even though his team wasn't known for delivering anything. He was a horrible person and everyone in the office knew his work would go nowhere even though he had a fancy title and pretended he was single-handedly saving Glam. But I wasn't going to let go that easily.

'What concerns?' I said sharply, collecting my thoughts and preparing myself for a fight with Harsh.

'Well, your peer feedback was appalling, to put it mildly. Every single person rated you 'Needs Improvement'. We decided you needed more direction, and someone with strong people skills could coach you on that.'

'People skills!' I burst out. 'That peer feedback was because people thought I was responsible for the insane deadlines, but that came top down!'

'Good people managers know how to manage upward, as well as delegate,' Harsh said. 'The peer feedback is reflective of the fact that you did not handle that level of responsibility well. Or at all.' This was ironic coming from a man whose own team evaluation scores were abysmal, and had been so for years.

'But Harsh, I was able to get the team together and deliver on an impactful project . . . '

'Performance is just one part of leadership,' he said. 'As you become more senior, your people skills are far more important. And I will not let the culture of my team get impacted by having someone with such poor peer feedback scores!'

I couldn't believe my ears. Harsh himself hadn't delivered anything in years and he held the office record for having the worst team evaluation scores, and yet he was sitting here with a butter-wouldn't-melt-in-my-mouth expression while saying this?

'Harsh, if this structure goes into effect, what happens with my project? I came up with that idea and I proved its viability,' I said with gritted teeth.

'There is no I in "team",' he said grandly. 'If only you realized that and paid attention to the feedback you got during the Circle of Success programme, your peer scores would be better. Dhruv has expressed interest in a product role, and he gets along fabulously with the team. He was also part of the launch, so he is the perfect candidate to scale the subscription programme.'

The penny finally dropped. This wasn't just about Harsh, this was also Dhruv's revenge. Even though I'd got my promotion, I was being shifted into a role where I would disappear. It was the equivalent of banishing me to a forest in the middle of nowhere, while he stole my project. He would scale the subscription programme, get promoted and then be on the fast track to future leadership roles. In time, everyone would forget I had anything to do with this, and all my hard work would be wasted.

'Harsh, I don't want to be on Anirban's team,' I said.

'In that case, find a role that suits you. As of today, you're no longer on my team,' he dismissed me.

I left his office fuming.

I went up to the terrace, the only place I could spend some time alone. As alone as I could be with the crows and pigeons that hung out there. I took deep breaths in a wasted attempt to calm myself down. I was fuming at the unfairness of everything that had just happened. I closed my eyes thinking of everything I had done to get this promotion. Which of course brought me back to Abhimanyu and his horoscope, and how I'd managed to drive away someone who truly cared. I couldn't believe just how much my life had spiralled out of control within the span of a month and a half.

When you thought about it, it was such a short period of time, and yet so much had changed. After all the change, things were still somehow the same. Career-wise I was back to square one, and once again, I didn't have a friend named Abhimanyu. The only difference was, instead of thinking he was a dick, I now knew he was the best person I'd ever met. And he now thought I was a manipulative bitch. But I missed him. I missed his voice, I missed the way he ran his hands through his hair when he was stressed, I missed the way he was like the earthing wire to my fiery moods, I missed the way he made every problem seem non-existent. Thanks to Harsh and my new role, I would probably never run into Abhimanyu at work again, and he would avoid me too. Maybe I should quit so I'd never have to see him again?

I wondered if he would ever forgive me. I could remove every trace of him from every online platform, avoid him, but how could I turn off my feelings? Forgetting him would be like forgetting to breathe. Over the past month, he had been there for me whenever I needed someone, and now I couldn't get him out of my mind.

Suddenly, I felt the urge to take matters in my own hands.

I swept out of the terrace in such a tizzy that the pigeons scattered and the crows began to caw in rage. I banged the door shut and stormed down to Ash's office. Luckily for me, he wasn't in a meeting. I took the opportunity to barge in.

'Ms Srinivasan,' he said, looking up. 'To what do I owe this pleasure?'

'Thank you for the faith you've shown in me, Ash,' I began.

'You proved yourself worthy of it,' he said, as he looked at me somewhat warily. I sensed he wanted to cut to the chase. After all, people didn't just storm into his office purposefully to talk about his faith in them.

'Did you come in here to praise my people management or do you want to discuss your new role?'

'I did,' I said and straightened up. This wasn't a conversation where I could afford to feel sorry for myself. This was a 'Sitara Srinivasan, ready to kick ass and take over the world' conversation. I knew exactly what I needed to do, and I was going to do it with full confidence.

'As Harsh probably told you, he doesn't think you're a fit for his team,' he began. 'You could do really well on Anirban's team. They need innovative thinkers like you. I'm happy to discuss how you can be most effective there . . .'

'The subscription programme is mine,' I said cutting him off. 'Ash, I'm most suited to expand the programme. I already have a detailed plan for scaling it.'

'That may be,' Ash said. 'But your reviews showed you're not ready to manage a cross-functional role like this. You're an asset to Glam and I want to ensure you're able to achieve your full potential.'

And there it was. Time to forget wheedling, horoscopes, other political manipulations and do what I should've done from day one. It was time to bet on myself.

'And what if I say I can achieve my full leadership potential by expanding the subscription programme?'

'Some of the senior members of the team are dead set against that. It wouldn't work,' he said. 'Just take the new role, Sitara.'

'Let me explain.' I sensed he was still curious to see what I'd come up with, and I did not want to give up without a fight. I took it as a good sign that he hadn't dismissed me yet, nor was he looking at his laptop and avoiding my gaze.

'We start a new vertical for the subscription programme, which I lead as senior manager reporting to you. You give me six months to show you how I expand the programme, as well as improve my peer feedback. This way, I'm focused on a product that gives me the best growth potential and I'm not on Harsh's team.'

'Six months is a long time,' he said. 'And reporting into me isn't easy.' I suppressed a grin. If only he knew just how well I knew that reporting into him was no cakewalk.

'I'm ready for a challenge,' I said. 'You can think about it and let me know. I really do not want to take my ideas to a competitor.' I stressed on the word competitor, hoping he would pick up on the not-so-subtle hint that I was willing to resign over this.

'I'll give you three months,' he said, ever ready to negotiate. 'And if your peer feedback doesn't improve, you will move to Anirban's team. I'm only taking a bet on you because of the impact of your work so far.'

'Done,' I said and stuck out my hand. I couldn't believe my gamble had paid off.

Every problem had a solution. I couldn't turn off my feelings for Abhimanyu without some kind of *Eternal Sunshine of the Spotless Mind* type mind wipe out. That didn't exist in the real world so I would need to find a more constructive solution.

If I could get the promotion in spite of all odds, if I could get everyone to forgive me, if I could get a second chance to prove my worth at Glam, why couldn't I get Abhimanyu to forgive me?

I got back to my desk and sent an email saying I had some personal work and left the office. I called Kavya on my way home.

'Can you help me get in touch with The Sherlock Homies?' I asked. Kavya was a great online stalker and someone who always seemed to have only two degrees of separation from anyone, so I knew that with a little effort, she would be able to easily locate all the phone numbers.

'Why?' she said curiously.

'I won't give up,' I said. 'I know what to do now . . .'

'Yay,' Kavya cheered. 'Tell me more!'

'Let's just say that the answer is written . . .'

'In the stars?'

'On a cue card.'

I held my breath and thought about what I was about to do. If it didn't work, I'd make a fool of myself in the most public way.

But then, I had nothing to lose.

30

Venus Brings Forth the Jewel in Your Crown

I stumbled into Last Call in a manner very reminiscent of my first meeting with Abhimanyu. I was extremely late and I had an important handoff to make. Every second I sat in the Uber, my blood pressure rose, taking minutes off my life. I had to run the last few metres, and of course I'd broken my slipper yet again. So there I was, dripping wet, holding a slipper in my hand as I stumbled into the pub.

This time, the only person I saw when I walked in was Abhimanyu. He was at The Sherlock Homies's usual table, studiously avoiding my eye and staring into his phone as though it was hazardous to life if he looked up. I handed off the pen drive I was clutching in my palm to George and walked to our table.

'You're insane,' said Kavya, peeling off a wet curl away from my forehead.

Upasana dug through her bag and silently handed me a clutch.

'Do you think he'll go for it?' Shirin asked. She began pouring out drinks for everyone at the table.

'Let's see,' I said.

'Welcome to tonight's edition of Thirsty Thursday, ladies and gentlemen,' George boomed. 'After the spectacular success of the knockout rounds a few weeks ago, we're going to do that again tonight.'

We cheered, even though 'spectacular success' wasn't quite how the knockout rounds could be described, after the brawl we'd caused. George shot us a look to get us to quiet down.

'The first round in today's knockout will be between Whiskeypedia and The Sherlock Homies. This is an audio round,' he announced, gesturing to the set-up in front of him.

There were two chairs facing each other, and the ever popular buzzer. He had learnt from the last time and skipped the weird floor lamps.

I held my breath. There was a bit of an argument at The Sherlock Homies table. I watched Abhimanyu shake his head vehemently, as his teammates pushed him out of his chair. He reluctantly made his way to the stage.

This was my cue. I went up to the stage and sat on the chair opposite Abhimanyu. I nervously smiled at him, but he continued to avoid my eyes. He was busy glaring at his friends who had now moved to the front of the pub. They were joined by my friends.

'Let's begin,' George said.

He played the familiar strains of the Airtel signature tune. 'What was the first song the composer of this jingle composed for his movie debut? Bonus points if you can name it in the original language, and not the dubbed version.'

BUZZ!

'"Chinna chinna aasai", from the movie *Roja*,' Abhimanyu replied. He looked mildly suspicious.

Satish whooped, 'Go *macha*', as the rest of the team softly began humming the song.

'Next question. This popular singer couldn't even make it to the top five on a popular music reality show in 2005. Today, nobody remembers the winners. Name the singer and for bonus points, name this song,' he said, as the opening bars of the song began to play.

BUZZ!

'Arijit Singh and *Raabta*,' said Abhimanyu.

'Sing it,' yelled Zaina, as a blush crept up his cheeks.

'Yes, sing it,' George said.

Abhimanyu started to demur but then, the entire pub erupted in cheers and shouts of 'SING IT.'

He was still studiously avoiding my gaze, but began to sing. When he got to the line '*tera nazaara mila*', our teams joined him to yell out in unison '*roshan SITARA mila . . .*'

His face was now a 'flaming fire engine' red as he finally looked at me. I felt goosebumps on every inch of my skin. But I was suddenly too nervous and shy to look up.

He stopped singing abruptly and looked at George. 'Shouldn't we get on with trivia?' he asked pointedly.

The crowd booed, clearly wanting to hear more of his singing.

'OK, let's move on,' George agreed. 'M. Balamuralikrishna sang the Tamil sections of this song that was telecast for the first time after the prime minister's Independence Day speech in 1988. It featured Indians from all walks of life and was meant to be a message of national integration. Name the song.'

BUZZ!

This time, I picked up the mic and began singing, 'Mile Sur Mera Tumhara.' The crowd went wild, as they all joined in.

Abhimanyu was now glaring at his friends, who looked like they were the very pictures of innocence. Mine, on the other hand, were trying hard and failing to hold back their smiles. I stopped singing and looked at him. There was a glimmer of a smile tugging the corners of his mouth, and he was struggling to control it.

'Next question,' George smoothly interjected. He was thoroughly enjoying himself. 'This one's a movie clip so look carefully at the projector.'

The clip began to play, as my heart sped up.

A man in a blue shirt leaned into a mic and said, 'I'm afraid you did it again, Bill.'

The camera panned to an upset looking Billy Mack who said, 'It's just, I know the older version so well.'

The man in the blue shirt replied, 'We all do. That's why we're making the new version.'

The clip faded.

'Remember the question is, name the movie,' George said. 'Also a good reminder that sometimes the new version is better than the old.' Some folks booed.

I looked up, and I was staring directly into Abhimanyu's eyes. My heart was pounding in my ears.

BUZZ!

'*Love Actually*,' he said. He could no longer avoid my eyes. He looked at me as I slowly mouthed 'I'm sorry!'. I hoped it would remind him of his apology from a few days ago.

The ghost of his smile was slowly becoming broader.

'Patience reaps rich rewards,' George said. 'I know some of you are having a little too much fun with this round, but we're almost at the end. Next question: This 1994 movie only did moderately well when it was released, but became a cult classic in recent times, with Raja Sen calling it 'one of the greatest comedies in recent times'. There's a song picturized on one of the lead couples, where they're on a horse cart. Name the song, the movies and for bonus points name your favourite dialogue from this cult classic.'

There were loud whoops.

BUZZ!

I picked up the mic, and in a shaky voice I said, '"*Ello ello*" from *Andaaz Apna Apna*.'

Before I could name a dialogue, my team began singing the song and gesturing at me to join in. I threw all caution to the winds to join the racket and sing, '*Ello ji sanam, hum aa gaye, aaj phir dil leke . . .*'

Krish had jumped on the stage and begun doing a dance on my behalf, replete with gestures to say '*ab itna bhi gussa karo nahin jaani*'.

When I ended the rendition by quoting the dialogue '*galti se mistake ho gaya*', for the bonus points, Abhimanyu couldn't hold it back any more.

He smiled. It was like the sun had come out from behind the dark clouds. I slowly smiled back. George was looking back and forth between us, seeming extremely pleased with himself. Every single person in the pub was singing and clapping.

Abhimanyu opened his mouth to say something, but I gestured him to wait.

'The last question is a toughie,' George said. 'The two books the singer is reading in this song are *Love at First Sight* by B.J. Daniels and *Skylar's Outlaw* by Linda Warren. Name the song.'

BUZZ!

'This one looks like it's a tie, folks,' George said. 'Both teams pressed the buzzer at the same time, so maybe they can answer together?'

Abhimanyu blushed as the opening strains of the song began playing. We stared at each other as we began singing the chorus of 'Call Me Maybe'. The pub went wild as our friends all jumped on to the stage to mime the hook step of the song.

'You've got to forgive a girl who can accept your love for Carly Rae Jepsen,' Zaina yelled.

'And one who's taught you the Tamil version of Rahman songs,' Satish added.

I took a deep breath. By this point, every single person in the pub knew this was not a regular trivia night. And it didn't seem like anyone cared that they weren't going to participate in a trivia competition today. George grinned as though he had spent all his time as a quizmaster training for this very moment.

My entire body felt like it was on fire. Every eye in the pub was trained on me. In the past, this had happened because I'd given stupid answers, started a pub brawl or otherwise embarrassed myself. I didn't know what I was going to be doing today.

Abhimanyu looked into my eyes. I cleared my throat. My face was completely red, and resembled an apologetic tomato.

'I messed up! I was a complete idiot . . .' I started.

'You made me look like a fool,' he replied, matter of factly. He still looked a little miffed, but he was finally talking to me. A little fizz of hope burst into butterflies in my stomach.

'No, I was the fool! I never should've done what I did . . .'

'Sorry isn't enough,' he said. 'How do I know you really want to be with me?'

'How did I know you really wanted to be with me?' I shot back. 'I trusted you when you said you loved me. Now it's time for you to trust me!'

'I don't know . . .' he said, still staying a safe distance away from me.

'Abhimanyu, I love everything about you,' I said, echoing his outburst from outside my balcony. 'I know you rake your fingers through your hair when you're stressed. I know you love apple slices and pesto pasta, and hate pineapple on your pizza. I know that you listen to Carly Rae Jepsen to destress and that you've translated the Backstreet Boys in Hindi. I know you'd do anything to help a friend . . .'

He grinned and finally stood up. He came towards me and I stood up too.

'I did something incredibly stupid because I was angry and competitive. Those aren't my favourite things about myself, but I'm asking you to forgive me. To trust me.' I took a deep breath, ready to plead my case further.

I was one step away from breaking into dialogues from every romcom I'd ever watched in a hope to convince him.

'You should've told me about following my horoscope as soon as we confessed our feelings,' he said, as he looked into my eyes. 'It was the fact that you kept it a secret that killed me, not what you did.'

'I swear I didn't look at it after I realized I had feelings for you. The promotion didn't matter to me, only you did.'

'Forgive her,' someone shouted from the audience.

'Yes, forgive her,' the crowd echoed.

'She dedicated an entire trivia round to you. She deserves a chance,' someone else shouted. Slowly, sounds of cheers and claps began emanating from various corners of the pub. There were a lot of glasses clinking, and I wondered if someone had spun up a drinking game out of this very public confession.

He took a deep breath. Suddenly, I spotted something on his face. He was desperately trying to stifle a smile.

'I suppose . . . ' he began, as he ran his fingers through his hair.

'Go on, say it,' The Sherlock Homies heckled in unison.

'You're not angry,' I said, with a wide grin.

'I was,' he shrugged. 'But then, you burned every bridge with Harsh by standing up for me. I didn't expect you to give up on winning just for me,' he took a step forward. People in the pub were now whistling.

'If I could go back and change how I approached everything, I would. I would never download that app. I would do anything to take it all back. I can't begin to imagine my life without you!'

I told myself to stop speaking. He was now standing really close to me. As he faced me, I looked deep into his eyes. They were so big, bright and honest that I could barely breathe. I had spent hours looking at him over the past few months but in that moment it was like I was seeing him for the first time.

This was Abhimanyu, a horoscope obsessed, 1990s Bollywood aficionado, listener of Carly Rae Jepsen, translator of music and a part-time cycling enthusiast. He was so many things, and there was still so much more for me to discover.

He leaned towards me, and I tingled with anticipation. He reached out to hold my hands. And then it happened.

I forgot that we were in a crowded room with a hundred people staring as he bent down and kissed me. The kind of kiss that makes your leg spring up, where fireworks go off in the background, where the world stops spinning, where the censor board inserts two flowers in front of your face and where a group of back-up dancers magically appear behind you to synchronize their steps to yours. I did not want the moment to end. As we broke apart, the entire pub cheered.

'And that, ladies and gentlemen, is probably the most entertaining trivia night I've ever hosted,' George boomed. 'If anyone else fancies a trivia proposal, you know where to find me!'

We smiled at each other. We both wanted to go straight home and continue where we'd left off, without an audience.

A month and a half ago, at this very pub, I had met him for the very first time. A month and a half ago, I didn't even know someone called Abhimanyu existed and now I couldn't imagine a version of my life that didn't have him in it.

'I'm all in,' I said.

'I'm all in too,' he replied. 'This feels so right, as right as breathing. Besides, my horoscope said that today is the perfect day for a romantic fairy tale ending.'

Acknowledgements

Amma, Appa and Adi for being my most ardent cheerleaders. Appa, I promise that someday soon I will take your suggestions for what I should write next.

Surabhi A.R. and Varsha V. Rajan for volunteering to read my early drafts and giving me such insightful feedback. I couldn't have done this without you.

Gurveen Chadha, my editor, who pushed me to get this book to where it needed to be, without ever making me feel like I was being pushed. I'm glad I got to work with you again. Thanks also to the team at Penguin Random House India—Devangana Dash, Saloni Mital, Sumangla Sharma and Vaishnavi Singh—for all your hard work and support.

Archana Iyer and Chandhrika Venkataraman for being the inspiration behind Kavya. You'll always be my 3 a.m. friends. After all, you know too much!

Navia Shetty, my favourite trivia partner, for being a part of my most fun (and embarrassing) trivia memories.

Someday, there will be a question where the right answer *will* be 'The Statue of Liberty's husband'.

The Singhs, the 'Soul Sante Sisters', Soumya Sampath, Gayathri Arumugam and my US family for keeping me sane and always giving me something to laugh about.

Friends who made dreary days at work fun: Prerna Kapoor Sonkar, Abhineet Sonkar and Kaushik Mitra. Adithi Murthy and Tushna Mistry for the giggles, the stress snacking and inspiring some of my best comics. Credits also to Tushna for the mint-chocolate-macchiato recommendation at Starbucks.

Zarreen Khan, whom I first met in the corporate world but is now the author friend I'll always lean on for advice, laughs and encouragement while I plod through a manuscript.

My amazing husband, Vivek, for all his enthusiasm, encouragement and the much needed critical feedback—you make my writing what it is. Of all the friends I've made at my various workplaces, you'll always be my forever friend.